## TAKE ME HIGHER

"Enough play. I need you now."

She blinked up at him, trying not to squirm. "Okay."

He held her gaze with his blue, blue one and entered her as though he were entering a cathedral, quietly and reverently.

Okay, now she was scared. No woman should feel so intimately connected to a man she'd just met. That spelled danger.

She shouldn't look into his eyes while he loved her so sweetly; that was more dangerous still. She should crack a joke, change positions, she should . . . With a quiet sigh, she arched her hips to take him deeper, increasing the connection between them.

She gasped at the heat that flared, each slow, deliberate stroke driving her both higher and yet deeper into something that was outside her experience. He felt it, too, she was certain. His gaze was hot with more than sexual desire.

*from* "Going After Adam"
by Nancy Warren

# BOOK YOUR PLACE ON OUR WEBSITE AND MAKE THE READING CONNECTION!

We've created a customized website just for our very special readers, where you can get the inside scoop on everything that's going on with Zebra, Pinnacle and Kensington books.

When you come online, you'll have the exciting opportunity to:

- View covers of upcoming books

- Read sample chapters

- Learn about our future publishing schedule (listed by publication month *and author*)

- Find out when your favorite authors will be visiting a city near you

- Search for and order backlist books from our online catalog

- Check out author bios and background information

- Send e-mail to your favorite authors

- Meet the Kensington staff online

- Join us in weekly chats with authors, readers and other guests

- Get writing guidelines

- AND MUCH MORE!

**Visit our website at
http://www.kensingtonbooks.com**

# Bad Boys to Go

## Lori Foster

## Janelle Denison

## Nancy Warren

KENSINGTON BOOKS
KENSINGTON PUBLISHING CORP.
http://www.kensingtonbooks.com

KENSINGTON BOOKS are published by

Kensington Publishing Corp.
850 Third Avenue
New York, NY 10022

All Kensington titles, imprints, and distributed lines are
available at special quantity discounts for bulk purchases for
sales promotion, premiums, fund-raising, educational or in-
stitutional use.

Special book excerpts or customized printings can also be
created to fit specific needs. For details, write or phone the
office of the Kensington Special Sales Manager: Kensington
Publishing Corp., 850 Third Avenue, New York, NY 10022.
Attn. Special Sales Department. Phone: 1-800-221-2647.

Kensington and the K logo Reg. U.S. Pat. & TM Off.

First Trade Paperback Printing: November 2003
First Mass Market Paperback Printing: June 2005
10 9 8 7 6 5 4 3 2 1

Printed in the United States of America

# CONTENTS

BRINGING UP BABY

by Lori Foster

7

THE WILDE ONE

by Janelle Denison

105

GOING AFTER ADAM

by Nancy Warren

203

# BRINGING UP BABY

Lori Foster

# Chapter One

Gil Watson was both nervous and excited—an odd combination he hadn't experienced since his first years of college. These days he was confidence personified, commanding even, an in-charge guy perfect for the corporate world. He prided himself on his professional demeanor, his calm outlook on life. He had a business to run for his family; they relied on him and he enjoyed that.

He'd grown up—and in the process permanently buried all wild inclinations.

But today, the figures blurred on the computer screen in front of him. He wasn't getting much work done, which seemed to be the norm of late, rather than the exception. It had taken only one phone call to throw him off track, but then, it wasn't every day a man learned he had a daughter, a daughter he hadn't known of until two weeks ago.

He hadn't been the same since.

Would she look like him? At two and a half years, was a child developed enough to look like anyone? What he knew about babies wouldn't fill a thimble. At thirty-two, he concentrated on knowing business, family responsibility, and finances. And not to brag, he also knew women.

But he knew zilch about being a father.

It still boggled his mind that Shelly had never said a word. He saw her two or three times a year, whenever business took him to Atlanta. He'd been to her office, to her home, met her coworkers and friends. Right after his father's death three years ago, he'd been so sick at heart that he'd done things he wasn't proud of.

Like using Shelly.

Not that she hadn't been willing. She'd sent him one of her looks and he'd reciprocated, and within the hour they'd gone from business associates to lovers. He still remembered the wild, frenzied way she'd taken him. For two days, he kept her in his motel room burning up the sheets. She'd catered to his sexual needs, his fantasies, and even his less than orthodox demands—*the demands he'd thought well under control.* She'd been everything he'd physically wanted and needed at the time.

In truth, she'd wrung him out and left his body and mind thankfully blank for an entire weekend, relieving his sense of loss for his father, obliterating his concern about taking over the family business and the overwhelming responsibilities he'd accepted as his own.

It was when he'd awakened and saw her looming over him, smiling with too much emotion for a mere sexual coupling, that Gil had realized his mistake. Shelly wanted a husband and apparently saw him as a prime candidate. But he didn't want the burden of a wife added to the new load he already carried.

His oldest brother was a cop, his youngest brother still in school, and his mother had never involved herself with the company. Taking over the successful family novelty business and keeping them all financially solvent had naturally fallen to Gil. Outwardly, he was the most staid, the only one who'd shown an interest, his father's protégé.

No, the last thing he'd wanted was a wife to further

muddy the waters, so he'd done what he considered wise and responsible. He'd gently explained his lack of interest and had never again touched Shelly sexually. Yet she'd had his baby and continued to associate with him as a close friend. Without once ever telling him.

Gil's stomach clenched over such a deception. He hadn't known, damn it, but that was no excuse. Shelly had taken care of their baby alone and now she was gone. He couldn't make things right by her—but he could raise their daughter. And he would.

Giving up, he closed out the computer program and leaned back in his chair, his mind churning with regrets and curiosity and that persistent nervousness. A baby, his baby. Jesus.

A small commotion in the outer office drew him forward again in his chair. He grew alert, his brows drawn in confusion when the door opened and his assistant stuck her head in. Her frown rivaled his own. "Gil, you have . . . company."

At fifty, Alice wasn't prone to melodrama. Her expression had Gil rising from his desk in a rush. "Who is it?"

"Well, the young lady introduced herself as Anabel Truman. And the youngest lady is Nicole Lane Tyree, as I understand it, although all she's done is suck her thumb."

Every muscle in Gil's body went rigid. His brain cramped. His daughter was here—*with Anabel*—two weeks early. He rounded his desk with a long stride.

Damn Anabel; he'd offered to come to her, to buy her airline tickets, to pay for their transportation. As contrary and outrageous as ever, she'd refused, telling him it'd be at least ten days before she could leave. Ten long days before he'd get to meet his baby.

Yet she was here, at his office, where he didn't want her to be, rather than at his home where he might keep his private business private for a little while longer. At least until he could figure out what to do, how to proceed . . .

Arms crossed and eyebrows lifted, Alice moved out of his way as Gil charged forward. If this was a deliberate ploy on Anabel's part to discredit him, he'd—well, he didn't know what he'd do yet, but he'd think of something. Because Anabel had been Shelly's roommate, he'd known her as long as he'd known Shelly. She was always there when he visited, always twitting him, picking at him. Her presence was always unnerving; she made him think things he shouldn't think, things he had tried not to think now that he had new responsibilities to consider.

As Shelly's best friend, she'd been off-limits then. But no more.

He threw the door wide and then froze, his heart shooting into his throat, his stomach dropping, his knees almost giving out. Damn it, why did Anabel have that effect on him?

She looked the same as always: seductive. He'd never really liked her. She was too outspoken and pushy. Too overtly sexual and in your face. Too . . . hot. She was one of those women you just knew would be incredible in the sack and it made him nuts.

It wasn't just her jewelry, her overdone makeup and risqué clothing that had made her far too difficult to ignore. There'd been something about the way she watched him, too, her close attention, the carnality in her gaze that made him wonder if their basic natures might mesh.

That thought had kept him on edge whenever he was around her.

Now he realized that she might have watched him for the simple reason that he was Nicole's father and didn't know it. He might have totally misread her.

When she'd called, her tone had been devoid of accusation, empty of any real emotion when usually she teemed with emotion. She'd told him of Shelly's death, of his baby girl, all with a detachment that had left him bewildered and floundering—a situation he didn't like one bit. He was used to being in charge, of knowing what he did and why and having no doubts whatsoever.

Did it matter to Anabel that he hadn't known of the baby?

She stood there now in low-slung, faded jeans, a clinging stretch top of bright pink and . . . oh God, she had a belly button ring. He fixated on that for what seemed like an inordinate amount of time before he heard her low, throaty laugh. He jerked his gaze up to her face.

The woman was beyond outrageous, and in the months since he'd last seen her she'd only grown more so. "Anabel." Thankfully, his tone was even, polite. "This is a surprise."

"I know." She grinned, and that grin was so teasing that Gil felt it like a tactile touch. Then he saw the exhaustion she tried to mask, the utter weariness in every line of her body.

Sudden worry overwhelmed every other emotion. "What's happened?"

At the sound of his voice, a pale face surrounded by dark curls peeked out from behind Anabel's knees. Until that moment, Gil hadn't noticed the tiny hands hugging around her legs, the little bare feet behind hers.

The baby, his baby, was hiding.

At his very first glimpse of her, Gil's heart turned over. He couldn't get enough oxygen into his starved lungs. She was so tiny, he hadn't expected . . .

Without really thinking about it, he went to one knee, putting himself more on her diminutive level. "Nicole?"

The little girl blinked enormous chocolate brown eyes

framed by long lashes. Her rosebud mouth crumbled and she tried to climb up the back of Anabel's legs, saying, "Mommy!"

*Mommy?* Taken aback, Gil lifted a brow and looked to Anabel for some explanation.

Anabel pulled Nicole around to her front and playfully scooped her up, holding her to her breasts and laughing. "Hey, little rat, remember what I told you? I promise you don't need to be afraid."

Little rat? But the child had a stranglehold on Anabel that she couldn't pry loose, so it didn't appear she'd taken offense at the less than complimentary endearment.

Anabel glanced at Gil and shrugged in apology. "It's been a long trip and she's tired."

Disappointment shook him, but Gil hid it. At least he hoped he did. He rose slowly to his feet again. "Come into my office." Stepping back, he held the door open until Anabel had swept past him. He could feel her energy, detect her light flowery scent. Behind on his office floor she'd left a large colorful bag overflowing with a tattered stuffed bear, a faded print blanket, a squeeze bottle of juice, and other baby paraphernalia.

Blank-brained, at an utter loss, Gil looked at Alice.

In her typical no-nonsense manner, Alice lifted the bag and pressed it into his hands. "The child might need this."

"Of course." The damn thing weighed a ton. "Hold all my calls and cancel any appointments."

"You were meeting your mother and brother for lunch."

His brain scrambled in panic mode before settling on a course. "Call Sam. Tell him Anabel is here. He'll understand."

"You're the boss." Alice hesitated. "Gil, if you need anything else . . ."

She'd been his father's secretary, and now his. She was protective and loyal, and Gil sent her a smile of gratitude. "Thanks. I'll let you know." Then, on second thought he added, "How about some coffee, Alice?"

"I'll bring it right away."

"Thank you." Gil stepped into his office, shut the door, and tried to figure out what to do next. He silently tallied the facts at hand: Anabel was here, a woman he shouldn't have wanted, but did. His daughter was here, a child he'd only just found out about but already cherished. His life was about to undergo some drastic changes. He had to do *something*—but all he managed was to stand there, watching the two of them.

Anabel had sprawled in his black leather desk chair, the child on her lap, and she was whispering in Nicole's ear, kissing her downy cheek, and rubbing her narrow back.

Gil wanted to hold her. He wanted to cuddle his child and know her and let her know him. The feeling was so alien, yet so powerful, Gil naturally shied away from it.

"We're starving." Anabel glanced up at him. "You got anything to eat?"

Finally having a purpose, Gil strolled to his desk to perch on the edge and pushed the intercom button. "Can we order up some lunch, too, Alice?"

"Sandwiches, pizza, soup."

He turned to Anabel, leaving the choice up to her, and she said, "Pepperoni pizza. Maybe some salad for me, too. And a Mountain Dew if it's available—I could use the caffeine kick. I have juice for Toots, here."

Alice said, "Give me fifteen minutes."

With that accomplished, Gil settled back, linking his fingers and resting his hands on his thighs. The pose was relaxed when he felt anything but. He made note of so many things at once. The dark circles under Anabel's green eyes, the windblown disarray of her short, fawn-colored hair. The row of hoop earrings in her left ear, each increasing in size. Five total, he counted, the largest about as big as a quarter.

A tattoo circled her upper arm. It appeared to be a horizontal flower vine, but it was too delicate for him to be sure without leaning forward for a closer look. And he wasn't about to get that close to her.

Nicole twisted slightly to see him, but she kept her nose stuck in Anabel's neck, her arms locked around her. Her round eyes were huge and wary.

Gil tried for his gentlest smile. "Hello there."

" 'Lo."

He badly wanted to touch her, and he didn't deny himself. Slowly reaching out with only one finger, he stroked the silky soft hair over her temple. His heart threatened to punch through his chest.

She shied away, going back into hiding and gripping Anabel with new fervor.

"Give her time, Gil. She's been through a lot."

The idea of what she'd been though smote him clean through to his soul. He was her father; he should have been there for her, protecting her, making her feel safe and secure no matter what else happened. He cleared his throat. "And you, as well. I know you and Shelly were close."

She looked away. In a whisper she said, "Toward the end, I barely knew her at all."

Toward the end? The end of what? Shelly had died suddenly of a car wreck, Anabel had told him. What did she mean, then? But his questions would have to wait until Nicole wasn't listening. He didn't know how much a child her age might comprehend, and he wouldn't risk adding to her trauma.

Alice knocked before stepping in with a tray of coffee and cups. "This will get you started before the lunch arrives. The little girl has something to drink?"

Anabel shoved to her feet with Nicole still clinging like a determined monkey. "Juice—never leave home without it."

"Juice," Nicole mimicked. She stuck out one skinny arm in demand, grasping at the air with her tiny fingers.

Gil wanted to melt on the spot. She was by far the most precious thing he'd ever seen. "I'll get it for her."

"Thanks." Anabel hoisted her small burden a little higher in her arms. "Methinks naptime is closing in." She winked at Gil, then moved to the leather couch and pried Nicole loose to sit her on the cushion next to her. "You're giving him a complex, rat. Say hi again, like you mean it this time."

Nicole sat there, her pudgy bare feet sticking off the couch cushion, sizing him up with an unblinking stare. To Gil's surprise, she suddenly treated him to a beatific smile, wrinkling her little pug nose and scrunching her whole face up. "Hi."

"Good girl." Anabel accepted the coffee that Alice handed to her and took a long sip, groaning in pleasure. "Wonderful. You're an angel, thank you."

"My pleasure." Alice retreated from the room.

Cautiously, not wanting to startle her, Gil handed his daughter her juice. "Is it cold enough for you?"

"She doesn't like it cold, do you, Nicki?" Nicole didn't answer. She had the squeeze bottle tipped up, guzzling away until juice ran down her chin. Anabel quickly put her coffee aside to relieve her of the drink. Eyelids drooping, Nicole turned to her side, put her head in Anabel's lap, and just that easily, dozed off.

"She's run out of gas." Anabel smoothed the dark curls, straightened the wrinkled T-shirt. "She's been up all morning, poor little thing. Long car trips make her nauseous. We're lucky we got here with only one barfing episode."

Gil drew himself up. "You drove?"

"Wanna keep your voice down? She konks out fast, but she's a light sleeper. If she's back up after only ten minutes, she'll be a hellion. You'll boot us out before she can show you her sweeter side."

Boot out his own daughter? Never.

"Hey, can you maybe produce some music? Background noise would help her sleep, and then we can . . . chat about things."

Annoyed at both her censure and that the child had been ill, Gil went to a console and turned a switch. Doors slid open to reveal a state-of-the-art television, and CD and DVD players. He glanced through his collection, picked out a classic Beach Boys CD, and put the volume on low.

Once the music filtered into the room, he turned to face Anabel Truman, his emotions boiling too close to the surface.

She beat him to the punch, blinking green eyes in horror and whispering, "What the heck is *that?*"

"What?"

"That . . . noise." She gave a theatrical shudder.

"The Beach Boys?" He should have known she'd take exception to his choice. In the past, she'd taken exception to everything.

"I forgot that you have the most deplorable taste in music." She snorted. "You listen to crap that a fifty-year-old guy would like."

Gil drew himself up. He would not be sidetracked by her ridiculous insults. "Forget my preference in music. Let's talk about how you got here."

Shrugging, she said, "I drove."

"All the way from Atlanta?"

"Yep." Unconcerned, Anabel stretched out her long legs and slumped back in her seat, nursing her coffee like a drunk nursed a whiskey. The pose exposed more of her soft belly, making it hard for Gil to concentrate. "We left at five this morning, stopped several times, and now we're here."

Forcing himself to look away from her negligent and somehow provocative posture, Gil went back to his desk, but he didn't seat himself in the chair. Again, he chose to rest his hip against the surface. He was a mature man, calm and collected, always with a purpose. A peek at a woman's belly did not waylay him. "Why, Anabel? I offered to fly you both in."

"We New Age gals like to have our transportation with us. Who knows when you might piss me off and I'll have to leave? No way will I be dependent on you."

She said all that in such an amicable, even tone that it took a moment for the words to sink in. Once they did, anger washed away his calm façade. "We should be very clear with each other, don't you think, Anabel?"

"Sure." She rested her head back against the couch and closed her eyes.

Damn it, Gil couldn't help but notice her belly again, how cute the colored stone looked there. He also noticed her breasts and the lack of a bra. Her nipples were smooth and soft right now, but he imagined a woman like Anabel could be easily aroused with a soft, leisurely suckle. She was so open about things, so casual about her body and her thoughts . . .

It'd been too damn long since he'd had a woman.

It'd been years since he'd had the raw, uninhibited sex he preferred. Not since that night with Shelly . . .

Again, he reined himself in. "She's my daughter."

"You don't have to growl it." Looking boneless and

exhausted, her eyes still closed, Anabel said, "Anyone who sees you two together will know you're her dad. In case you haven't noticed, she's the spittin' image of you."

Gil glanced at the toddler, but in her slumber, her adorable little face was smooshed up against Anabel's denim-covered thigh, making it impossible to assess her features. How could she look like him? He was a two-hundred-pound man, dark enough that he had to shave twice a day to avoid beard shadow. Nicole was petite and precious and sweet. He recalled the way her dark brown eyes had assessed him, the same color brown as his own. Her hair was as dark, too, but silky soft and curly, unlike his own. So the coloring was the same, but there the similarities ended.

As he stared at Nicole, he felt that elusive yearning again, expanding inside him, almost choking him. How long would it take before his daughter accepted him? He cleared his throat. "You brought her to me."

Anabel's eyes snapped open. "Whoa, big boy. I brought her to meet you. We'll see about anything else."

"She's mine, Anabel." He wasn't certain about everything, but he had no bones about that. "She belongs with me."

Her breasts rose on an anxious breath. Carefully, she straightened and slid the child over so that she curled on her side, forming a small adorable lump on the couch. Anabel pushed to her feet. Gil knew she wanted to look in calm control, but her eyes had darkened to a forest green and her hands were curled tight in restraint. "Nicki loves me, Gil. I'm the one who's cared for her. I'm the one who's raised her so far. I'm the one who's loved her."

Where had Shelly been if Anabel raised Nicole? Gil shook his head. "I didn't even know about her."

"That was Shelly's decision, not mine." She strode to him, her body rigid, desperation pulsing off her in waves.

"If I'd told you, she said she'd take Nicki from me. I couldn't let that happen. In every way that is most important, Nicki is mine."

Feeling as though he stood on the edge of a deep cliff, Gil waited.

Anabel drew a breath, collecting herself. She tucked in her chin, met Gil's gaze squarely. "There's only one way you can have her."

Narrowing his eyes, Gil played along, knowing damn good and well that he'd never let her go, not now, no matter what. "And that is?"

She licked her lips, but her hesitation lasted no more than a few seconds. "You can marry me."

The timely arrival of pizza saved Anabel from saying any more. Not that she'd be able to get a single word out with Gil standing there, stunned mute, his expression leaning toward incredulity. *Well, what had you expected, Anabel? Open arms and gratitude?* She twisted her mouth in a grimace, wanting to cry, to sleep, wanting to grab Nicki and run as far and as fast as she could.

Those options weren't open to her.

While Alice bustled into the office with a fragrant box of pizza and a salad, Gil turned away to the window. He looked stiff, outraged, confused. He looked . . . well, delicious.

With a fine trembling making her unsteady, Anabel reseated herself behind his desk in his cushy chair. The fancy office hadn't thrown her. She'd known he was well off, just from the fifteen-hundred-dollar suits he wore whenever he visited Shelly. He was always well-groomed, well-spoken, polite and polished.

He hid his true nature well. But she knew, oh yeah, she did. She knew and she understood, and hopefully that'd be her ace in the hole.

Before she bungled this more, she needed to eat and she needed to sleep. Gil didn't look ready to let her do either. Damn her big blabbermouth. The stress had taken its toll and she wasn't thinking clearly to have just blurted that out. Now she'd have to retrench, laugh it off, give him a little more time to get used to her.

Maybe seduce him.

Alice put out napkins. "Sam said he expects a full accounting tonight. He'll speak to your mother for you."

"Damn it . . ."

"No. He said he'd keep her from visiting until you invited them, but he also said not to press your luck."

"Meaning my mother isn't known for her patience."

Alice just smiled. "Let me know if you need anything else." After she'd again left them, Gil strolled to the front of the desk, facing Anabel. She sat there, mostly numb, not quite daring enough to meet his gaze, while he served her a slice of pizza and the salad she'd ordered. "You can eat while you explain that outrageous comment."

She wished he sounded more passionate and less reasonable. If she read him wrong, if Shelly had mistaken things, then she'd blow this for sure.

Reaching for calm control, which wasn't really her forte on her best day, Anabel said, "Not much to explain." She took a huge bite of pizza and groaned at the mingled delights of melted cheese, tomato sauce, and spicy pepperoni. "Oh God, that's good."

Gil stared at her mouth, making her self-conscious. "Have you eaten since this morning?"

"I packed some stuff for the rat, but no, I didn't take much time to eat." She'd been too rushed, too desperate to find an alternative to the unthinkable, and far too nervous about her improbable success.

His antagonism thickened. "Must you call her that?"

"What?" Anabel peeked at him, then indulged in another large bite. He was every bit as autocratic as she remembered, and just as contained. Gil Watson never voiced his temper, never made public mistakes, was never indecisive or uncertain.

"Rat." He said it like a dirty word. "It's insulting."

From the day she'd met him, Gil had made his disapproval of her known. Oh, he wasn't mean-spirited enough to say anything, and he was never cruel. But the way he looked at her, the rigid way he held himself in her presence, told it all.

He disliked what he assumed to be her laid-back lifestyle. He disapproved of her choices, choices he knew nothing about.

He judged her and found her lacking—but he wanted her anyway. She could tell as much, whether he admitted it or not. She wanted him, too, so she had no problem with that. Even in the face of his condemnation, she'd always liked him. A lot. By necessity, he'd never known the whole story, not about her or the basis for her choices. Would it matter? She hoped so.

He'd make a good father to Nicki, and if it all worked out as she hoped, he'd make a passable husband so that they could be a family, the type of family Nicole deserved. Gil might not ever love her, but that didn't matter at this point. He would care for his daughter. He would protect them and give Nicki everything she needed.

He deserved the truth, so she mustered her wavering courage and bared her soul. "I love her more than life. She knows that. Rat is just a pet name for her."

"I don't like it."

Anabel grinned and saluted him with her cola. "Already the protective father. Remember that when she's demanding and whiny and stubborn."

He glanced at Nicole's sweet little face with disbelief. "You're just being snide and there's no reason for it."

She laughed. Oh, was he in for a surprise if he expected Nicki to be the perfect child. She was delightful and precious, but also as cranky and contrary as any other toddler. "Sorry. Just let me have two more bites before I faint from hunger and I promise I'll magically transform into a pleasant being."

He appeared doubtful at that, but nodded. "What about Nicole? I thought you said she was hungry, too." He stopped beside the couch, his hands shoved deep into his pants pockets, his head down as he watched his daughter. Her T-shirt had ridden up, showing her pale, soft back and the top of plastic-covered training pants above the waistband of her shorts. His expression was fixed, clouded with emotions.

Watching him watch Nicole made Anabel's heart hurt. He'd missed out on so much. Anabel could almost feel his desire to pick Nicki up, to hug her. It had been wrong to keep the baby from him, but what choice had she been given?

Softly, suffering smothering regret, Anabel said, "I guess she was more tired than hungry." She cleared her throat. Getting sentimental at this point would blow everything. "She'll eat when she wakes up."

"How long does she normally nap?"

"Maybe an hour if we're lucky." Anabel stared at his broad back, visible through the perfect fit of his tailored dress shirt. "Where will we sleep tonight?"

Gil's head snapped around and he stared at her over his shoulder. His piercing attention settled on her like a thick blanket, further unnerving her.

"I mean Nicki and me, not . . ." Damn her exhausted state. She sighed, laughed a little at herself. "Is your place big enough for us? I don't exactly have the funds to start staying in motels for an extended visit, and I assumed you'd want time with her. Where she goes, I go, so—"

"I get it." He turned away from the couch to fully face her, still holding her in that unrelenting stare. "Yes, I have room. Don't give it another thought." He went to the phone on the desk near her and dialed a number. A second later he said, "Candace, this is Gil. Prepare the guestroom please. And stock the refrigerator with juice—" He covered the mouthpiece and said to Anabel, "What type of juice does she prefer?"

Candace? Who the hell was Candace? If he had a girlfriend or, God forbid, a wife, what would she do?

"Anabel?"

Her heart pounded in dread but she forced herself to answer. "Mixed fruit. And milk. And she likes fresh vegetables and bananas and crackers of just about any kind."

Gil nodded and relayed the list to Candace. When he hung up, he crossed his arms over his chest and surveyed her. He was so close Anabel could smell his cologne. It was spicy and warm—like Gil. Of course, he didn't want most people to know just how spicy he could get.

But Shelly had talked. A lot. And so Anabel knew him better than he might imagine. "Are you married?"

It came out sounding like an accusation, and Anabel winced. But Gil didn't look offended. "No."

In for a penny . . ."Engaged? Involved? Serious about anyone?"

"No."

Her breath came out in a long sigh of relief. "So who's Candace?"

At her inquisition, his gaze sharpened the tiniest bit. "She's the housekeeper."

"No kidding? You have a maid?" She knew he was well-to-do, but that just seemed so . . . extravagant.

"A housekeeper. Part-time. She comes three days a week."

"Just to clean up after you?" Anabel raised one brow, surveying him from head to toe. "And here I thought you were a pretty fastidious fellow."

His expression didn't change. "I like a certain amount of order in my life, and I like things clean and neat. Candace sees to it."

Order, neatness? Oh boy. With a falsely bright smile, Anabel said, "And now you have a very active toddler. Imagine the fun."

Gil straightened away without replying to that. "I have a few more things to do here and then we can head to my place." His attention drifted over her face before softening with concern. "You look like you could use a nap yourself."

That little bit of sympathy about did her in. She was so physically and emotionally spent that it wouldn't take much to have her bawling. She drummed up a cheery smile. "Yeah, I'm pooped. But there's no need to interrupt your day. If you want to just give us directions . . ." She could get there and get a lay of the land before him.

"I don't think so." He crossed his arms over his chest. "Tell me what's going on, Anabel."

His stance said it all. He wouldn't be put off, not a second more. She shoved one more forkful of salad into her mouth, then pushed her plate away and propped her elbows on the desk. She hoped she looked unconcerned with everything she had to dump on him. If he knew how desperate she was, would he use it against her? She didn't think so, but couldn't take the risk.

"Shelly got strange after she had Nicole." His left eyebrow shot up, and she said, "Yeah, yeah, I know what you're thinking. Who am I to talk about strange, right?" With one finger, she fluttered her row of earrings.

He didn't comment, just gave specific notice to the narrow tattoo circling her upper arm.

Anabel resisted the urge to defend herself. "What I

mean is that she wanted little to do with Nicole. She spent all her time partying, trying to prove to herself that she was sexy, that men wanted her."

"She was sexy. And I know she didn't want for dates."

"No, but you rejected her and that really took a chunk out of her self-esteem." Anabel didn't want to add to his guilt, so she said, "You might not know this, but Shelly didn't have a very happy home life." *What an understatement.*

"And that made her a less than perfect mother?"

"There is no such thing as a perfect parent. But no, I just meant that it made her very insecure. I think in her own way, she loved Nicole, but she didn't want to be tied down with her. She thought having a baby made her somehow less appealing to men. She thought they'd see her differently if they knew she'd given birth. So she kept it a secret."

"From everyone?"

"Most people." Her parents had known—and vehemently disapproved. "I work at home, so I took care of Nicole." This was the part where she had to convince him, had to make him understand. "I'm the only real mother she's ever known, Gil."

He looked her over again, and Anabel just knew he found her lacking. Not that she blamed him. When she'd taken over the task of caring for the baby, she'd worried, too. She loved Nicole and always did her best. For a while, it had been enough.

But not anymore. Now she needed Gil.

He said only, "You took care of her all by yourself?"

"For the most part." And in more ways than he could imagine. "Nicole was covered by Shelly's medical insurance, and occasionally, when she thought of it, she contributed financially. But she spent almost no time with her. When she did, it was more like Nicole was a stranger to her, not her own daughter."

He stood silent, not looking particularly convinced or skeptical. When Gil Watson chose to keep his thoughts hidden, he did an admirable job of it.

Anabel stared down at her hands. "I wanted to tell you about Nicki." She swallowed down her guilt and her reservations to give him another truth. "I always thought you'd be a good father and things would have been so much easier with your help. But Shelly was insistent. She said you'd take Nicole away."

"From her—or from you?"

Her gaze jerked up to his. "I would have been willing to share her." Her heart raced fast and her palms were damp. "I know it sounds strange, but Shelly hoped to win you over someday and she wanted to know it was for herself, not because of Nicole. You . . . you were the only man who ever dumped her."

He ran his hand over his face and began to pace the office. "We were only friends."

"You were lovers, too."

He stared at her hard.

"Shelly told me . . . things." Anabel shrugged awkwardly, wishing she knew his thoughts, but his look was too inscrutable for her to decipher. "She talked about you a lot."

"I see." He made no effort to hide his displeasure.

Leaving her chair in a rush, Anabel strode to him. "She died in that damn car wreck because she'd been drinking. I think she might have been high, too. She was getting worse and worse, losing her focus." She stopped in front of Gil, hating to remember just how bad it'd gotten, how she'd been so afraid for Nicole. "After she died, her parents stepped in and took her business to sell, but they said there wasn't much money left once they'd paid her debts and taken care of the funeral."

Gil folded his arms over his chest, his face set. "So now you need money."

He made her sound like an opportunist. In a way, she supposed she was. She wanted Nicole, and she needed him—in more ways than one. "Yes. On my own, I can't afford to give Nicole everything she should have. I've always chosen to work at home so I could be with her and now . . . well, my income isn't something to brag about."

"You're still doing web pages?"

Her chin lifted. She remembered the time Gil had walked in on her while she'd been working on an extensive adult site. He'd considered it porn, while she'd only seen it as one of her better paying jobs. "I make enough to keep up with the rent and monthly bills, but I don't have insurance for myself or Nicole. Babies get sick a lot, they need vaccinations, checkups." Please let him understand. "They need two parents."

Gil stepped closer, casually intimidating her with his size. His eyes were such a deep, fathomless brown, framed by thick lashes, awesomely direct and always serious. "So I'm supposed to marry you so that you can keep *my* daughter."

It wasn't easy, but she nodded. Then added, her voice soft, "Yes."

He took another step closer until she thought she could almost feel his heartbeat mingling with her own. Staring at her mouth, he said, "Tell me, Anabel. What's in it for me?"

BRINGING UP BABY 31

with a man's thoughts of sweet and... no. No. 32.

# Chapter Two

Gil watched her small pink tongue come out to wet her dry lips, saw the nervous flutter of her long eyelashes, the rapid pulse in her smooth throat. After her bold declaration about marriage, he was surprised anything could discomfort her.

He did want her. Hell, the wanting burned just beneath his skin every time he looked at her. In his younger days he would have damned the consequences and jumped on the opportunity afforded him now. But he was no longer that wild, impetuous youth ruled by his dick. He was a well-respected businessman—and his last uninhibited escapade had landed him with a daughter.

And Anabel.

He'd never thought much about settling down with one woman, but if he had, he wouldn't have envisioned a wife like her. No, if he had to consider it—and he didn't, not yet—it'd be with the idea of an elegant woman, subtly feminine, very refined and polite. A woman who would fit into his new corporate life, who could attend the business parties and cultivate new connections.

It would not be with a woman whose body language screamed sex, whose every smile had his guts twisting with raunchy thoughts of sweat and moans and wet, sliding pleasure.

It wouldn't be to a woman who threatened his self-control with every breath she took.

"You'll have your daughter living with you," Anabel said in a low, soft voice that seemed contradictory to the casually sexy clothes and mod tattoo. "I think you want that."

He tipped his head in acknowledgement. "I do." She started to relax, until he added, "But I can have that without you."

*"No."*

Gil didn't change expression, but he felt himself softening. With her bottom lip quivering, Anabel met his stare, and she looked so small and vulnerable and . . . her damn earrings were blinding him, the way they reflected the fluorescent office lights.

His tension grew, making it nearly impossible to disguise. "It's not up to you, Anabel. She's my daughter."

"And for all intents and purposes, I'm her mother."

"And yet," he reminded her gently, "you're not."

Stark pain stole over her features, quickly replaced with iron will. "Don't con me, Gil." Her small hand came up to rest against his dress shirt directly over his heart. Her breath came fast and shallow. "I know you too well. You won't do that to her. You won't break her heart that way."

The trembling of her lips kept snagging his attention, until he wanted to warm them with his own. "Actually, you don't know me at all." He started to turn away.

Her hand fisted, wrinkling his expensive shirt, pulling him back around. She didn't raise her voice when she said, "I've known you three years."

Three years that he'd thought of fucking her, imagining how wild she'd be, how she'd taste and feel. Three years of doing his best to ignore her and her carnal appeal. Three years of resisting her because that was the right thing to do. "We've been no more than acquaintances."

Now *she* stepped closer, staring up at him, her chest heaving, her expression resolute. "We've debated business and politics and society. We've talked about the weather and clothing and music. We've argued and teased and I've . . ."

Her breath hitched and she pinched her lips shut.

She was so close he could smell her, a subtle fragrance of perfume and the headier scent of warm woman. "You've what?"

"Nothing." She released him and stepped back, moving to his desk before turning toward him again. Seconds passed like the ticking of a bomb. "Do you know, Nicki was always there when you visited. It gave Shelly a thrill to have her that close to you, without you knowing it."

Unable to comprehend such malicious machinations, Gil shook his head. "Why?"

"I don't know." She looked as dumbfounded by it all as he felt. "I had a hard time figuring her out. I think she sometimes hoped that Nicki would wake up or make a fuss and you'd find out. The matter would be taken out of her hands, so to speak. But she didn't, and so you never knew and Shelly chose not to tell you."

She kicked off her sandals and hopped her rounded behind up onto the edge of his desk. Hands in her lap, shoulders slumped, she stared down at her bare feet and said, "I wanted to tell you, Gil. I swear. But Shelly said if I ever did, she'd run off with Nicki and no one would ever find her. I couldn't bear the thought of that. Shelly birthed Nicki, but she wasn't her mother. I kept my door open at night, always listening with half an ear, always wondering if . . ."

"If?"

She looked up, her eyes sad, hopeless. "I was so afraid she'd take my baby, that she'd run off and I'd never find her." Anabel rolled her shoulders, shrugging off the melancholy to give him a small smile. "I heard her first word."

"Mama?" He couldn't mesh the image of this woman with that of a mother. Impossible.

She laughed. "No. It was 'bird.' She loved watching the birds out the window. From the time she was a tiny baby, it'd make her squeal. I put a feeder outside the window so they'd come up close and it'd keep her entertained for a long time."

Wishing he could have seen her enjoying the birds, Gil said, "I have a wooded backyard. Lots of birds and other animals to see."

Her expression was distracted, a little sad. "I stayed up nights with her when she cut teeth. I'd hold her, and she'd drool on my shoulder until we were both soaked, but I could never bear to hear her cry. I bought her clothes, mostly at secondhand shops, but I made sure everything was clean and cute, and she always looks adorable." She turned her face up to his, her eyes pleading with him to understand. "I've changed all her diapers, bathed her and fed her, and I've loved her with all my heart. You can't take that from me. I *know* you won't take that from me."

Gil rubbed the back of his neck, lost in turmoil. It was the damndest thing, an onslaught of emotions and considerations and needs. Nicki was his daughter and now that he knew about her, he'd never let her out of his sight again.

He hadn't realized how he'd feel about a kid, so he couldn't have prepared for the strange bombardment on his heart. The more Anabel spoke of her, the richer his love for Nicki seemed. It crushed him that he and his family had already missed so much of her young life.

Questions about her birth, her personality, her preferences, seemed to be building up inside him, demanding answers the same way his lungs demanded air. He didn't just want to know. He *had* to know.

Yet mixed with that was the undeniable urge to protect Anabel—an urge he couldn't seem to stifle no matter his anger or his common sense. Never in his life had he indulged macho displays of chest beating. He left that sort of chauvinistic behavior to his older brother, Sam. As a supercop, Sam filled the role to perfection and then some.

But in Gil's world of business, women were not delicate creatures that needed a man's protection. They were intelligent, savvy, capable—and sometimes ruthless. He'd never felt like the all-powerful, superior male with any woman. He'd never felt that a woman needed him to shelter her.

But now he did.

Anabel Truman, with her multiple earrings and tattoo and come-get-me smile was tugging at his heart in a way no other woman ever had.

Damn her; she'd kept his baby from him. She was as responsible as Shelly for deceiving him.

And he still wanted to cuddle her close and hold her and make outrageous promises that weren't at all in his best interest. If he encouraged her now, what type of example would she set when his daughter started forming her own decisions? Would she emulate Anabel? His heart skipped a beat at that awesome thought, and he swallowed hard. Would Nicki want a tattoo, too? Oh God, the very idea made him cold inside.

No two ways about it: Anabel just wasn't proper mother material. He thought of mothers as being like his own—no-nonsense, understated, ready with a hug and advice. His mother *looked* like a mother. Soft, a little rounded, casual and comfortable.

Anabel looked like . . . not a mother. He couldn't label her, but there was nothing comfortable about her. Exciting, yes. Hot, definitely. But not maternal.

Even while she'd been pouring her heart out to him, a part of his mind kept thinking how sweet it'd be to push her to her back on his desk, to tug those threadbare jeans down her hips and thighs so he could . . .

Suddenly she slid off the desk and started toward him. "I know what you're thinking, Gil."

Along with the look in her eyes, that throaty tone brought him out of his reverie. "You haven't got a clue." If she did, she sure as hell wouldn't get so close to him.

"Wanna bet?" He caught his breath when she leaned into him, her hands sliding up his chest to rest on his shoulders. Her cool fingertips brushed the heated skin of his nape. Eyes direct, even challenging, she whispered, "You're thinking about sex. With me. I've seen that look on your face before."

He didn't back down. "What look?"

Her smile curled, lighting up her eyes, flushing her cheeks. "Well, the look before you just went blank. It's this sort of heated expression, very direct and interested and naughty."

He caught her shoulders to hold her away—and instead, he just held her. His heart thundered and the muscles of his abdomen and thighs pulled tight. "You're mistaken."

"Oh really?" She went on tiptoe to brush her nose against his throat. "Mmm. You smell good, Gil."

Her breath whispered over his skin with the effect of a lick. Her breasts, shielded only by a clinging shirt, brushed his chest.

"Anabel." He meant his tone to be chastising, and instead it reeked of encouragement.

Her hand left his shoulder to glide down his chest, down, down to the waistband of his slacks where she lingered, making him nuts, causing his lungs to constrict. Her lips moved nearer to his, and at close range she stared into his eyes.

"You want me, Gil. Admit it."

He wouldn't admit a damned thing. But neither could he deny it.

The darkening of her eyes should have given him warning. But when her slender fingers drifted lower, cupping his testicles through his slacks, he was taken completely off guard. To call her brazen would be an understatement. To call him unaffected would be an outright lie.

She held him, gently squeezed, expertly stroked. "You're already hard," she whispered.

Yeah, from his ears to his toes, but did she have to sound so pleased about it?

Still in that soft whisper, she purred, "Gil, I want you, too. I always have." As she said it, she moved her fingers up to his throbbing cock, teasing his length, deliberately arousing him further, pushing him. "We would be good together. I know you, know what you like and what you want. I'll do anything, Gil. Any time you want, any way you want. I'll—"

The bribe finally registered, dousing him in ice water. He felt used, repelled, and he automatically sought to distance himself by pushing her back. She was taken by surprise and would have fallen if he hadn't grabbed her shoulders to steady her. Just as quickly, he released her again.

Her eyes were wide, dark. *Aroused.* "Gil, please . . ." She started to reach for him.

"No." His lip curled, disgust at himself and her boiling up to choke him. She acted in the role as Nicole's mother, and yet she'd just offered to prostitute herself. He said again, "No."

What he felt must have been plain to see, given the

lack of color in her face. Devastated, appearing somewhat lost, she faced the desk and braced her hands
there. Gil could see her shaking, could hear the choppy
unevenness of her gasping breaths. She was going to
cry and he couldn't bear it. He had to do something,
say something.

"We'll leave now." His own hands weren't that steady
when he went to his desk and snatched up the phone,
quickly dialing his brother's cell phone. When Sam answered, Gil could hear restaurant noise in the background. He closed his eyes. "Don't let Mom know it's
me, but I need a favor."

"Shoot."

"Come by the company and get my car. I'll leave a
key in the office, top desk drawer. Bring it to my house
later tonight or tomorrow morning before I have to get
to work. By yourself."

"You can only fend them off for so long. I speak from
experience, Gil."

Gil well remembered Sam's recent relationship sna-
fus with Ariel. No, his family was not the type to stand
idly by. They liked to get involved. He glanced at Anabel
and wanted to groan. Her shoulders were slumped so
that she curled in on herself. Her exhaustion, her desperation, was enough to flatten him.

"I just need a few days." At least he hoped he'd be
able to figure something out in a few days.

"Sure thing. See ya then."

Sam hung up, and Gil knew he'd come up with some
good excuse for the phone call. Sam worked under-
cover—he was great with lying. With that worry now in
Sam's capable hands, Gil faced Anabel.

Keeping her back to him, Anabel wrapped her arms
around herself. "How will you get to your house if you
don't take your car?"

"I'm going to drive yours."

She jerked around. "Mine?"

There were no tears in her eyes, thank God. In fact, that unwavering resolution still remained, contradicting the slump of her narrow shoulders.

Gil caught her wrist. She was fine-boned, soft. "You just offered to sell yourself to me, Anabel. I'd say that makes you pretty desperate. No way in hell am I letting you out of my sight with my daughter."

A second ticked by, then two and three. She drew a shaky breath and looked at his hand on her wrist. "I offered to marry you."

"In exchange for raunchy sex."

Her gaze swept up, clashing with his. She half laughed, from surprise or disbelief, he wasn't sure. "Raunchy, sweet, hot and fast or slow and easy." She shook her head. "I've wanted you since I first met you. Something about you draws me, something dark and impossible to ignore. I go to sleep every night thinking about you inside me."

Gil closed his eyes, wishing like hell that she'd shut up, that she didn't seem so determined to turn him inside out.

Her free hand touched his jaw. "I didn't offer to have sex with you as a trade to keep Nicole. I was just trying to show you how compatible we'd be. Marriage or no marriage, I'd still want you. I'm starting to think I always will."

Sincerity rang in her tone, once again knocking Gil off-kilter. "I don't fucking believe this."

She smiled. "You should know that Nicki repeats everything she hears. Good thing she's sleeping through this, huh?"

Gil let her wrist drop to tunnel both hands through his hair.

"I know it's a lot to take in, Gil. First Nicole and now me. Even if you decide against marrying me, I'd still like to have you."

*Have me?* Speechless, Gil could only stare at her. He couldn't imagine a woman more outrageous than her. And damn it, it made him want her more.

"But . . . before you completely reject the idea of marriage, will you at least give me a trial run?"

"A . . . ?"

"Trial run." She nodded. "I could take care of your daughter while you're at work, and then take care of you at night, in bed."

He squeezed his eyes shut. "I don't think I want to hear this." He was still hard, getting more so with every insanely sexual thing she muttered.

Her words rushed out in her attempt to convince him. "I'm sorry I have to push you like this, but we only have a few days to decide. I'm hoping that if you enjoy sex with me—"

He would. He knew it down deep in his bones. He'd known it for three years, which was why he hated being around her.

"—then maybe the idea of marriage to me won't be so repellent. Maybe you'll see that Nicki loves me and is happier with me around. Maybe you'll even see that you like me well enough to keep me."

With very little effort, she drove him over the edge. "You make yourself sound like a stray dog."

"I want you. I want Nicki. I'm a woman trying to have it all."

He began to feel desperate. "I don't love you, Anabel. Doesn't that matter?"

World-weary cynicism shadowed her smile. "In my position, I can't let it matter."

Something she'd said struck him, making Gil frown. "You mentioned that we only had a few days to decide. To decide what? And why the time limit?"

She chewed her bottom lip, then went to the diaper bag and dug through it until she found a small diary. "I don't expect you to take my word for it. I mean, you don't even like me, so why believe anything I have to say?"

"I never said I didn't like you." It was her effect on him, the feelings she drew from him with a mere look, that he didn't like.

"Shelly told me." She said that with far too much acceptance.

"Then she lied. We never even discussed you."

"Really?" Her brows lifted. "Why would she?"

"I have no idea." He accepted the book she handed to him. "What is this?"

She swallowed hard, leveled her shoulders and her gaze. "Shelly's parents want custody of Nicole."

His jaw locked. Over his dead body.

"They're not warm people, Gil," she added in a rush. "They've never paid any attention to Nicki. Whenever they were in the same room with her, they ignored her."

Glancing at his daughter, he found that hard to believe. Who could look at her and not fall instantly in love?

"They wanted Shelly to give her up."

"What?" Gil felt a cold sweat break out on his forehead. If that was true, then he might not ever have known about Nicki. That thought was too awful to contemplate.

"Even when Shelly brought her home from the hospital, they refused to get close to her in the hopes that one day she'd change her mind and put Nicki up for adoption. They thought of her as a . . . a blot on their good name. They talked about her like she was nothing more than a mistake."

On several occasions, he'd spoken with Shelly's parents. Not in depth, just superficial pleasantries common to business introductions. They'd seemed average enough to him. But they hadn't cared about their own grandchild?

Anabel touched his arm. "It's all in Shelly's diary."

He held the small, flat journal at his side, tapping it against his thigh. "But now, with Shelly gone, they want Nicole?"

"That's what they said. I don't understand it, but I don't trust them. They didn't want me to tell you about Nicki. They . . . well, they offered to pay me off."

Gil's chest swelled with anger. "What the hell does that mean?"

"They're rich," she told him. "They offered me money to keep quiet. They said you didn't ever need to know, that Shelly hadn't wanted you to know and I should abide by her wishes. But I couldn't do that."

Thank God.

She licked her lips. "Gil, by tomorrow morning they'll know I left with Nicki and they'll assume I came here."

Meaning they, too, would show up on his doorstep? Gil turned to to stare at his precious little dark-haired daughter. By the second, things became more complicated.

Anabel's hand tightened on his arm. "I won't let them have her, but I can't fight them on my own. You and I need each other. As a married couple, we stand a chance in the courts. Otherwise, we might both lose. And Nicole would lose more than anyone."

At least in this instance, he could reassure her. "I'm not going to let anyone hurt her, Anabel."

His confidence didn't alleviate her worry. "You don't understand." She pulled on him, forcing him back around. "Nicki is used to love, to hugs all day long and lots of kisses and playtime and . . ." She stopped to collect herself. "She wouldn't be happy with a cold, detached nanny and private schools and disdain from her grandparents.

She wouldn't be happy without *me*. Just read the diary tonight, and then we'll talk."

Because she looked so upset, Gil gave his promise. "All right. In the meantime, don't worry about anything, okay?"

She breathed hard in her upset. The seconds ticked by. "And the trial run?"

He wished like hell that she'd quit talking about sex. "I'll consider it." What *was* he saying?

Tension drained from her body, making her shoulders loose, her frown even out. "Thank you."

At her relieved gratitude, Gil could only shake his head. Everything that had transpired in the past hour was too unbelievable for words, culminating with that absurd *thank you*.

"So," Anabel said with new purpose, "you want to carry the little rat down to the van? Not that I can't. She's light as a feather. But I know you're dying to hold her and now's as good a time as any. If she wakes up, though, give her to me quick. You don't want her to start screaming her head off. Nicki's got a shout that can peel paint." As Anabel spoke, she stepped back into her sandals, took the diary from him and tucked it, with Nicki's juice bottle, into the diaper bag. Her movements were fluid and efficient, practiced in that way exclusive to mothers.

She hefted the bag over her shoulder. When he just stood there, she said, "Well?"

Gil took the few steps to the couch—and hesitated again. He hadn't known about her long, but already Nicole Lane Tyree had a permanent spot in his heart.

"Scoop her up, Gil. She won't break."

Being very gentle, he lifted her, and his precious bundle gave an indelicate juice belch into his shirt. Charmed, Gil positioned her against his shoulder, felt her stretch, and patted her back until she went boneless again. Holding his daughter against his heart felt more right than anything ever had in his life.

He glanced up—and his eyes met Anabel's. Seeing the way she smiled at them both felt right, too. What the hell was he going to do?

First, he'd read the diary. He needed all the facts before making decisions based on emotions—or worse, on lust. At the moment, he was feeling an excess of both, one thanks to a tiny little daughter now snoring in his ear.

The other thanks to a very sexy little bombshell currently swishing her delectable ass in front of him, on the way to moving into his home.

Life as he knew it had just been turned upside down.

Anabel jerked awake with a start when she felt Gil's fingertips brush her cheek. For a single moment, she misconstrued that tender touch, leaving her lost in a dream world where he actually wanted her. Except that she wasn't in a bed, the sun was bright in her eyes, and Gil stood outside the van, beside her open door.

Reality hit just as Gil's big hand settled warmly on her shoulder. She watched his gaze wander from her belly to her chest and finally to her face. He didn't smile, and wow, there was an inferno of heat in his eyes.

"You awake, sleepyhead?" he asked in a low, somewhat gravelly voice.

Oh no, she hadn't. Anabel's head slewed around, taking in her surroundings. She saw that they were parked in front of a very lovely home. She had passed out on him.

In the next instant, panic hit and she turned in the seat—but there was Nicole, smiling away at her, wide awake and bubbly.

"Since she's awake," Gil explained, "I didn't want to chance invoking that scream you warned me of."

It took Anabel a second to realize that Gil meant Nicole. "Oh, yeah." She pushed her hair from her face and rubbed her tired eyes. "You never know with her."

As if his patience had suddenly ended, Gil reached into the van and unfastened her seat belt. His knuckles brushed the sensitive skin of her belly and she caught her breath, startled by his forwardness. He ignored her reaction, catching her arms above her elbows and literally hoisting her out of her seat.

She stumbled into him and was struck anew at how solid and comforting he felt. He was a big man who hid his ruggedness behind a suave exterior. But she knew the truth. She knew that down deep inside, Gil Watson was a wild, carnal man.

He let her lean on him for a moment while she collected herself, and oh my, it felt nice. Her life had gotten so complicated, so scary lately, and uncertain, that borrowing some of his solid strength was more than necessary. She could have stood there feeling his heat and heartbeat, breathing in his scent forever, but Nicole laughed and Gil set her a few inches away.

She'd kicked her sandals off almost as soon as they'd gotten in the van and now she felt how the warm sunshine had heated his concrete drive. She also felt her own awkwardness. Had she snored? She hoped not, but given how long it had been since she'd had a restful sleep, she couldn't be sure. "Sorry I nodded off."

His expression enigmatic, Gil reached inside for her sandals. "No problem. You were exhausted. I'm just glad this jalopy got us here safe and sound. You need new . . . everything on it."

"Yeah." She couldn't very well take offense when it was true. "But it gets us where we're going."

He held her arm as she stepped into her sandals. "It got you here. We'll see about more reliable transportation in the morning."

Her defensive hackles rose. She didn't want him to think he needed to buy her things. But then she noticed him smiling at Nicole and realized his thoughtfulness was for his daughter, not her. Naturally, he wanted the little rat safe during transportation. "You want to get her out of her seat?"

Anticipation brightened his expression. "You think she'd mind? I don't want to frighten her."

"With me here, she'll be fine. Go ahead."

Gil nodded, then leaned through the open back door. He moved slowly, spoke softly. "Hello, Nicki. You ready to come on inside?"

"Juice." She reached out her small arms to Gil, and Anabel thought he might very well melt on the spot. It amused her to see him so affected by such a tiny person.

He unfastened Nicki's car seat and lifted her out.

Nicki put one arm around his neck, leaned back to frown into his face, and demanded again, "Juice."

Anabel laughed. "Patience is a virtue, rat. Let's get inside first, okay?"

At that moment, Nicki noticed several squirrels scurrying from limb to limb in the big elm trees in Gil's front yard. She started hopping up and down in Gil's hold, flailing her arms and kicking her pudgy legs. "Look! Look!"

"Squirrels," Gil told her while smiling ear to ear. "And lots of birds and some deer and occasionally a skunk or possum."

Anabel started to unload the van, but Gil took the diaper bag from her and turned her toward the walkway. "Come on. I'll show you around and then unload."

Nicki was still bouncing against his chest, trying to see everything at once while Anabel studied the expansive dimensions of his sprawling ranch house. "Gee, you think there'll be room for us?"

"Don't be facetious. It's actually modest."

"Uh-huh. Like the Taj Mahal, right?"

He grinned, a beautiful, bone-melting grin that made her want to lick his mouth. Luckily, Gil was too occupied hanging onto an energetic toddler to notice her reaction. "Candace is already gone by now, but she should have your room ready for you."

"Thank you."

"The basement's finished, with a workout room, hot tub, and home theater. I'll have to put a lock on that door so Nicole doesn't try to go down the steps."

"Good idea." He already showed a willingness to adjust, giving Anabel hope that it'd work out. "Usually she sits and scoots down on her fanny, but I worry. And since I didn't know what kind of house you'd have, I brought some baby-proofing stuff. Gates, rails for a bed, outlet covers . . . stuff like that."

Gil shifted Nicki, unlocked the front door, and pushed it open. "Does she get into a lot?"

"Only everything." Anabel took two steps inside and froze. "Holy sh—" She peered at Nicki, who watched her, wide-eyed. "Um, wow. I don't think we can baby-proof everything in here."

Gil just shrugged. "I'll move things around however you think is best."

Through the wide tile foyer, she could see into the living and dining rooms. They were huge, with eleven-foot ceilings that all but echoed her surprise. His tables were heavy marble with sharp corners and glass tops, complemented by the snowy white carpeting, drapes, and walls. *White,* Anabel thought with a sick feeling, already imagining the spills and spots and fingerprints soon to occur.

His furniture, thank heavens, was gray leather, so probably a little more resistant to two-year-old terrors. But all in all, his home looked like what she'd imagine—an expensive bachelor's pad not in the least suited to kids.

Nicki squirmed to be let down, and Gil, not knowing any better, obliged. The second her feet touched the floor she was off like a shot, tottering this way and that, careening dangerously close to hard corners, almost but never quite losing her balance.

"Oops!" Anabel raced after her, barely managing to snatch her up just before she crashed into a pewter-fronted fireplace. "You little speed demon," she teased Nicki while squeezing her close. Smiling, she turned to face Gil—and found him immobilized with shock.

It amused her how poleaxed he looked and she started to laugh.

"It's not funny," he wheezed, color just beginning to leech back into his face. "We need a padded room. Inflatable furniture. She should be wearing a damn helmet or something."

Nicki said, "Damn helmet."

Gil blinked, horrified, while Anabel said, "Damn is not a nice word, Nicki. Only adults can say it, okay?"

Nicki scowled at Gil.

"It's uncanny," Anabel told him, "how she can pick out only the curse words."

Holding a hand to the top of his head, Gil again looked around his home, and this time he appeared sick, drawing Anabel's sympathy. "Really, Gil, it's okay." And when he just stood there, she said to Nicki, "Tell your daddy it's okay, squirt."

Gil jerked around so fast, he nearly threw himself off balance. "She knows?"

Losing her smile, Anabel nodded. "I told her we were coming to meet her daddy. I wanted her to be excited about the trip. But right now, it's just a word to her."

Very gently, Anabel added, "It's up to you to make it more than that."

Nicki squirmed to get down, trotted over to Gil, and patted his knee. " 'S'okay," she said with so much exaggerated sympathy that Gil swallowed hard, dropped to his knees, and smoothed her hair with a shaking hand.

Concerned, Nicki looked back at Anabel. "Mommy?"

Anabel joined them. She crouched down next to Nicki. "Daddy looks like he could use a hug, huh?"

Nicki nodded. " 'S daddy sick?"

"No, munchkin, he's just so happy to meet you. You want to give him a hug?"

"He give me juice?"

"I'll get your juice."

" 'kay." She opened her arms and wrapped them around Gil's neck, squeezing with all her puny might before treating him to a loud smacking kiss on the cheek. She pulled back and wrinkled her nose. With her little hands holding his face, she stared into his eyes at close range and said, "You better now?"

Gil nodded. "I'm very good now." He swallowed. "Thank you."

She rubbed his cheeks experimentally then gave Anabel a wide grin. "He tickles."

Anabel put her palm to Gil's cheek, smoothing with her thumb. He had a five o'clock shadow and his jaw was rough, warm, and oh so masculine. "Yep, he's whiskery."

"Whiskery." Nicole nodded, and with an abrupt about-face, said, "I want my juice."

Gil drew a calming breath and stood. "Take a look around, make yourself at home. I'll go unload everything."

Because he still appeared to be in shock, Anabel worried. "Thanks."

"Hold onto her."

"I will."

He hesitated a second more, then turned and went outside again, carefully closing the door behind him. If he was this shook up in the first five minutes, how would he feel after a week? Anabel said a quick prayer that the joys of little Miss Nicole Lane Tyree outweighed the inconvenience, otherwise they were both in for a lot of trouble.

# Chapter Three

By suppertime, Gil's house looked very different. Bumpers covered all the sharpest corners of his furniture and gates cluttered every entryway. What used to be an open, airy space was now carefully sectioned off to contain a toddler's energy. Clean lines had disappeared, replaced with toys strewn into every conceivable corner. His once immaculate, state-of-the-art chrome kitchen now sported a variety of knee-high fingerprints.

Nicki touched everything. A lot.

Next to his ebony enamel dinette table was a colorful red and yellow highchair, looking much like a spring flower blooming on blacktop. Among his trendy black dishes, set behind clear glass cabinet doors, were several sipper cups of crayon-bright red, blue, and green. There was also a stack of equally bright bowls with hideous cartoon faces on them.

Nicole had recited her colors and counted her bites while eating. Judging by Anabel's praise, that was quite an accomplishment. She put a lemon yellow potty chair in the guest bathroom, explaining that Nicki no longer used regular diapers, but pull-ups that worked like diapers, but looked a lot like little girl panties. In a few more months, Nicki would be in regular underwear, but Anabel said she didn't want to push the issue right now with everything else going on.

Gil decided he needed to get a book or two to figure out some of this stuff. He had no idea what kids did, or when.

His daughter talked a lot about everything. Her sentences were endlessly long and he caught . . . oh, maybe every third or fourth word. The rest sounded like gibberish to him, though Anabel seemed to understand her just fine.

Nicole also hugged a lot. And kissed a lot. She was such a sweet little girl. Anabel was right about that. Nicole thrived on the love she gave and received.

There hadn't been much time to talk or discuss the issues while Anabel and Nicole settled in, but Gil enjoyed just watching her. Her expressions were priceless, the way her small face scrunched up in annoyance or anger, how she always squinted her eyes shut and lifted her chin when she smiled real big.

When she was sleepy, she sucked her thumb and tugged on a curl of hair. When she was sad or mad, her bottom lip stuck out and she crossed her arms tight over her chest. And she was a master at manipulation. She'd ask for something by punctuating the request with a hug or kiss and an innocent smile.

She delighted him, more so every minute.

Gil was busy setting up Anabel's computer in the bedroom he'd given her when Nicole came streaking through, shouting, "Daddy, Daddy, Daddy!"

His little angel was naked.

Grinning, Gil sat back on the floor and caught her as she hurled herself into his arms.

Anabel, carrying a disposable pull-up diaper and a T-shirt, rounded the corner hot on her heels. When she saw Nicki tucked close to Gil's chest, she pulled up in relief.

"Sorry. Sometimes she's like greased lightning." She flopped down next to Gil, propping her back against the wall.

"I don't mind." Just the opposite. He loved hugging her, and he especially loved being called *Daddy.*

"Nicki's a true nature child," Anabel told him while reaching out to pat the baby's butt. "Give her half a chance and she loses the clothes. She learned how to strip a few months ago, and she's been doing it ever since."

Gil rubbed Nicki's soft back and kissed her downy head. "Let's hope she outgrows that."

Anabel laughed. "At least before she hits her teens, huh?"

"Oh God." Gil squeezed her closer. "I can't think that far ahead. I'm still getting used to the idea of her being a baby. A teenager—no, it's too much to take in."

Anabel leaned into his shoulder in a show of camaraderie that felt far too intimate—and far too comfortable. She wasn't the type of woman he could ever treat like a pal, not when every cell in his body stayed on alert status whenever she was near.

But Anabel seemed unaware of his dilemma. She kept touching him, leaning into him, getting too close. She hugged his right biceps now and said, "One of the first things I bought when Nicki was born was a video camera."

Balancing Nicki against his free arm, Gil looked down at Anabel. "You have tapes of her?"

"Hours' and hours' worth. Her birthdays, Christmas, even some everyday stuff. There's a really funny one of her in a bubblebath—"

"Bath!" Nicki echoed, jumping up and down within the secure hold of Gil's arm. "Bath, bath!"

The shrill squeals of excitement almost pierced Gil's eardrums. "I take it she's fond of bath time?"

"Are you kidding? I think she was a fish in another life." Anabel released Gil to push to her feet. "And speaking of that, I better get her ready for bed before she gets her second wind. Bath, book, and bed—that's the routine, and a smart woman doesn't mess with success."

A new complication occurred to Gil. "Damn. The connecting bath in the room I gave you only has a shower."

Nicki gave him a beatific smile and said, "Damn."

"Nicole Lane, that is a bad word."

She stuck her finger in her mouth and glared at Gil, making it difficult for him to contain his smile. "I'll learn," he promised Anabel before handing Nicole up to her. "Give me just a second to finish connecting things here and I'll take you to my bathroom."

"Your bathroom?"

"It's the only tub." He had two and a half bathrooms, but only one tub—in the private bath off his bedroom. And he wasn't altogether sure it'd work for Nicole, being that the tub was so huge.

He quickly connected the rest of the cords on Anabel's computer system and plugged everything into a surge protector. "That should do it."

Anabel switched on the computer, watched her monitor light up, and nodded. "Looks like everything's working. Thanks. I don't have anything pressing, but if I want to meet the deadlines on my new website designs, I can't take too much time off."

The second Gil stood beside her, Nicole reached for him again. "Daddy."

"So I'm to be your mule, am I?" He felt her skinny arms go around his neck, her bare butt settle on his forearm, and thought to ask, "She can . . . ah, control herself, can't she?"

"Most of the time."

When his eyes widened, Anabel burst out laughing. She was as exuberant and carefree as his daughter. He liked that about her. "You're teasing me?" he asked, watching the way her green eyes twinkled.

"Yeah, I'm teasing." In a too familiar way, all things considered, she hooked her arm in his and started him toward the hall. "Without her pull-ups, she'll tell you if she needs to go."

They went down the hall and into his room. It struck Gil just how close Anabel would be to him during the night. The spare bedroom was at the far end of the hall on the right, with Gil on the opposite side and down a bit. His room was twice as big, but then, he hadn't been selfish when choosing it because there'd been no one else to consider. The third bedroom was mostly used for storage and to house his many bookcases filled with books. He'd already considered how he could rearrange things, fitting the bookcases into his den and changing the room into a playroom for Nicole. But in the meantime . . .

"I wonder if we should switch bedrooms. It might be better for you to have my room since it has a bathtub—for Nicole, I mean."

She looked flabbergasted by the offer. "Our room is fine."

He scowled. "But you might be more comfortable in the bigger room."

"No, I'd feel lost in a room that size." She grinned, but added, "Sometimes Nicki showers with me, but I try to keep that to a minimum. There are times when I want my privacy, too. So as long as you don't mind us trooping through here every now and then, we'll keep what we've got."

The idea of Anabel naked and wet flitted through Gil's mind before he could squelch the image. Maybe during her trial run, he'd get the opportunity to shower with her.

*What was he saying?*

Annoyed with his wandering thoughts, Gil shook his head and realized that Anabel had stopped in the middle of his bedroom to look around. She stared pointedly at his king-size bed. Candace had made it earlier so that the plump down quilt was smooth, the matching gray pillows placed just so. Anabel cocked a brow, but refrained from comment.

When they stepped into his black and gold bathroom, though, her mouth fell open. "It's as big as your bedroom."

He shrugged. "I like my luxuries." Like the immense tiled shower with five separate showerheads that could reach every aching muscle. And the heated towel bars, the double sink, the high ceilings.

"You call that a tub?"

Gil went straight to the partially sunken square bath and turned on the water. "You don't like it?" He knew that wasn't her problem, but decided he could tease, too.

"It's . . . decadent. And it could easily pass for a swimming pool." She, too, sat on the edge of the marble ledge surrounding the tub. "Wow. This is amazing."

With the temperature adjusted, Gil turned a knob that tightened the plug and the tub began to fill. Nicki tried to squirm loose, but Gil held onto her. "Will she be okay in there? I've never bathed a baby before."

Still a little bemused, Anabel shook her head. "I don't know. Let's don't fill it up too much."

He turned the water off when it was still very shallow. Keeping his eyes on Nicki as he lifted her inside, he said to Anabel, "If you'd like to take a soak sometime, feel free. With the whirlpool jets on, it's really relaxing."

"Hmm." She trailed her fingers through the water. "There's plenty of room for two." Her eyes slanted his way. "But then, I bet you already knew that, didn't you?"

Her not so subtle digging amused him. If she only

knew how long it'd been since he'd had a woman, she wouldn't worry. "Actually, this is the first time a female has been in my tub." Nicki, who remained oblivious to the undercurrents between the adults, managed to splash and thrash and soak them both. "And I'm not sure the little rat here counts." The second the words left his mouth, Gil wanted to choke himself. Damn it, now she had him calling Nicki a rat.

Anabel laughed while lathering Nicki's hair. "Oh, I dunno. I think it tells a lot about you."

Gil didn't like the speculative way she said that. "It tells you only that I'm a private man who tries to keep my relationships with women as simple as possible."

"Well, this relationship won't be simple."

He didn't know if she meant with Nicki or with her, and he decided not to ask. Anabel was so good with his daughter, so natural about the whole mother thing that he almost felt the need to reassess. If he hadn't already known her, if she looked different, he'd think she was born to be a mother.

"Get in," Nicole demanded of Anabel.

Gil raised a brow.

With a crooked smile, Anabel said, "Not this time, Toots."

Nicole aimed a calculating eye at Gil. "Get in."

Gil sputtered. "Uh, no. Thank you."

Stubborn determination brought a comical scowl to Nicki's face. "Get in, get in, *get in.*" She emphasized each demand by kicking her legs and slapping the water with her hands. Gil noticed that when she wanted something, his little angel spoke very clearly indeed.

Anabel had to scurry to support her so Nicole didn't slip in the tub. She got drenched in the bargain. The front of her T-shirt clung to her breasts and water dripped from her nose. "Bath time is over, rat." Laughing, she caught Nicole beneath the arms and lifted her out onto a thick, soft towel. "Look at what you did. You got me and your daddy both soaked."

Gil hadn't realized he was wet until Anabel said that. He'd been too busy studying the way her nipples puckered from the drenching and how clearly he could see them beneath her soaked tee.

He straightened abruptly. "If you can manage on your own, I have a few things to take care of."

Anabel looked hurt by his abrupt withdrawal. "I've been managing just fine all along. Go ahead. I don't want to interrupt your routine." She did a double take at that, and shrugged self-consciously. "Any more than we already have, I mean."

He started to tell her that she wasn't interrupting at all, but Nicole was already busy trying to play and Anabel was laughing at her—and stupidly, Gil felt left out. He shoved his hands in his pockets and walked from the bathroom, unsure what to do with himself. On a normal night, he'd have gone through some paperwork, maybe watched ESPN for a bit or worked out, then retired. But tonight wasn't normal.

He remembered the diary and fetched it from Nicole's diaper bag, then headed to the den. His desk here was smaller, but his chair was identical in size and color to the one in his downtown office. He settled in and began skimming the pages.

It didn't take him long to realize just how unhappy Shelly had been. She chronicled all the ways she'd disappointed her parents; it seemed that from an early age their expectations for Shelly had been so high that she'd never been able to please them.

Time and again, Shelly's parents let her know that she hadn't quite measured up. They even criticized her business skills, which was absurd. She ran a chain of novelty stores and was quite successful with it. Gil had met Shelly through business, and she was as professional and able as anyone. She was one of his best buyers, and she could negotiate prices like a shark.

They also berated her on her friends, namely Anabel. That made Gil wince. Anabel had read the diary, so she knew how disparaging Shelly's parents had been. Unfortunately, many of their remarks were on a level with his own personal thoughts. Only now, he knew he was wrong. Anabel might appear free-spirited with her earrings and tattoos and laid-back manner, but she'd still managed to take care of his daughter all on her own.

Worst of all, Shelly's parents hated it that she'd "shamed them" by having Nicole without benefit of marriage.

Guilt got a stranglehold on him when he read her next scrawled words: *They'll definitely approve of Gil for a son-in-law.* She'd obviously been counting on him to come back to her and profess his love.

But Gil hadn't asked Shelly to marry him. Instead, he'd broken off any romantic ties, and so, just as Anabel claimed, Shelly's parents had pressured her to give Nicole away. Given what he'd just read in her diary, they'd continued to press her right up until the day she'd died.

They were Nicole's grandparents, but they hadn't wanted her, had never warmed to her. Not once.

Why the hell did they want her now?

Gil closed the journal, unable to read any more. He already knew how his family would react to Nicole— they'd love her as much as he did. She'd be welcomed with open arms and assured of unwavering support. She'd be doted on, cherished, and protected.

It enraged Gil to think of what Shelly had gone through, and at the same time, he was awed at the steps Anabel had taken to make things right for Nicole. Shelly hadn't known how to be a mother, but Anabel had never let Nicole feel slighted in any way. His daughter had been well loved and cared for—by Anabel.

Gil stood to pace for a few minutes, chewing over complications and procedures, deciding on a course of action. The grandparents would have to be dealt with, and that meant he'd need to cancel all his appointments tomorrow. He wouldn't take the chance of leaving Anabel in case they arrived unannounced. She'd handled enough on her own already.

Once he'd made up his mind, Gil felt urgent need to put his plans in action. He called Alice's answering machine at work and left her instructions to clear the next couple of days for him. She'd rearrange his schedule the moment she arrived in the office.

Next, Gil called his lawyer, Ted Thorton, at home. He wanted all the legalities out of the way. He gave Ted Shelly's name and last address so he could look up her parents and inform them that Gil was claiming permanent custody of his daughter. He then requested that changes be made to all of his investments, as well as his will. He wanted Nicole noted as his beneficiary in every regard. Ted promised to get right on it, and once he had the papers in order, he'd meet with Gil to get the necessary signatures.

One decision led to another, until he could no longer put Anabel from his mind. She had a stake in everything, whether he wanted her to or not. Throughout the day, he'd watched her with Nicole and now he accepted the truth—he couldn't separate them.

Anabel would accompany him to meet the lawyer, Gil decided, so that she knew his plans. He would put her mind to rest on that score, at least. She, as well as his daughter, would be taken care of.

At that moment, Anabel stepped into the room. Her wet shirt still clung to her breasts, her light brown hair was still mussed, and she looked beyond wary. She put her hand on top of Nicole's head. "You busy?"

"Not at all." Gil slipped the diary into a drawer and

slid it shut. "I was just contemplating fate." He gave her a smile he hoped would ease her.

It didn't. "I usually read Nicki a story before bed, but since I still need to shower, I thought maybe you'd do the honors."

Nicole held up a thick book with both hands. "I want dis one."

Gil strolled forward and stood staring down at this tiny person whose life would have been so different if he'd only known about her. It wouldn't, he realized, have necessarily been better. Not with Anabel Truman guarding her like a mother hen.

Nicki's freshly washed hair had dried into tight ringlets around her cherubic face. Her nightgown was a soft, pale yellow and dragged the floor, almost hiding her itty-bitty toes. She was a happy, carefree, and well-loved child, and he owed Anabel more than he could ever repay her.

"I'd be honored," Gil told them both with grave formality, and then, as naturally as if he'd been doing it forever, he scooped up his daughter and held her against his chest. Again, with a naturalness that surprised him, he slid his other arm around Anabel's waist. For only a moment, he appreciated her slenderness, her softness, before steering them all toward the hall. "Take your time. Soak in the tub if you want. We'll be fine."

Anabel shook her head. "No, not this first night. I want to make sure she's settled."

Gil knew it would do no good to argue with her. "I'm sure you know best."

She gave him a disbelieving, wide-eyed look.

They stepped into the spare bedroom. The blankets on the bed had been turned down and temporary rails, attached by sliding fold-out poles beneath the mattress, lined each side. Anabel intended to sleep with Nicole tonight, but Gil considered that a very temporary situation. How he'd remedy it, he didn't yet know.

On impulse, he kissed Anabel's forehead and left her open-mouthed and speechless at the bathroom door, then pretended to drop Nicole in the bed. She squealed and laughed, and Gil knew this was a routine— with mother and daughter—that he could quickly grow accustomed to.

Anabel stood there a moment longer, until Gil had pulled a chair over to the bed, then she turned and went into the bathroom, closing the door behind her. Gil heard the shower start, but he refused to picture her stripping, or wet, or soapy . . .

"Daddy read."

"Right." Shaking his head to clear it, Gil took the book and flipped through the pages, looking for a story.

Nicole scampered to the end of the bed, slid out, and came around to crawl up on Gil's lap. She poked him in the throat with a pointy elbow and stepped on his testicles twice before settling herself. Gil grunted, dodged a third stomp, but didn't chastise her. He let out a sigh of relief when she quit squirming. "Comfy now?"

She nodded, pushed on his chest, and said, "Mommy's softer."

He'd just bet she was. And then because he couldn't help himself, he asked, "Anyone ever read to you besides your mommy?" Like any other men that Anabel might have dated.

"No. Jus' Mommy." She carefully turned pages in the big book until she reached a particular story. The book had a lot of pictures and Nicole focused on one. "Dis is the mommy bear. Dis is the daddy bear. And dis is the brudder bear."

Gil gave her a squeezing hug. "Very good."

"Now you read." She curled into his shoulder, closed her eyes on an enormous yawn, and stuck her thumb in her mouth.

"All right, sweetheart. I'll read." And he did. Unlike the children's books Gil remembered, this one was more detailed. Before long, he found himself engrossed in the story.

He was still reading some fifteen minutes later when he felt Anabel's presence. He glanced up to find her in the bathroom doorway, a crooked smile on her face and fat tears in her green eyes.

He started to speak, but she put a finger to her mouth. "The rat is out for the night," she whispered.

Startled, Gil glanced down, and sure enough, Nicole was boneless against him, her head dropped back on his arm, her wet thumb now against his chest.

Gil made a wry face. "I guess this means I don't get to see how the story ends?"

Anabel sauntered away from the bathroom. "I'll tell you all about it later." She lifted Nicole from his lap. As she bent close, Gil could smell the lotion on her dewy skin, the shampoo scent in her still damp hair. She wore another T-shirt, this one of soft cotton and long enough to hang to midthigh.

She laid Nicole in the bed on her side and pulled the sheet up to her waist. Her hand lingered, smoothing Nicole's hair, stroking her small shoulder. The love that Anabel felt for Nicole was almost painful to witness.

Gil couldn't recall ever seeing a baby put to bed, and he noted how small Nicole looked among the bed-clothes. "Should she be in a crib?"

"No, not anymore." Her smile was teasing. "Your daughter is like a monkey—she likes to climb. Something closer to the ground is safer." Anabel switched on a night-light, then turned out the brighter lamp.

Shadows filled the room, leaving no more than a soft

glow to see by. Gil still stood there, unable to pull himself away. He hadn't seen Shelly grow big with the pregnancy, hadn't felt his daughter kick or watch her be born. Despite all that, he felt such an unbreakable bond to this child of his, he knew he'd die for her if necessary.

Anabel touched his shoulder. "I know how you feel, Gil, because I feel the same."

Startled, he stared at her. Could she read his mind?

"She's pretty incredible, isn't she?" Anabel's smile wobbled the tiniest bit. "Even when she's being a hellion, yelling because she's too tired or she doesn't get her way, I just marvel at what a miracle she is and thank God that I have her, that she *can* yell and that she feels safe and . . ."

The rest of her words got choked off. Anabel shook her head in embarrassment and slipped out of the room.

Yes, she knew how he felt. Gil bent to place a barely there kiss on Nicole's head, then went to find her mother. They had some issues to resolve, and no time seemed better than the present.


Anabel stood in the formal dining room, her arms wrapped around herself, staring out the patio doors. Gil's yard was immaculately kept, displayed by decorative lighting. It was a big yard for one person. Perfect for a swing set or playhouse—things she'd always wanted for Nicole but couldn't give her.

She knew the second that Gil stepped up behind her.

He was far too close, his warmth touching her back, when he said, "I left the door open a little."

Anabel nodded. Somehow, she'd known he would.

"She'll sleep through the night?"

"I hope. Usually yes. She's a sound sleeper. But here . . .

I don't know." *Great way to give a straight answer, Anabel,* she grumbled to herself. She hated showing her nervousness and anticipation.

Gil's hands settled easily on her shoulders, making her catch her breath. "Will it frighten her," he asked very near her ear, "to wake up in a strange place?"

Anabel turned to face him. Earlier, he'd lost his tie and opened several buttons on his shirt, but he hadn't changed. He seemed very comfortable in the professional suit, whereas she smothered in anything dressier than jeans. "I won't let her be afraid. Ever."

The right side of his mouth curled up in a crooked smile, while his gaze moved over her face, lingering on her lips. "You're ferociously protective of her, aren't you?"

She couldn't get a single word out, not with him looking at her like that. She shrugged.

Cupping her face, Gil smoothed his thumbs over her cheeks and across her bottom lip. She knew what was about to happen and her heart hammered in her chest.

"About that trial run," Gil murmured.

Anabel started to say "Yes," but his mouth covered hers, warm and firm. Oh God, he tasted good. Better than good, and if he thought she could be cavalier about this, he was sadly mistaken.

She clutched at him, relishing the feel of firm muscles in his shoulders, the heat of him. She pressed closer, aligning her body with his, trying to absorb him. She opened her mouth and accepted his tongue and groaned with the pleasure of it.

Two big steps and Gil had her pressed to the patio doors, on her tiptoes, his mouth eating at hers. She tried to get the rest of his buttons undone so she could touch his bare flesh, but her hands felt clumsy and she heard one button ping against the doors.

Breathing hard, his body taut, Gil lifted his head.

"Come on." He took her hand and practically raced her to his bedroom. The second they stepped inside he closed the door, quietly clicked the lock, and reached for her again.

"Wait." Anabel flattened both hands against his chest. She'd dreamed of this moment for three long years. "Just . . . wait."

Gil stared at her, breathing hard, his impatience palpable.

Slowly, Anabel backed him into the door. She took her time now, carefully sliding each button from its hole, tugging his fine shirt out of his slacks, stripping his chest bare. Gil closed his eyes and let his head drop back against the door. Anabel heard him swallow, heard the racing of his breath.

She pushed the shirt off his shoulders and down his arms. His chest was incredible, lightly covered in dark hair, hard and wide, rippling with lean muscles. She stroked the crisp hair, learning the feel of him, then found his nipples.

His breath caught, but she ignored it, toying with him a moment, then leaning forward to taste him with her tongue.

"Jesus." His muscles knotted tight.

But she didn't stop there. She dropped to her knees and went to work on his shoes.

"Anabel." His shaking hand touched the top of her head, his fingers threading into her damp hair.

"This is my fantasy, Gil. Let me have it."

He didn't say anything else, just lifted each foot as needed so she could strip off his shoes and socks. He braced his feet apart and reached for his belt buckle, but Anabel brushed his hands away. Looking up at him from her submissive position, she smiled suggestively. "*My* fantasy."

His hands dropped to his sides.

She loved the sound his belt buckle made as it clinked free, the rasp of the leather sliding through his belt loops. Beneath his fly, his erection swelled and throbbed, enticing her. She wanted him naked, but she also wanted to savor each moment. Leaning forward, she brushed her cheek against his cloth-covered crotch, inhaling deeply of his rich, aroused scent.

Gil gave a low groan and stiffened.

Pleased with that reaction, Anabel slid her hands around to hold his muscled backside and teased him with her teeth. She nipped carefully, grazing his length through the light wool material.

His hands fisted and pressed to the wall at either side of his hips.

She groaned, too, loving him so much it hurt. Quickly, before he decided to take over, she opened his pants button and drew the zipper down, allowing the metal teeth to slowly part over his swollen erection. His patience shot, Gil shoved his slacks and underwear down and off, then kicked them away.

He was naked.

Awed, overwhelmed, Anabel sat back on her heels and took in the sight of him.

He made a low growling sound. "Anabel, I want you naked, too."

"Soon."

"Now."

The smile came without her permission. He was every bit the commanding man of authority. "All right." She rose to her feet. Holding his gaze, she reached under her shirt and skimmed her shorts and panties down. "But I'm not done with you yet."

His gaze burned over her, urging her to haste. "We'll see."

She dropped her shorts to the side and reached for

the hem of her shirt. "Promise me you'll let me taste you first."

As if pained, his eyes closed. "Anabel."

"You know you want me to," she taunted, and pulled the shirt free.

His eyes snapped open and he went very still as he looked at her, taking an extra long time to study her belly and the small decorative jewel in her navel.

His jaw locked. "You like giving head?"

If he thought to disconcert her, he could forget it. "I'll like sucking on you."

In a heartbeat, he went willing, resting back against the door again, his limbs deliberately loose while his cock twitched and his chest swelled with his laboring breaths.

Feeling wicked and sexy, Anabel knelt in front of him again. She tasted the firm flesh of his abdomen first, dipped her tongue in his navel, bit his hipbone— then curled her hand around him, held him still, and swallowed him deep.

His head tipped farther back, his knees locking tight. *"Yes."*

It was better than she'd imagined, the sounds he made, the way he fought to hold still, the explosive moan when he gave up, grasping her head and moving with her mouth, thrusting in, feeling the hollows of her cheeks with his thumbs.

"I'm going to come," he whispered harshly.

Anabel drew him deeper still, letting him know what she wanted. At the same time, she cradled his balls, very gently squeezing, urging him, and with a low shout, he exploded.

Slumped against the door, his eyes closed and his chest heaving, he curled his hands around her head and drew her away. Anabel gave one last, lingering lick to the head of his penis, felt him flinch, and smiled.

For the moment, she was content to enjoy her victory, to sit there and peruse his gorgeous body and think about what was to come next. Her entire body felt alive, warm and soft in some places, ripe and swollen in others.

She licked her lips, tasting him again, salty and rich, and she wanted to start all over.

Gil was watching her. His face was flushed, his thickly lashed eyelids partially open. "Should I come down there," he murmured, "or are you going to come up here?"

Anabel reached a hand toward him. He hauled her up, proving that he might be winded, but was far from spent. He further made that point by scooping her up as easily as he had Nicole.

"What are you doing?"

"Putting you in my bed so I can give a little payback."

"Yeah?" She could hardly wait. And in fact, she didn't have to.

The second her back touched the mattress, Gil settled on top of her. He took her mouth, stifling her moan as his hands found and kneaded her breasts. He sucked at her tongue—and tugged at her nipples.

The pleasure was so acute, Anabel arched her back. Gil slid one arm beneath her, keeping her positioned that way so he could kiss a path down her throat to her breasts.

"I always wondered if you had sensitive nipples. Do you?"

"I don't know." At the moment, she barely knew her own name.

"Let's find out." He drew her left nipple into his mouth, suckling softly, stroking easily with his tongue. He was being so gentle, it startled her when he increased the pressure, drawing hard, pressing her nipple to the roof of his mouth.

His fingers at her other breast mimicked the sensation, squeezing just so much, pulling and tugging.

Anabel twisted, fighting against the dual sensations while at the same time wanting more. It did her no good. Since he'd already come, Gil was in no particular hurry. Instead, he seemed determined to drive her crazy, spending so much time on her nipples while other parts of her body grew hot and wet.

He moved to the side of her, propped himself up on one elbow, and stared at her belly. "So?"

Anabel could barely breathe. No way could she hold still. "What?"

"Are they sensitive?"

He sounded utterly unaffected while she was going insane.

"Yes."

"Good." He bent again, licking each nipple in turn while wedging one big hand between her thighs. She caught her breath, waited, but he didn't do anything other than hold her. The warmth of his hard palm was stimulating, but she wanted his fingers inside her. She needed his fingers inside her.

"Gil?"

"Shhh." He licked his way down her body to her belly. "You are so fucking sexy."

His tongue dipped, teasing her navel, nudging the tiny belly button jewelry, tickling her so that she tried to turn away.

"Hold still." He anchored her by sinking his middle finger deep into her, drawing her to an immediate stillness. Just that, just that one finger, and she felt ready to come. Her inner muscles clamped tight around him, but other than that, she didn't move.

"That's better," Gil whispered, teasing her again with his tongue. Her nipples were wet and tight from his mouth, her belly twitching with the tickling, teasing licks and prods of his tongue, and she had to fight the urge to lift her hips, to thrust against that thick, invading finger.

He stared up her body at her face, making certain she understood. "Good girl."

"I . . . I need to come now, too."

"And you will. More than once." She started to let out her breath when he added, "But not yet," then nibbled his way down to her hipbones.

It seemed he was determined to taste her everywhere. Her thighs, the backs of her knees. And all the while, his finger was inside her. Just when she thought she couldn't play his game anymore, Gil situated himself between her thighs. "Open your legs for me."

She did, immediately. He stared down at her sex, his expression intent, determined. His finger pressed more firmly into her, and with his other hand he smoothed her pubic hair, touched her clitoris with a light stroke of his thumb, and said, "You can come now."

And oh God, she did. The pleasure washed through her, rippling through her thighs, twisting inside her. Gil watched, his thumb brushing her very gently while his finger filled her. She could feel his breath, heard the smile in his voice when he said, "That's good . . ."

Anabel couldn't believe what had happened. She was still numb, her body heavy and sated when Gil shifted, sliding his hands under her to raise her hips.

"Gil?" She lifted her head and stared down at him. He was between her thighs, his dark hair mussed, his mouth damp, his expression hot.

"Time to come again, Anabel. Then I'll get a rubber and make love to you proper. But first . . ."

She felt the damp stroke of his tongue and dropped her head back against the pillow with a low cry. She was already sensitive from her orgasm, her vulva hot and full. Gil wasn't timid about tasting her. He licked and sucked and stroked deep with his tongue until she was crying out, twisting and shaking, and just when she knew it was too much, he closed his mouth around her clitoris and sucked.

A tidal wave of sensation rushed through her, making her thighs shiver and shake, her belly hollow out, her back arch. He kept it going, sliding two fingers into her, back out, in again. She didn't know if it'd ever end and didn't really care.

Her mind was still blank of cognizant thought when Gil very gently kissed her cheek. "You still with me, Anabel?"

"Mmm."

His mouth smiled against her jaw. "That's good. Because I'm not done yet."

A groan erupted. She honestly didn't know if she could muster up any strength to accommodate him.

"You were awfully easy. But then, so was I." He continued to press tiny, affectionate kisses to her cheek, her ear, her temple. His big hand rested on her belly, one hairy thigh over hers. "It had been a long time for me," he admitted. "I guess too long."

Anabel forced her eyes open. "Why?"

His gaze went from her eyes to her mouth. "Who knows? I thought I'd lost interest. I said I was too busy. Maybe it's just that no one really appealed to me."

She lifted a hand to his sweaty shoulder. "It's been three years since I was with anyone else."

Beneath her hand, his muscles stiffened. "Three years?"

Anabel shrugged. "Shelly was pregnant and upset and I spent a lot of time with her. Then Nicole was born. I didn't really have a baby-sitter, and I was afraid if I left her with Shelly . . ."

"That she'd take her away." His voice was low, a little angry, somber and accepting. He cupped her cheek and turned her face toward him. He wore a frown, but as he bent his head and kissed her, she felt his grave gentleness, and his silent thank you.

Amazingly enough, the second his mouth touched hers, Anabel felt revived. She loved him. For her, loving Gil was the biggest reason that she'd been celibate so long. True, she always put Nicki first, but it hadn't been a hardship to give up men when Gil was the only man she wanted.

She turned toward him, sliding her arms around his neck and pressing her belly to his. Gil rolled to his back and pulled her atop him, adjusting her legs so that she straddled his hips.

"I want you to ride me, Anabel. I want to play with your breasts and belly while I'm inside you, and I want to watch you come."

Just hearing his intent was almost enough for her. She said, "All right. Just tell me where to find a rubber."

# Chapter Four

Three years, Gil thought, unable to fathom such a thing, especially for a woman as sensual and open as Anabel.

Holding her hips with one hand, he reached past her to the nightstand and pulled open the top drawer. Anabel saw the packet of condoms and pulled one out.

She flipped it like you would a fan. "I'm out of practice, so let me know if it doesn't feel right." After tearing the silver package open with her teeth, she held his cock and teasingly rolled the rubber on.

Not feel right? Gil considered the touch of her small soft hand around him, the glint in her eyes as she concentrated on the task, wonderful, mind-blowing torture.

"On your knees."

She lifted up, bracing her hands on his chest. "Like this?"

Gil didn't answer. With two fingers, he stroked her, making sure she was wet enough, opening her, preparing her. "Now ease down."

Her smile taunted. "You like to give orders, don't you?"

He met her gaze. "Sit down, Anabel."

She laughed, and slowly sank onto him. The head of his cock passed her delicate lips, then got hugged by the hungry clasp of her body. She paused, drawing a breath, closing her eyes.

"A little more," he urged through clenched teeth. He held her hips and pressed up while drawing her down. They both moaned with the incredible sensation of him sinking inside her, stretching her a bit, fitting snugly. Her fingers curled against his chest, leaving half moons from her nails. Her head tipped back and she thrust her breasts forward.

Gil drew her down so he could latch onto a tightly drawn nipple—then he began to thrust. He wanted to be easy but he couldn't manage it. Never mind his own long abstinence; knowing Anabel had been three years without sex drove him wild. He loved seeing her shifting expressions, how her teeth bit into her bottom lip, the way her belly drew in, how her thighs gripped him. He squeezed her soft ass, guiding her until she found his rhythm, then slipped one hand around the front of her and wedged his fingers between their bodies.

She was hot, wet, gasping and making low, sexy sounds deep in her throat. Using the tips of his fingers, Gil applied pressure where he knew she'd need it most. Far too quickly, she started to come. She dropped forward to take his mouth, and Gil rolled, putting her under him again, slowing so that her climax was suspended.

*"Gil."*

"Shhh. Easy now." He kissed her again, long, deep, wet kisses while slowly sliding in and out, giving her only shallow thrusts, keeping her on the edge.

She tried to lock her legs around him, probably in hopes of taking over. Gil caught her knees and pressed them forward and out, opening her completely, leaving her vulnerable. Anabel went still, a little apprehensive, he knew, but nowhere near ready to call it quits.

"Am I hurting you?"

Breathlessly, she said, "No," but she strained against him, trying to hold him back.

"Good." He eased her legs farther apart. "Then relax."

She drew two deep breaths, trying to do as he asked.

Very slowly, Gil pressed forward, deeper, deeper . . .

*"Oh God."*

"Relax for me, Anabel." He no sooner growled the words than he felt the start of her climax. Gil marveled at her. Her eyes had darkened with trepidation, and still she enjoyed him. She quit holding him off and instead embraced him with a soft, throaty, vibrating moan of surrender.

Gil lost it. He thrust hard, fast, aware only of the draining release, the powerful rush of scalding sensation. It was more than he had ever experienced—more than he'd known existed.

Some moments later, utterly sated, he became aware of Anabel squirming beneath him. "Gil? My thighs are killing me."

Oh hell. He realized he still had her legs caught up in his elbows. He groaned, straightened away from her, and fell to his back. His bedroom smelled of sex. It smelled of Anabel. He took a deep breath, then let it out on a sigh. "Sorry," he murmured.

"All things considered," she teased, "you're forgiven."

Gil turned his head on the pillow to look at her. "What things?"

Her eyes were closed, but she smiled. "Three orgasms?"

"Ah." Knowing he had to do the manly thing, he pushed himself from the bed and stumbled on shaky legs into the bathroom. He disposed of the condom, washed, and filled a glass with water. When he returned to the bedroom, his door was open and his bed was empty.

Frowning, he stepped out into the hall and found

Anabel peeking into Nicole's room. He noted with some disappointment that she'd pulled her tee and panties back on. But with a toddler in the house, he supposed some sacrifices were necessary.

He didn't own any pajamas, but he went back and got his boxers, then joined her. "She's still asleep?"

"Snoring like a bear cub." Anabel turned to him with a smile. Her gaze skipped over him head to toe and back again. "I just wanted to make sure."

*Like any good mother would.* Gil took her arm and guided her back to his room. This time he left his door open but turned the lights out. Without a word, he urged her into his bed, then climbed in beside her and pulled the sheet over them.

She immediately curled into his side. That felt right. More than right. He closed his eyes and said, "Sleep."

She was silent a moment before asking, "Here?"

It was fast, but Gil didn't care. "Yeah, here."

Anabel said nothing more. She just snuggled against him and quickly drifted into deep slumber. And like his daughter, she snored.


Sometime late in the night, Gil woke to the feel of damp breath in his face. He opened his eyes, then started with surprise. Nicole was on the bed beside him, leaning on his chest, her nose almost touching his.

"I'm wet," she explained in a loud stage whisper.

"Oh." Gil's brain scrambled at such a predicament. He was in his underwear. Did two-year-olds notice or care about such things?

"I can't find Mommy."

She sounded ready to cry. Gil quickly got over his squeamishness. This was his daughter, for crying out loud, and Anabel was exhausted. "She's right next to me," Gil told her.

"Why?"

*Why?* "She . . . got cold."

"Oh."

"Do you want me to change you? That way we can let your mommy sleep."

No answer.

Gil carefully caught Nicki and lifted her away so he could get out of the bed. Her gown was soaked, but he still cradled her close to his chest. "Let's be real quiet and sneaky, okay? Won't your mommy be surprised?"

Nicki had no comment on that, but she rubbed her little hand on his chest. "You're whiskery."

"Not too much."

"I'm not whiskery."

"No, and neither is your mommy."

"Only daddies?"

"That's right." He slipped out of the room and quietly pulled the door shut behind him. "Do you know where your nightgowns are?"

She tugged experimentally on his chest hair. "No."

Wincing, Gil untangled her fingers and set her down in her room. Together, they rummaged around until she approved a soft shirt to sleep in. The pull-up diaper was thankfully easy. He wasn't altogether sure he could have managed the other kind, not without any practice to his credit.

After he'd changed her wet sheets and was ready to tuck her in, Nicole stuck out her bottom lip. She looked half asleep on her feet, but still she said, "I want a story."

So he'd get to hear the ending of the book after all? Gil could handle that. He settled in the chair with Nicole in his lap, and had barely finished one page before he heard her breathing even out in sleep. Feeling very paternal and proud, he slipped Nicole into her bed, stood there a moment to make sure she wouldn't awaken, and then headed back to his own room.

Anabel had slept through it all, proving just how little rest she'd gotten lately.

He, on the other hand, was now wide awake and very aware that he had a warm, sensual woman curled up in his bed. Not just any woman, but Anabel. He'd always been drawn to her, no matter how he fought it. But now he liked and respected her, too. She'd done so much. Without complaint, she'd taken on responsibilities that weren't hers, and managed them admirably.

She was not only sexy, but strong. She wasn't just outrageous, she was also bighearted. She was . . . beyond appealing. Physically and emotionally. And now she was here, in his bed.

Moonlight flooding through the windows formed a halo around her face. He could see her soft hair tangled on the pillow. She had one hand tucked beneath her cheek and one slender leg bent at the knee, drawn up in what Gil saw as an invitation. Of course, in his frame of mind, even her deep, even snores seemed inviting. He was in a very bad way.

What the hell, he decided, and again locked his door.

Moving silently so that he didn't disturb her yet, Gil pulled the blankets off the bed. Anabel shifted, but didn't awaken. She had beautiful legs, slim and sleek, but it was her fanny that caught and held his attention now.

Gil pushed his boxers off. Given it hadn't been that long since he'd come twice, he stared at his boner with some chagrin, then donned a condom before getting into bed behind Anabel. He leaned close and smelled her hair, a familiar smell now, arousing and comforting at the same time. Gently, he brushed his nose against her, over her ear, her temple, down to her nape. He wallowed in the pleasure of having her near. She slept on.

Using only one finger, Gil traced her graceful spine down to the small of her back, continuing to her bottom, and on still until he found the incredible warmth between her legs. He lightly stroked, using only the tip of that one finger, and felt her soften, swell.

She made a sound in her sleep, one that sounded of growing urgency and awareness.

Gil continued to tease, to arouse her. He wanted to take her from behind. It was nice that way, giving him easy access to her breasts and sex. He could push deep while fingering her, teasing her nipples.

Biting off a groan at those erotic images, he slid one arm under her so he could keep her close, in just the right position, at the same time kneading a soft breast. "I want you, Anabel."

She fluttered awake. "Gil?"

Roughly, he stripped her panties down far enough that he could get inside her. He positioned himself, held her still, and with one firm thrust, he was there.

*"Gil."*

His heart pounded with the excitement, the power of it. "Push back against me, Anabel."

And with a welcoming moan, she did.

Oh yeah, his life was different now. As far as Gil was concerned, it was infinitely better.


Anabel felt a hand on her breast and groaned. Did the man never rest? Okay, so she knew he was sexually uninhibited, but no one had said anything about insatiable. "Go away."

A husky, male laugh sounded in her ear; solid morning wood nudged her hip. Against her ear, he whispered, "How late does Nicki sleep?"

Oh, good grief. She was actually sore. Deliciously sore, but still, she needed a little time to recoup. He'd really taken the whole trial-run thing to heart. "Um . . . what time is it?"

"No, you answer first."

Knowing he was on to her, Anabel grinned. "Gee, I expect her any minute."

"Liar." Gil turned her to her back and rose over her, smiling with sensual intent.

And Nicki shoved the door open. Vaguely, Anabel remembered Gil unlocking the door after making love to her again. "Time to get up!" Like a small whirlwind, she burst into the room and scrambled up onto the bed, bursting with morning cheer.

In a flash, Gil jerked back to his own side of the bed and pulled the covers all the way to his chin. "Nicole . . ."

"Daddy!" Nicki landed between them, liked how the mattress bounced, and began to jump.

Laughing, Anabel pushed herself to a sitting position and caught Nicki. She dragged her over her lap and gave her a resounding smooch on the cheek. "Did you sleep well, rat?"

"Daddy changed me."

"He did?" Anabel noticed then that Nicki's nightgown was gone, replaced by a tee. She glanced at Gil.

He, too, had sat up, and now he had one of the plump bed pillows over his lap. "It was a small matter of a wet nightgown. Nothing too difficult."

"He read to me."

"Twice in one night?" It sounded like they'd been up having a good time without her. "Aren't you the lucky little girl."

Nodding, Nicole confided in a loud whisper, "Daddy's whiskery *all* over."

Gil sputtered. "She commented on my chest. She also pointed out that you aren't whiskery."

"I see." But she didn't, not really. It made her feel odd to know that Gil had managed a midnight crisis without her. Why hadn't she awakened? Why hadn't *he* awakened her?

But she knew why. Gil was a very capable man. She'd been fooling herself to think he needed her. For anything.

And she trusted him. It was why she'd come to him in the first place. Not only was it the right thing to do, but in her heart she'd known that he'd be a terrific father. He wouldn't completely remove her from Nicole's life, but would he let her stay in his?

As if he'd read her mind, Gil put a hand on her shoulder. "We decided to let you sleep. You were pretty wiped out."

Anabel nodded. After all her worries, she'd finally felt safe enough to sleep soundly. She didn't doubt that if Nicki had wanted her, she'd have come awake in a rush. But Gil had handled things, proving he was not only a sensitive, astounding, *tireless* lover, he was also considerate beyond belief.

She felt lost, unsure what to do next.

Very gently, Gil smoothed her hair. "If you'll throw blinders on the little monkey there, I think I'll escape into the bathroom to shave and dress. Then we can start on breakfast."

"Stay put," Anabel told him. "We'll head out and give you your privacy."

She rose from the bed, but rather than follow, Nicki threw herself against Gil and said, "I want pancakes." She ensured obedience by giving him a sweet kiss on the cheek and a tight hug. Only after finishing that did she allow Anabel to lead her from the room. Gil, the sop, looked ready to rush off in search of his griddle.

She had just finished helping Nicki dress when a knock sounded on Gil's front door. He hadn't come out of his bedroom yet, so with Nicki racing beside her, Anabel went to the living room. Before she could reach the door, a key rasped in the lock and it opened.

In stepped two big men. One looked to be in his late

thirties. He had hair as black as Gil's, but the bluest, most piercing eyes she'd ever seen. He seemed startled to see her, then in one quick sweep, he took in all the changes to Gil's home. One glossy black eyebrow shot up.

Another man, this one a younger version of Gil, pushed his way in past the first with a grin. "Hey. You must be the mystery lady, huh?"

Painfully aware of her mussed hair, slept-in clothes, and lack of makeup, Anabel cleared her throat. "I'm Anabel Truman. I take it you're Gil's brothers?"

The friendly one nodded. "That's right. I'm Pete and the thundercloud is Sam. He's thundering, by the way, because he wanted to bring Gil's car back here without me, only I was too curious to wait. Sam hates it when things don't go his way."

Sam rolled his eyes. "Is Gil around?"

"In the bathroom. I'll just go get him . . ."

Nicki, who didn't like to be ignored, stepped forward and mimicked Sam's pose by crossing her arms over her chest and bracing her feet apart.

Both men stared down at her.

Clearing her throat, Anabel said, "Nicki, these are your uncles, Pete and Sam. They're your daddy's brothers."

"Daddy's brothers," Sam repeated, somewhat poleaxed.

Pete nudged him with an elbow. "Uncle Sam. Now ain't that a kicker?"

Anabel urged Nicki forward. "You want to say hi to them, rat?"

Nicki scrunched up her face, thinking about it for some seconds before saying, " 'kay." She marched forward—and sat on Sam's foot. "You do the horsie."

"Do the—?" Sam looked at Anabel for help.

Pete started snickering uncontrollably while Anabel

rushed to explain. "She rides on my foot sometimes. It's a game we play."

Sam said, "Oh," while standing there with that one leg stuck out comically, as if he feared he might hurt her if he moved.

Gil chose that moment to appear. He was freshly shaved, smelled wonderful, and wore only jeans. He scooped Nicki up with a grin. "You're terrorizing my brother, sweetheart. Look at him."

"I want pancakes."

"All right." Gil tucked her up against his hairy chest and turned to Anabel. "Why don't you go do . . . whatever you have to do and I'll take the brood into the kitchen."

That sounded like a fine idea to Anabel. Not only was she hung over from too much sex the night before, but now she had two family members to face. "Do you think you could produce some coffee?" Caffeine would hopefully kick-start her thinking processes.

"It'll be ready when you are."

As Anabel made her escape, she heard Nicki ask, "Are you as whiskery as Daddy?" She didn't know which brother Nicki addressed, and she didn't wait around to hear the answer.

What would Gil's brothers think of her? She was an interloper, a deceiver, and now a seducer. She knew she loved Gil, that she'd been in love with him almost from the day she'd met him. But they didn't know that.

In record time, Anabel washed her face, brushed her teeth, applied her makeup, and chose clean jeans and her most conservative tee to wear. Barefoot, she hurried back to the kitchen. She'd barely been gone ten minutes.

Sam and Pete were sitting at the table and Gil was at the stove. Nicki, bless her heart, was perched on Gil's foot, getting hauled around as he prepared her pan-

cakes. No one noticed Anabel looming in the hall outside the room.

"So she showed up, asked you to marry her, and now
you're sleeping with—"

Gil cut Sam off with a pointed look at Nicki. "That's
about it."

"What are you going to do?" Pete asked.

"I'm taking legal measures to make sure Nicole is financially noted as my daughter. There shouldn't be any
question of custody, but I'm addressing that, too, just in
case."

"I meant about the woman."

Gil shrugged while measuring out batter onto a hot
griddle. "I've known Anabel for three years, and I'll
admit I've thought about her in a lot of different ways."

Pete bobbed his eyebrows and Sam grinned.

"But not once did I ever consider her the type of
woman to marry."

"Why not?" Pete asked.

"Did you see her earrings and that damn tattoo?"

"Damn tattoo," Nicki repeated, making Gil groan
and giving both Pete and Sam a chuckle.

"Sweetheart, you can't say damn." Nicki just stared
up at Gil until he sighed. "Do you want to go look out
the patio doors at the birds?"

"Birds!" Like a flash, Nicki left the dubious enjoy-
ment of Gil's foot to study the backyard. He'd have finger and nose prints on the glass, but Anabel knew he
wouldn't mind.

From his position at the stove, Gil could still see
Nicki, but now that she was out of hearing range, he
had more freedom to talk to his brothers—much to
Anabel's discomfort.

Gil shook his head. "The thing is, I kept thinking
about the influence she might have on Nicole. She's not
like any mother I've ever seen before, that's for sure."

And then, with a thoughtful frown: "She even has a belly button ring."

"Yeah?" Pete's interest rose. "Those are sexy."

"You think everything on a female is sexy," Sam pointed out.

"And you don't?"

Ignoring Pete, Sam said, "You don't have to marry her to keep your own child."

"I have to do something with her. But it's a complicated situation, so I'm not going to rush things."

They discussed her like an inanimate object instead of a person. Anabel had heard enough. Pasting on a smile, she stepped into the kitchen. "My *damn* tattoo is part of a business agreement."

Spatula in hand, Gil jerked around to face her. His gaze was cautious, concerned. "You were listening in?"

"Nasty habit of mine, I know. Almost as bad as wearing body jewelry."

"Anabel." He sounded very put out with her.

She turned to Pete and lifted her shirt a bit. "There it is, that offensive belly button ring. Disgraceful, isn't it?"

Pete's Adam's apple bobbed as he swallowed hard. His gaze stayed glued to her stomach. "Um, cute."

"Thanks, but don't you mean sexy?"

Chagrined, he said, "Somehow I think it's in my best interest not to answer that."

Sam crossed his arms over his chest and rested back in his chair. "And you all thought my romance was entertaining."

Gil wasn't amused. "Put your shirt down, Anabel."

"Why? Am I embarrassing you?" She dropped her shirt, but only because she saw no point not to.

"No, but Pete is bright red."

She rolled her eyes. The last thing she wanted to do was explain herself to Gil and his brothers, but her situation didn't afford her the luxury of pride. "I do web page designs. It was about the only thing I could figure out that'd pay enough and still let me work from home so I could be with Nicki. Most of my work is for small businesses, and those include some that are just starting out. I let Dixon, the guy opening the tattoo shop, practice on me. He tattooed my arm, took pictures, and we used those to put up at his shop and on the website that he hired me to do. Same thing with the jewelry. Dodger gave me the earrings and the belly button ring to advertise his business. He didn't have to hire a model, and I got paid to design his website."

"So you didn't even want the tattoo?" Sam asked.

"I had never really thought about it, but no, I wouldn't have spent the money on a tattoo because my budget was too tight." She traced a fingertip over the delicate flowering vine. "But now I kinda like it. It suits me. And we know it helped Dixon get new business because it's his most requested design."

Pete said, "Got anything else pierced?"

She shook her head at the same time Gil said, *"No,* she does not."

Sam leaned over to Pete. "Gil's going to serve you for breakfast if you don't pipe down."

Gil turned off the stove. In very precise terms, each word carefully enunciated, he said, "You're telling me that pictures of your belly are on the *Internet?*"

Anabel couldn't help but laugh. "Is that the only part you heard?"

"Are they?"

"Yep. I got body parts flashing all over the Web."

Gil fell back against the sink counter. "Dear God." He looked incapable of doing or saying more.

Sam pushed from his seat and relieved Gil of the spatula. "You're burning our breakfast." Like an expert chef, he began filling the plates that Gil had set out. "And for the record, I like her tattoo, too. It's not like she's got a giant rattlesnake or the words 'I love Killer' emblazoned on her arm. It's tasteful and feminine."

"Maybe I'll suggest that Ariel get one."

"Try it, and I'll kick your ass." Sam turned to Anabel. "Ariel is my wife, and she's dying to meet you and Nicole. In fact, I'd be surprised if she and my mother didn't finagle an invite for later today."

Pete interrupted to ask, "What's the url for the sites where you're at?"

Gil rounded on him. "Forget it, Pete."

"All right, all right. Sheesh. No reason to breathe fire on me."

Sam began serving up breakfast. "Hey, Nicki, Uncle Sam has your pancakes ready."

Gil glared at him. "Way to hog all the credit."

"Hey, I gotta make a good impression while I can."

Nicki came barreling back into the kitchen, jabbering ninety miles a minute about the birds and pancakes and uncles who cooked. *She* felt right at home with Gil's brothers, so Anabel gave up. After all, it was just her feelings that were hurt, and she had to get over that real quick because it was bound to happen a few more times. She'd known from jump how Gil felt about her. Just because he enjoyed sex with her didn't mean he'd suddenly have a personality transformation. They were as different as night and day—except in bed. And Gil could certainly find another woman to fill that role if he chose to.

She'd have liked to tell him to go to hell—but she couldn't. She couldn't even really argue with him because it might mean she'd lose Nicole. An ominous dread had skated down her spine when he said he planned to take legal action to bind Nicole to him. If she didn't make headway soon, he'd probably kick her out and she'd lose Nicole as well as Gil. She couldn't let that happen.

But what could she do?

Suddenly Gil was beside her, the consummate gentleman, holding out a seat for her with one hand and offering a cup of coffee with the other.

Anabel would never understand him. "Thank you."

He kissed her forehead, saying very softly, "You're welcome."

Nicki grinned and reached up for him. "Tank you."

Gil lifted her into her high chair, then kissed her, too, before reaching for his own seat. When he turned around, Pete puckered up as if waiting his turn, but Sam wielded the spatula like a weapon, saying, "Keep those lips on the females."

Nicki thought they were hilarious; Anabel just thought they were nuts. Breakfast, she discovered, was a circus— and quite thoroughly enjoyable. The brothers were anxious to hear all about Nicole's preferences and peccadilloes, but they asked just as many questions about Anabel. As far as she could tell, Gil's brothers had no problem with her at all. Now if only Gil would feel the same.


After his brothers had gone and the kitchen was cleaned, Gil pulled Anabel into his arms. "Hi."

She blinked at him. Gil knew she was very uncertain, that she had no idea what the future might bring. Well, she'd just have to go on wondering for a little longer. He was no dummy; he'd already decided that Anabel deserved more than a trial run, and more than a marriage of convenience. How to convince her of that was the question plaguing his mind. He didn't want her to feel like a convenience, not when she was so much more. He had a plan and he'd stick to it.

"Can I have a kiss?"

Her brows came down in suspicion. "Why?"

"Because I enjoy kissing you and you look sexy as hell this morning."

Ever the doting mother, Anabel glanced around for Nicole.

"She's busy dressing up a near bald doll with crayon marks on her face. Ugly thing."

Anabel grinned. "That's her baby."

"So she told me. It looks older than dirt."

"It's not *that* old. I gave it to her for her first birthday."

Gil wasn't surprised, but he was touched. Again. "Perhaps," he whispered, "that's why it's a favorite."

Anabel's smile faded in nostalgia. "A few months ago, the little rat decided it needed makeup, and she did a job with her crayons. Then she decided she didn't like the look after all and insisted I wash the poor thing. Most of the yarn hair fell out—but Nicki still takes that doll with her everywhere."

Without waiting for permission, Gil caught Anabel's chin and tipped her face up. Deliberately, he kept the kiss tender instead of sexual. It wasn't easy.

"Do you like my brothers?"

She dropped her forehead to his chest. "The more important question is whether or not they like me."

"They do—not that it matters. I don't have to have their approval for anything I do." He held her shoulders and bent his knees to see her face. "Besides, what's not to like?"

She snorted at that. "Body jewelry? Tattoos?"

Gil grinned. "What else have you traded on the Internet? Nothing too risqué, I hope." He rubbed his thumb over her lips and his voice dropped. "You haven't traded this pretty mouth, have you?"

She slugged him in the stomach, but he held her so close that it was an ineffectual punch. "Nicki's old room was painted by a mural artist that I worked for. I used her room as the background for the website. She had birds and trees on all her walls. It was beautiful. I've had different hairdos to help advertise for a beautician friend." She ran a hand through her short curls. "I remember you came around once when it was red."

"Yeah. I liked it."

"You did?"

He just grinned. He wouldn't tell her yet that he liked everything about her—even her belly button ring. He needed to show her first. "Why don't we take in a movie? Would Nicki like that?"

"I don't know. I've never taken her before."

Because she couldn't afford it? Gil decided they'd spend the day out. He wanted to give Nicki everything she didn't have, to watch her experience new things with him. But he was also driven to treat Anabel to a few luxuries, as well. She'd given much of herself and it was time she got something in return.

A few hours later, at the matinee show, Gil began questioning his wisdom. With so many kids in attendance, the chattering was nonstop. "I've never been to an afternoon movie before," he remarked to Anabel over the drone of crying babies, fussing toddlers, and cajoling moms. "I'm not altogether sure I like it."

She leaned into his shoulder and laughed. "You're just disappointed that you can't make out."

"True." Then he whispered, "But there's always tonight." He felt Anabel's shiver before she could move away.

They had lunch at McDonald's, but by then Nicki was getting cranky. Her constant whining was trying, more so because Anabel looked horrified that his little angel wasn't being all that angelic.

"She's tired," Anabel explained.

"And loud," Gil agreed. "But she's also a toddler and I suppose they all get this way on occasion."

Anabel rushed to give Nicki another french fry. "Just some of the time."

Gil shook his head. "Don't sugarcoat the reality. I can take it. Besides, it doesn't matter how she fusses, I can still see that you're an excellent mother."

Wary hopefulness darkened her eyes. "You really think so?"

Gil lifted Nicki from her high chair. "Of course. And I think I'll make an adequate father once I get the hang of it."

"You're already a wonderful dad and you know it."

She sounded disgruntled about it, making him fight a smile. "Thank you." He hoisted Nicki up to his shoulders. She liked that enough that they got her out of the restaurant and into his car with nothing but cheers and squeals of happiness.

But once in the park, she fell asleep on the blanket they spread beneath a shading tree. Gil smoothed her short dark hair. "I wanted to show her the different birds."

"There'll be plenty of other days for that."

"Thanks to you." He picked up Anabel's hand and kissed her palm. Together they leaned back on the tree, still holding hands. It was peaceful. And nice.

They were a family.

Gil hadn't realized how much was missing from his life until Anabel showed up. After his father's death, he'd buried himself in his work. At the time it had been a necessary escape, a way to cope with his grief. But he was done with that. He was ready to move forward.

On the drive home from the park, Gil considered all the changes that still needed to be made. Anabel could use a minivan to replace that heap she currently owned.

And he should have one of the bathrooms remodeled to include a tub that Nicki could use. Perhaps Anabel would even want to do some redecorating.

Gil was contemplating the various ways he could tie Anabel into his future when they pulled up to his house and found a black BMW in the driveway.

"Oh no." Anabel stiffened in alarm. "It's Shelly's parents."

"So I assumed." Gil noted the older couple waiting on his porch, and smiled in anticipation. "I wonder if my lawyer has spoken with them yet? No matter. I'm glad we'll be able to get this settled." He parked the car and started to get out.

Anabel reached for his arm. "What are we going to do?"

"I'm going to talk to them. You're going to wait with Nicki in her room."

"No. You can't just shut me out—"

"Yes, I can." Gil walked around the car to her door. The grandparents watched impatiently from the porch. "Leave it to me, Anabel. It has nothing to do with you."

"That's not true!"

He gave her a stern look and dropped his voice to a whisper. "You're too emotional. You came to me, now let me handle this." He reached in and lifted Nicki out. She stretched awake, immediately slipping her thumb into her mouth. "Go to your mommy, sweetheart."

Nicki was too tired to argue.

Anabel squeezed her close. "Gil . . ."

He put his hand at the small of her back and urged her forward. "Trust me. Everything will be fine."

The grandparents looked beyond rigid. With no sign of welcome, Gil said, "Mr. and Mrs. Tyree. I've been expecting you."

Mr. Tyree, tall with dark brown hair showing no signs of gray, cleared his throat. "We're here to discuss—"

Gil cut him off. "We'll talk in my den." He opened the door and ushered a miserably silent Anabel inside. Nicki, bless her heart, had her head on Anabel's shoulder, her thumb in her mouth, watching the intruders warily.

Gil kissed both mother and daughter on the forehead. "This won't take long." He left Anabel standing there and led the Tyrees down the hall.

"We're here about Nicole," Mr. Tyree said the moment the door closed.

Gil ignored his opening salvo to say, "I was very sorry to hear about Shelly. She and I were good friends."

Mrs. Tyree curled her lip. "More than friends."

"Once, yes." Gil indicated the chairs. "Would you like to sit down?"

They did so reluctantly. Gil saw the weariness, the grief, still etched in their faces. Their relationship with Shelly might not have been ideal, but it could never be easy to lose a child.

Gil decided to end things quickly, for everyone's sake. "Nicole is mine. Shelly wrote of that fact in her diary, which I have, so no blood tests are necessary. I never knew about her until after Shelly's death."

"Anabel ran to you, didn't she?"

"Yes. A wise decision on her part. She loves Nicki as much as any mother would love a child. She wanted only to do what was best for her." He looked at each of them. "This is best for her. Nicole will be well cared for."

"We're her grandparents."

"Yes, I know. Any involvement you have with her will be up to you, but you won't, under any circumstances, try to take her away."

Mr. Tyree stood. "You don't even know her."

"As I said, Shelly never told me about her. But I am her father and that's something you can't challenge."

"You intend to keep her here, with you?"

"I realize it's a long way from Atlanta, but arrangements could be made for visitation—"

"No." Mrs. Tyree joined her husband, standing at his side. "We have a reputation in the community, Mr. Watson. Losing our daughter was hard enough. I don't want to have to deal with the scandal of an illegitimate grandchild as well."

Gil's sympathy for these people went right out the window. "If you don't want a relationship with Nicole, why were you going to take her from Anabel?" But then he knew, and the hairs on the back of his neck stood on end. "You wanted to put her up for adoption?"

An aged, bejeweled hand waved the air. "Anabel Truman is a gold digger. She'd have come after us for money, possibly tried to blackmail us."

Stupid woman. "Anabel was your daughter's roommate, but you didn't get to know her at all, did you?"

"I know people, Mr. Watson. And I know it requires money to support a child. Anabel is a person with no ambition, no prospects."

"You're wrong. She has more heart, more courage and determination than anyone I've ever met."

"She's got you completely fooled, hasn't she?"

Shaking his head at such blind ignorance, Gil went to the door and opened it. He wouldn't waste his breath arguing with them. "I have money, so rest assured, I won't be contacting you for anything."

Mr. Tyree hesitated. "We had no reason to believe you'd want to take on the responsibility of—"

"Of my own daughter?" Gil's tone was flat in the face of such cynicism. "Good-bye, Mr. and Mrs. Tyree."

The older couple shared what appeared to be a look of relief, and seconds later they were gone. Gil stood there, unable to comprehend how someone could not want to take part in Nicole's life. She was a tiny, incredible, wonderful miracle.

Anabel touched his back. "I heard them leave."

Gil shook off his disgust and turned to face her with a smile. "Yes, and good riddance. I doubt we'll ever hear from them again."

Anable's eyes widened. "They . . . they won't press for custody?"

"They would have gotten her only to give her away." He looped his arms around her waist, pulled her body into his for a hug. "But I'm the father, all right and tight and no one can challenge that. You've got nothing else to worry about, Anabel." He waited for her to ask him what her role would be in it all, but she didn't.

She was probably afraid to.

Gil sighed. He'd give her a week, two at the most, to figure things out. But he'd use that time wisely. "I don't suppose Nicki went back to sleep?"

"No. She's busy renaming all her dolls, thanks to the characters in that Disney movie we saw."

"Well, if I can't engage you in a quickie, how about just necking with me a bit?" Gil noticed that her cheeks flushed with interest and a pulse raced in her throat. She reacted so quickly to him that she took his breath away. "At least until Nicki discovers us?"

"Here?"

"Mmm." He backed her into the wall. "Bedtime seems far too many hours from now."

Anabel licked her lips. "Yeah, okay." And then she was on her tiptoes, taking his mouth, stroking his chest, and, Gil hoped, loving him just a little.

# Chapter Five

As Gil moved to the side of her, each of them sweaty and breathing hard, Anabel wondered just how long the trial run would last.

It had been two weeks since he'd sent the Tyrees on their way, and it was getting harder and harder to bite her tongue, to keep her questions and her fears and, damn it, her love, hidden away. Especially since, by all appearances, Gil expected to keep her around. He'd offered to let her redecorate his home to make it more suitable for Nicole—but also to suit her, as if her preferences mattered in the long run. He'd put her name on his checking account. He'd dragged her along when he met with his lawyer to show her that he'd ensured Nicole's future, but also her own by giving her access to all his accounts.

It was like being married—only they weren't, and he hadn't mentioned anything about it. If he wanted her to stick around, but she wasn't to be his wife, then what? She'd done a lot to take care of Nicole, but she wasn't sure she could be a mistress.

With a wry twist to her mouth, Anabel wondered if she could somehow exchange that service for website business. It didn't seem likely.

Gil's big, warm hand settled on her belly. "Jesus, I think you've killed me."

Anabel turned her head to face him. It was late in the night, and Gil had just loved her twice. "Me? I was ready to go to sleep. You're the one who doesn't know when to quit."

"Moderation is overrated." His laugh was rough and winded. In the next instant, he rolled to his side and loomed over her. His dark eyes were teasing, hot, filled with tenderness. "Maybe if you didn't look so damn good . . ."

"I'm not wearing makeup. And after your . . . enthusiasm just now, my hair is a ratty mess."

He nuzzled her throat with a rumbling growl. "Then maybe it's the way you smell."

Anabel laughed. Gil had a playful side to him that she hadn't known about before moving in with him. But over the past few weeks, he'd grown more carefree, always smiling, always teasing. She liked it. She loved him. "I'm sweating like a pig, thanks to you."

His hand slipped between her thighs, pressing warmly. "You're sticky, too. But I like it." His voice deepened. "I like everything about you."

Anabel's heart gave an unsteady thump. He said things like that a lot. What did they mean? And how serious was he?

He kissed her mouth. "Do you like blue?"

The sudden change in topic threw her and she shrugged. "Sure, why?"

Again, Gil dropped to his back. "That's the color of your new minivan. I've been meaning to pick one out, but then it seems that between work and playing with Nicki and keeping you satisfied in the sack, I kept putting it off. Today during my lunch I went to a few dealers and—"

"You bought me a minivan?" Anabel knew she should

just say thank you, that the new vehicle was really for Nicki's safety. Whenever she left the house, Gil insisted she take his car. But his highhandedness was about to drive her insane.

"Yeah. We'll junk your van—if the junkyard will take it, that is. Not that I mind sharing my car with you . . ." He twisted to see her. "Would you want your own car, too? I mean, for when you get out without Nicki?"

Her jaw locked. "I don't go out without Nicki."

"You haven't up till now because you couldn't. Not that my family wouldn't be great as baby-sitters, but I can understand why you're not comfortable leaving Nicki with them yet."

He didn't understand at all. If Gil didn't need her to watch Nicki, he wouldn't need her for anything. "She's already been through so many changes, Gil. And she doesn't know them that well yet."

"She will soon. God knows, they come around often enough."

Too true. All of Gil's family was delighted with Nicole and she with them. At least twice a week Pete came to visit, and he was quickly spoiling Nicole with gifts. Sam and his wife Ariel doted on her, as well. And Belinda Watson, Gil's mother, was over the moon with her new granddaughter.

Gil reached for her hand and twined his fingers with hers. He did that a lot, she realized, held her hand, touched her face, gave her small, tender kisses.

"I'm going to interview some baby-sitters tomorrow."

Slowly, Anabel turned her head on the pillow so she could see him. "You're going to do what?"

"I want someone to come in during the day to give you a break so you can do your work or just go out, or soak in the tub. Mom recommends her beautician if you want to go get . . . whatever it is women get at those places. A manicure or facial or something. But don't change your hair. I like it."

Anabel's temper snapped. He was trying to phase her out. Little by little, her role in Nicki's life had diminished. Lately, Gil read to her more nights than not, and he'd become a regular hand at baths and pull-ups and everything else that affected Nicki's life. He was an excellent father—but damn it, she was Nicki's mother.

*She was.*

With fear lodged in her throat, Anabel pulled her hand away and sat up in the bed. She kept her back to Gil so he wouldn't see her ravaged expression. "What about me, Gil?" Was she relegated to bed warmer only? And if so, how long would that last?

She felt his stillness, what she perceived as empathy in his tone. "What about you?"

Her heart burned in her chest. "When I first came here, I made you an . . . offer."

"To sleep with me, I know." One finger trailed down her spine. "I love having you in my bed, Anabel."

She squeezed her eyes shut. "That's not the offer I mean."

The bed shifted as Gil sat up. He scooted around until he was beside her, one arm braced on the mattress behind her. For long moments, he just stared at her profile. "I don't *need* to marry you to keep Nicole."

There it was, the awful truth she hadn't wanted to face. "She loves me."

"A lot." She heard the smile in his tone, felt the love he had for Nicole. "You've been an incredible mother."

"I've done my best." But maybe her best wasn't good enough. No, she couldn't think that. Gil was a good man, a considerate man. Maybe he didn't want to marry her, but he would never keep her from Nicole. She knew that.

Problem was, she wanted them both. Forever.

Gil remained silent.

"I . . . I know we're very different." Could she convince him that their differences complemented each other?

"Remarkably so."

"But we both love Nicole."

"Yes, and we both have a place in her life."

That reassurance helped, but it wasn't all that she wanted. "Wouldn't that be enough for marriage?"

Gil wrapped his hand around her nape, put his forehead to hers. "I'm afraid not."

The bottom fell out of her world.

"I want a woman who loves me, too, Anabel, not just my daughter."

Her gaze shot up to his, searching, desperate. She put her hands on his chest to move him back so she could better see him. With her breath fast and shallow, she said, *"But I do.* I have for a long time."

His smile spread, slow and easy. "Yeah? You never told me that."

Frowning, Anabel punched his shoulder. "You had to know."

Tumbling her backward into the bed, Gil pinned her down with his body and caught her wrists. He grinned like a fool, confounding her further. "So you love me, huh? Damn, I'm glad to hear that."

"Gil . . . ?"

"As you said, we're very different." He stared at her mouth until she licked her lips. "I need a wife who can accompany me to business parties."

"And you think I can't?" He insulted her with his lack of faith. "I can dress up as well as any woman, I've just never had to."

"Why, Anabel," he said with mock surprise. "You mean

to say you'd wear a sedate little black cocktail dress for me?"

He was so amused, Anabel glared up at him. "I don't know if I'd go that far, but I'd find something appropriate. I'm not a complete social misfit." Grudgingly, she added, "I could even find a dress with sleeves that'd hide my tattoo."

"Now that'd be a shame."

What the hell did he mean by that? It almost sounded as though he liked her tattoo.

Gil rubbed his body against hers and said huskily, "I want a woman who's strong."

He turned her on so easily. How did he expect her to have a coherent conversation while he performed a full-body caress? Anabel pushed against him, but he couldn't be budged. "I'm strong," she promised.

"Could've fooled me." With almost no effort, he nudged her thighs apart and wedged himself against her. "The mouthy Anabel Truman I used to know was strong. She had an opinion on anything and everything, and God knows, she never hesitated to share it. But lately . . ." He shook his head with feigned regret. "Doesn't matter what I do, I can't get a rise out of her."

Suspicion rose and Anabel went still, her eyes narrowing. "Wait a minute. You know damn good and well that I've been trying to get along with you."

"No, you've been trying not to rock the boat. You had some harebrained idea that I'd kick you to the curb if you stepped out of line."

"You wanted me to step out of line?"

"No, I wanted you to be you."

Her pulse raced with hope. "You're not making any sense, Gil."

He leaned down and took her mouth. This was no sweet, gentle kiss but a tongue-thrusting, wet, hot kiss that completely stole her breath. "I've always been attracted to you, Anabel. I think you're about the most sexual woman I've ever run across. But the timing was never right, it seemed. My father passed away and things happened with Shelly that I used to regret. But not anymore."

"Because now you have Nicki."

His thumbs brushed her cheeks. "And I have you. When you brought my baby to me, when I saw how much she loves you, how could I not start to love you, too?"

Her eyes widened in disbelief. *How could he not . . .* "Now wait a minute—"

Gil's mouth smothered her protest, swallowed her questions. When she went limp, he continued. "You're a little wild and unorthodox, and I thank God for it. Not many women would take another's baby to raise. Not many would readjust their lives to do so. Not many would come to a man and make him the type of offer you gave me, just so she could go on being a wonderful mother."

Anabel decided on a full confession. "That wasn't the only reason, Gil. If it hadn't been you, I might have come up with a different plan. But I always wanted you."

"And now you have me." He said that with bright satisfaction. "But not because of Nicole, and not because it's convenient. I've tried to show you that I don't need you just to be Nicole's mother. I need you because I enjoy being with you, loving you, and laughing with you, more than any other woman I've known."

Her smile wobbled. Damn it, she would not cry like some ninny.

"You're pretty damn remarkable, Anabel soon-to-be-Mrs. Watson." He drew a slow, deep breath. "And I love you."

Anabel wrapped her arms around his neck. She felt

buoyant and carefree and so happy she wanted to burst. "Gil?"

"Hmm?"

"Now that I know I can speak my mind . . ."

His smile widened with anticipation. "Yes?"

"You won't expect me to listen to your Neil Diamond CDs, will you?"

"Not if I don't have to listen to Kid Rock."

Emotions rose up, almost choking her. "I love you, Gil." Now she got the tender, melting kiss. When he lifted his head, she cleared her throat. "One more thing."

"What's that?"

"I don't want a blue minivan."

He gave a short laugh. "No? And what do you want?"

"A red SUV." She kissed his chin. "Nicole." She wrapped her legs around his waist. "And *you.*"

Gil brought her closer, hugged her tight. In a voice rough with love, he said, "We'll pick out the SUV tomorrow. The others you already have."

# THE WILDE ONE

Janelle Denison

# Chapter One

Adrian Wilde took a long swallow of his beer in honor of the relaxing three-day weekend stretching ahead of him, and nearly choked on the drink when he caught sight of Chayse Douglas, the one woman he'd spent the past four months turning down and trying to avoid. Standing at the bar as she ordered a drink, she waggled her fingers at him in greeting and smiled in a way that made him feel like a hunted man.

*You can run but you can't hide . . .*

He all but heard the words conveyed in that determined look of hers, and his body warmed with a familiar lust he'd been fighting since the moment he'd met her, followed closely by annoyance. That she'd ventured into such a public place as Nick's Sports Bar to fight for her cause was enough to put him on full alert, and it didn't surprise him that she'd enlisted his hellion cousin, Mia Wilde, to help persuade him into agreeing to be a part of Chayse's beefcake calendar project.

He thought he'd finally convinced the pint-sized bundle of fortitude that he wasn't interested in posing half-naked for her Outdoor Men calendar. Since he knew she had a deadline to meet, he'd assumed she'd found another willing victim and he was off the hook. But having been the recipient of that purposeful gleam in those violet-hued eyes, Adrian knew, without a single doubt, that the delectable Chayse still had her sights set on him.

*Christ.* While he admired her tenacity to go after what she wanted and found her brazen pursuit too much of a turn-on, she was setting herself up for another dose of rejection, because there was no way in hell he was going to change his mind. He was doing her a huge favor by saying no. While she might think he was exactly what she wanted for her calendar, he was far from model material.

Frustrated by the entire situation, along with his unwanted attraction to Chayse that made everything all the more complicated, he returned his attention to his table mates and eyed them suspiciously. "Who the hell tipped off Mia that we'd be here tonight?" he demanded, because that was the only way Chayse could have found him so easily.

Three pairs of curious eyes glanced toward the bar, where he'd pointed his bottle of beer. His brother Steve sat next to him on the left, then there was Cameron, Steve's good friend and business partner, and their cousin Scott, older brother to Mia.

Cameron, who'd been fighting his own battle of the sexes with Mia, shook his head adamantly. "Not me, man. The last thing I'd do is invite the wild child to crash our little party and ruin my perfectly good evening."

Adrian believed him, though the fire and challenge in Cameron's eyes spoke a tale of its own. Cameron wasn't altogether upset about Mia's appearance. Not that he'd ever admit to the attraction that sizzled to life whenever the two were in the same room.

Adrian's gaze shifted to Steve, and his older brother held up his hands in defense. "Hey, I haven't spoken to Mia all week."

Which left Scott, and judging by the sheepish look on his cousin's face, Adrian rightly assumed the man was responsible for this interesting turn of events. " 'Fess up, Scotty-boy," Adrian said.

Scott shrugged. "Okay, so I was leaving the office today and casually mentioned I was coming here for a drink with some friends. When Mia asked who with, I wasn't about to lie."

"Your honesty is a refreshing and noble trait," Adrian drawled wryly, giving his cousin a hard time. "Next time, *lie.*"

Cameron and Steve chuckled in amusement.

Scott leaned back in his chair and absently stroked his finger along his jaw while regarding Adrian speculatively. "Why do I get the feeling that your problem isn't so much with Mia, but that hot little number she's with?"

Adrian downed the rest of his beer and motioned to the bar waitress for another one, wondering if he ought to order a chaser to go with it. "Because she's the photographer who's been dogging me for the past four months to do that damn beefcake calendar for charity, and she's having one helluva time taking no for an answer."

His male counterparts offered nods of understanding and grunts of sympathy, and a moment later Mia and Chayse were strolling across the establishment toward their table, each with one of those fancy, designer martini drinks in hand.

Despite himself, Adrian took in the long-sleeved, pink cotton shirt that clung to Chayse's petite curves and the snug jeans that outlined the gentle flare of her hips and the rest of her compact body. He'd noticed more than once that she had small but firm breasts, maybe a handful by his experienced estimation, and that was being generous, considering he had large palms and long fingers. Not that he'd ever get the opportunity to test the weight and size of those luscious mounds in his hands, except in his dreams. Oh yeah, in those nightly fantasies he'd caressed those soft breasts of hers, and a whole lot more.

"Hello, boys," Mia said cheerfully. "Mind if we join you?"

"Yes," Adrian and Cameron echoed at the same time Scott and Steve said graciously, "Not at all."

The women opted to ignore Adrian and Cameron and accepted Scott and Steve's invitation. Dragging two nearby chairs up to the table, Chayse flanked Adrian on one side with Mia on the other, which put Mia conveniently right next to Cameron. Mia, with her stylishly cut black hair and exotic silver eyes, slanted Cameron a smug grin full of her brand of sensual torment. He met her gaze unflinchingly, the instantaneous sparks of awareness between the two of them nearly tangible.

As was the feverish heat and undeniable hunger Chayse generated whenever she was near him, Adrian thought as the waitress delivered his second beer. He took a long drink of the cold brew, which did nothing to extinguish the fire that had started in his chest and was gradually spiraling its way lower.

Damn her, anyway.

Setting the bottle on the table, Adrian reclined back in his chair, glanced at the woman sitting next to him, and met that direct, sultry gaze of hers that never failed to unnerve him. It wasn't so much the rare, extraordinary violet color that disturbed him, but rather the way those eyes seemed to see past the footloose and fancy-free rules he'd lived by the past few years. Rules that kept his real emotions under wraps. Her pursuit felt personal, as if she found him much too intriguing to give up on. And quite frankly, her uncanny ability to unsettle him so effortlessly scared the crap out of him.

Thank God she had no clue how much she affected him. And she never would, he vowed, because he wasn't about to let down his guard, or allow her to rattle his control.

Then she smiled. A slow, sensual smile that affected him like a blow right to the gut. Just that easily, just that quick, he ached to kiss those pink, glossy lips of hers, wanted to eat her up, inch by delectable inch, and taste her in every hot, sweet womanly place. Most of all, he wanted to push her up against the nearest wall and let her feel exactly what she did to him.

Shrugging off his too stimulating thoughts, he lifted a brow her way. "What a coincidence meeting you here," he said, and didn't bother tempering the edge of sarcasm in his tone.

She laughed off his scorn, the lilting sound full of confidence. "What can I say? I'm a determined woman. When I find something I want, I go after it until I've exhausted every possible approach."

And what she wanted was him. "More like obstinate and too damned tenacious," he muttered, though loud enough for her, and everyone else, to hear.

"I think her persistence is very admirable." Scott lifted his beer to Chayse in a mock salute.

"Why, thank you." Chayse beamed at Scott for his support. "Being persistent has definitely served me well."

Adrian narrowed his gaze and pointed a threatening finger at his cousin, who'd dared to take her side. "Nobody asked your opinion, Scotty, so I'd appreciate it if you kept it to yourself."

Chayse turned her attention back to him, amusement dancing in her eyes. "If *you* weren't being so stubborn, I wouldn't have to be so persistent."

She ran her fingers through her permanently tousled, chin-length, honey blond curls, combing them away from her face, a habit of hers he found too damn fascinating, and tempting. Most of the rebellious strands sprang back into place, and Adrian's fingers itched to push them away again, just as an excuse to see if her hair was as silky soft as it looked.

He wrapped his hand tight around his bottle of beer and scowled at her. "Don't you have a deadline that's come and gone?"

"I got an extension." She took a sip of her green martini, and he caught the scent of apples just before she slowly licked her lips and his libido kicked into overdrive. "I have one more week, and I've decided that I'm going to make you my main priority and stalk you until you finally give in." Her tone was teasing, but her gaze told him just how serious her intentions were.

Well, he wasn't going to be around for her to stalk, thank God. For the next three days he'd be at the family cabin catching up on some R and R and enjoying a weekend of peace and solitude.

"Don't count on me changing my mind, sweetheart," he told her. "My answer is, and will always remain, no thank you."

"Aw, come on Adrian," Mia piped in, disappointment lacing her voice. "This is for charity, for crying out loud. I can't believe you'd say no to something that would benefit so many kids at the Children's Hospital."

Adrian's jaw clenched tight, but he remained quiet. Mia's comment made him sound cold and unfeeling, when his reasons for refusing had nothing to do with being selfish. Rather, he was self-conscious about baring so much of his less than perfect body to the thousands of people who purchased the calendar. But he wasn't about to reveal his personal, private reasons to Chayse, or anyone else for that matter.

Cameron slanted Mia an incredulous glance. "Contrary to popular belief, not all men are into being displayed as sexual objects."

"Since when?" Mia argued, and leaned closer to Cameron, clearly relishing a debate with him. "Come on, admit it, sugar. Being the object of a woman's fantasies is a nice stroke to the male ego."

Cameron frowned at her, impatience and something more heated smoldering in his gold-flecked eyes. "I'll admit to nothing, except that you're a female chauvinist."

She propped her chin in her hand and batted her lashes at him, unfazed by his accusation. "I'm a liberated woman, and proud of it."

Before Cameron could supply a comeback, Steve steered the conversation in a different, and unexpected, direction. "What about Scott here, Chayse?" Steve clapped the other man on the back. "He's in great physical shape, he's not bad on the eyes, and he's single. Maybe you could convince him to take his clothes off for your cause."

Scott looked mortified at the thought. "Uh, I don't think so."

Chayse laughed, and took another swallow of her martini. "Don't worry, Scott. While you'd make quite the eye candy for my calendar, you're off the hook," she reassured him, then shifted her unwavering gaze back to Adrian. She swirled the slice of apple that had accompanied her drink in the last bit of liquor, then popped it into her mouth and chewed. "You, on the other hand, are just what I'm looking for to complete my Outdoor Men calendar. Like the three other men who've posed for my project, you're the real thing. You're a sports enthusiast who takes it to the extreme, you own Wilde Adventures, which caters to outdoor recreational activities, and you epitomize everything an outdoor man should look like and be."

She scooted back her chair and stood; for a moment Adrian thought she was going to leave, and experienced an inexplicable combination of relief and disappointment.

"I need to run to the ladies' room," she said instead,

and flashed him a quick, I'm-not-done-with-you-yet look. "Maybe while I'm gone these guys and Mia can talk some sense into you."

With that bold statement, she sauntered away, hips swaying in those snug jeans of hers. He watched her stroll past the crowded dance floor to the corridor that led to the rest rooms, then finally glanced back at his brother, Cameron, and his cousins, who were all eyeing him with varying degrees of interest, anticipation, and amusement.

Mia opened her mouth to speak, and Adrian cut her off with a wave of his hand. "Don't *even* go there."

Steve wasn't so easily intimidated. "I have to admit, she puts up a convincing argument."

"I'm not interested. Period. End of discussion." He polished off his beer and refrained from ordering a third.

"Fine." Steve's stare was all too knowing. "But just for the record, I think the little spitfire has gotten to you, and maybe this is possibly about more than just posing for a beefcake calendar."

Adrian's first instinct was to deny Steve's very astute statement. But his older brother knew him well, knew what he'd been through in the past, and knew the emotional wringer one woman had put him through that had affected his views on relationships with the female gender and not letting any woman close ever since.

Steve sighed and stood. "And on that note, I'm outta here. I promised Liz I'd help her close up The Daily Grind tonight, and I'm hoping to get a caramel frappacino out of the deal." He waggled his brows, indicating that he was hoping for a whole lot more than just a cold coffee drink from his wife.

Scott grinned. "How's married life?"

Withdrawing a large bill from his wallet, Steve tossed it onto the table for his drink and tip. "A helluva lot better than this," he said, and indicated the singles scene behind him, gathered at Nick's to enjoy the band, play pool or darts, and generally attempt to pick up members of the opposite sex.

Cameron shook his head and rocked his chair onto its back legs. "You and Eric are something else, from sworn bachelors to domestic bliss. You're making us look bad."

"What can I say, boys. I'm living the good life." The broad smile on Steve's face attested to just how happy he was. "When the right woman comes along, then you'll understand the domestic bliss thing, and actually enjoy it."

With a chorus of "Good night," Steve left the bar, leaving Adrian to contemplate his brother's comment, and how the right woman had changed both Steve and Eric's bachelor lives. He'd never seen either of his brothers so mellow before, so content in their lives and the women they'd married. Adrian was beginning to feel like the odd man out lately, and restless in a way he couldn't shake. Which was why he'd decided to escape for the weekend to the family cabin—a quiet sanctuary away from work and the craziness of life. Not to mention the old, painful memories that had been nagging him ever since Chayse had made him a target for her pinup calendar and he'd realized he wanted her in ways that defied the keep-it-simple rules he'd set for himself four years ago.

Undoubtedly, he was an earthy, physical guy who loved sex and all the pleasures to be found in a woman's body, and he could always find a warm and eager female when the mood struck him. But that's all he allowed anymore . . . just hot, mindless sex with women who knew the score right up front and wanted the same thing. To that end, he didn't care what they thought of him, or how he looked in their eyes, because it was all about mutual give and take and carnal satisfaction, and they both walked away afterward with no expectations or regrets.

He scrubbed a hand along his jaw, forced to admit that even raucous sex with a ready and willing partner had lost its appeal over the past few months. And he had a certain stubborn, persistent blond-haired beauty to blame for his lack of interest in any other woman, and his celibate life of late.

Chayse was so under his skin, he couldn't get her out of his mind, his erotic dreams, his life, no matter how hard he tried. And whenever he felt the vibes between them, which was anytime they were in the same vicinity, it nearly devastated his senses and destroyed his restraint. Yet beyond their sexual attraction, she exuded warmth and a genuine caring he was inexplicably drawn to, especially when she talked about her project or the kids at Chicago's Children's Hospital, where she visited and was a volunteer.

He cast an irritable glance toward the rest rooms just as Chayse exited. She headed back in the direction of the table, only to be waylaid by a tall, good-looking guy who grasped her elbow. She stopped, surprised but not upset by the man's interception. He motioned to the dance floor with a charming smile and a nod of his head. She shrugged her shoulders in a "Sure, why not" kind of gesture and off they went together, mingling into the crowd dancing to the rock music the band was playing.

The pair started out innocently enough, with Chayse seemingly enjoying herself, but it didn't take long for Casanova to make a move, using their close proximity to initiate a little touchy-feely with her. His hands came to rest on her shimmying hips, then boldly slipped around to her backside.

Jealousy, a sensation Adrian hadn't experienced in

much too long, reared its ugly head before he could stop the emotion. His temper flared at the other man's predatory move toward Chayse, a possessive, unwelcome response he *refused* to act upon.

"Jesus, Adrian," Scott said, cutting through his dark, festering thoughts. "Would you stop glaring already?"

"That guy has his hand on her ass," he bit out, disgusted with himself for caring so much.

Cameron grinned with keen male insight. "And you wish it were *your* hand on her ass instead, don't you?"

Adrian couldn't argue the truth, so he didn't even try. Through a narrowed gaze, he watched as Chayse removed the other man's wandering hands from her bottom, but the chump merely grabbed her around the waist, jerked her hips to his, and ground himself lewdly against her. She stiffened and braced her hands against his shoulders to hold him away, but her partner wasn't letting go and used the crush of people around them to his advantage.

Adrian's hand curled into a fist, and the muscles in his arm bunched with tension. He wanted to pummel the guy, then tear him apart, limb by limb. "He's practically molesting her out on the dance floor."

"Then maybe you ought to go over there and do something about it," Mia suggested oh so helpfully.

"Maybe I will." Watching the other man ignore Chayse's attempt to slip from his grasp again, Adrian felt as though he'd been prodded with a hot brand, provoked beyond reason. Because it certainly wasn't any sort of reasoning that had him strolling across the room and into the fray of writhing, dancing bodies to rescue her.

Coming up behind the guy, Adrian placed his hand where neck met shoulder and applied a firm pressure with his fingers that immediately caught the other man's attention.

"What the hell?" The other man instantly let go of Chayse and tried to whirl around to face his accoster, but Adrian's unrelenting hold prevented him from moving freely.

"The lady's with me," Adrian said, low and menacing, and gave the guy a push to the side. "Touch her again, and I won't be responsible for my actions."

The other man straightened his shirt and shot Adrian a scathing glance. But after taking one look at Adrian's superior size and strength, the chump obviously thought better of challenging him and left the dance floor.

Adrian had every intention of dragging Chayse back to the table, but before he could do so she slipped her hands around his neck, ensnaring him with her arms and holding him in place with her sultry, disarming gaze.

She shook her head in wonder, causing those soft, disheveled waves to caress her cheek and jaw. "Talk about trading one bundle of trouble for another," she teased.

"Just say thank you," he said gruffly, and placed his hands lightly on her slender waist, because it was the safest place to keep them when he was so damned tempted to slide them elsewhere.

She swayed closer with the beat of the music, aligning their bodies even more intimately than she'd been with the previous guy. This time, of her own free will. "Thank you, though I didn't need the help."

His body responded to the warmth and softness of her supple curves, hardening him in a scalding rush of need. "What? You like being mauled by men?"

She laughed, the provocative vibration causing her breasts to jiggle enticingly against his chest. "Now that all depends on the man and the situation, though I have to agree that this wasn't the right man *or* situation. If you hadn't shown up when you did, he would have been the very unhappy recipient of having my knee jammed up against his groin."

He winced at that unpleasant image, and quickly realized that this sassy, spirited woman easily could have held her own with her dance partner.

"You, however, are the right man, in *many* ways." Her fingers played with the rebel-long strands of hair at the nape of his neck, and she tipped her head to the side. She smiled up at him flirtatiously, that lush mouth of hers displaying a wealth of erotic potential. "What is it going to take to change your mind about posing for my calendar?"

So, they were back to that again. "Absolutely nothing." He released a long exhalation just as an idea entered his mind, one that would benefit them both and finally end this agonizing situation for him. "Why don't I just write you a substantial check, donate it to your charity, and we can leave it at that?"

"I don't want your money, Adrian," she said softly, and glided her hands along his shoulders and down to his chest in a too arousing caress. "I want *you.*"

Her words held a dual meaning, one that encompassed her pursuit of him for her calendar, and the other holding a more seductive, sexual connotation. He would've liked nothing more than to take her up on that second offer, to finally slake the lust that had been riding him hard for the past hour and was increasing with each slow, rhythmic slide of her body along the length of his.

And if he wasn't careful, that lust was going to overrule his common sense. "You'd be better off taking the money, sweetheart, because that's all you're getting from me."

She mulled that over for a moment. "Tell you what, I'll make a deal with you."

He had to admit that he was curious to hear what she had to say, not that he'd agree to any kind of compromise. "What kind of deal?"

Her gaze captured his and searched deep, past those emotional barriers he'd erected and seemingly touching a piece of his soul in the process. "Tell me what you're really hiding from, and maybe I'll back off."

Adrian's lungs squeezed tight, making normal breathing difficult. How the hell she'd managed to hit him where he was most susceptible, he didn't know. And he wasn't about to stick around to find out, either. Needing to get away from Chayse and her too accurate intuition, he released her abruptly, pulled her arms from around his neck, and headed toward the men's room without looking back.

Once inside and certain he was alone, he slammed his fist against one of the steel doors, which did nothing to dissolve the reckless frustration gripping him—sexual and otherwise. He paced the length of linoleum floor like a caged animal, hating how Chayse so easily threatened his restraint when he was a man who prided himself on control—in his life, with his job and business, and especially with women.

At least until her, he acknowledged, and shoved his hands through his thick hair. Now he was constantly grappling for the upper hand between them, and battling an upheaval of emotion he had no use for. And the last thing he wanted or needed was the complication of a woman who got to him on such an innate level.

He heard someone enter the rest room and turned around, stunned to find Chayse standing just feet away from him. She locked the main door as if to keep him from bolting again, then leaned against it.

He jammed his hands on his hips and summoned his most intimidating scowl. "Just in case it's escaped your notice, you're in the men's rest room."

She ignored his sarcasm, and that direct, probing look was back in her eyes again. "Mia mentioned that your brothers nicknamed you the Wilde One, because you've always taken sports and other adventures to the extreme. Is that true?"

"Yes." Uncertain what she was getting at, he waved an impatient hand between them. "What's your point?"

"How wild and daring are you *really?*"

Furious at her audacity in challenging his manhood, he slowly closed the distance between them until he was looming in front of her. The little spitfire was attempting to pressure him, trying to eventually break him down so he'd give her what she'd been wanting from him for the past four months.

It wasn't going to happen.

He flattened his hands against the door on either side of her shoulders, trapping her against a hard slab of wood and his taut, unyielding body. His mouth twisted with a perverse smile. "You'd like to know just how daring I am?"

Instead of shrinking back from the bite in his tone, that stubborn, defiant chin of hers lifted. "Yeah, I would, because it seems to me you're not quite living up to that risk-taking reputation of yours."

Because he wasn't willing to do her calendar. He inhaled a deep breath, his nostrils flaring. God, she was bold and brazen, and incredibly brave to provoke him when he was feeling so hot, edgy, and resentful. "Well, let me show you just how wild and extreme I can be."

Before she could so much as utter a comeback or realize his intent, he captured her mouth with his. Her lips parted as she sucked in a quick, startled breath, and he shoved his fingers into her hair and held her head in his hands, rendering her immobile as he delivered a demanding, open-mouthed, tongue-tangling kiss she couldn't escape.

Knowing how tough and obstinate she was, he wasn't at all gentle with her, determined to instigate a bit of uncertainty in that confidence of hers so she'd back off. He was also hell-bent on making sure she knew what he wanted from her, what he'd greedily take given the opportunity—*her body*. He shifted closer and poured everything into the hot, ruthless kiss—aggression, dominance, and the desperate need to purge her from his mind, his dreams, his entire system.

Fire pooled in his belly, and lower, his anger mingling with an undeniable need to possess her in every way imaginable. She didn't resist him as he continued to consume her mouth the same way he wanted to ravish her body, with his lips, teeth, and tongue, and the craving for her grew stronger, a ravenous heat and hunger he was hard pressed to keep at bay.

His thick erection nudged her mound, and he slid a muscular thigh up between her legs until his knee pressed against her sex, forcing her to ride him. God, he'd never, ever needed a woman as badly as he ached for Chayse. Despite how she aggravated him, he wanted to worship her with his hands, taste her everywhere with his tongue until she begged him to let her come. Then he wanted to fuck her until she screamed with the pleasure of it, and he finally gave himself over to the hot, pulsing release he'd denied himself for too long.

She shuddered and moaned, and it was the pressure of her fingers digging into his arms that snapped him out of his carnal thoughts. He immediately let her go and stepped back so he wasn't crushing her against the door, so that he wasn't wrapped so intimately around her. They stared at one another, both of them breathing hard, panting. Her violet eyes were wide and dilated, her expression stunned and just a tad bit uncertain.

He should have been gratified that he'd finally managed to crack that resolve of hers, but instead his gut twisted with contrition for his barbaric behavior. He'd never treated a woman so roughly before, not that she'd tried to stop him. No, she'd let him have his way with her, accepting his penchant for being assertive and in control.

While he still had her off balance, he pressed his advantage. "If you insist on getting those pictures, you're going to have to spend the weekend alone with me at my cabin to get them. And I can just about guarantee that if *you're* enough of a risk-taker to join me, we'll finish what we started here tonight. Are you willing to take that chance?"

Still seemingly dazed by all that had transpired, she shook her head and whispered, "No."

He unlocked the door and eased it open for her. "Didn't think so, and trust me, you'll be better off, in every way, by finding someone else to pose for your calendar."

For the first time ever, she issued no argument and slipped out of the bathroom, and most likely out of his life. Just as he wanted.

He ought to have been overjoyed for accomplishing his goal. Unfortunately, the victory left a bitter taste in his mouth and generated yet another unwanted emotion—regret for what might have been.

# Chapter Two

Adrian wasn't going to be happy to see her, of that Chayse was certain. Lying in the large hammock secured to the thick porch posts of his family's small, cozy cabin while waiting for her outdoor man to arrive, Chayse basked in the warmth of the early morning sun on her face and bare legs. She was more than prepared to deal with his wrath, more than willing to spend the weekend with Adrian to get the pictures she wanted, and ultimately rise to his dare and show him just how much of a risk-taker *she* could be.

Especially after chickening out with him the evening before.

Chayse winced at the cowardly recollection of how she'd bolted, a moment of weakness she didn't plan to repeat. After spending most of the night berating herself for letting Adrian intimidate her with the hottest, most provocative kiss she'd ever experienced, she'd gotten up early this morning, her resolve rejuvenated and her fortitude stronger than ever. She hadn't gotten through life by shrinking from a confrontation, or allowing anyone to coerce her into backing down from something that mattered to her.

She'd learned the valuable lesson of being strong

and determined at the age of fourteen, after the death of her ten-year-old brother, Kevin. Her mother's emotional withdrawal had followed, and her parents ultimately divorced, leaving her floundering for a place to belong. She'd learned to depend on no one but herself, and developed the courage to take chances and fight for what she believed in, or wanted. And she believed in this calendar project that was a tribute to her brother, and she wanted Adrian's gorgeous face and sexy body to grace not only the cover, but the pages within.

She breathed the crisp, cool spring air, knowing she could have found another outdoor man to take Adrian's place. It sure would have been a much easier task than going head to head with the Wilde One himself—and she'd almost given up on him for good after he'd rattled her senses with his kiss last night.

There was also her own burning curiosity about Adrian and his true reasons for refusing her request time and again. She knew he was hiding something. She'd always had an eye for that kind of thing, for seeing deeper than the surface. She supposed that uncanny ability came from being a photographer, of being able to really look into a person's eyes, or read body language and recognize subtle nuances that nobody else seemed to notice. Adrian was much too defensive about a photo shoot most men would have fun doing in the name of charity, and she was here to discover why. She'd always relished a good challenge, and Adrian was one big complex puzzle that intrigued her.

She was back in the ring for another round, and this time she was doing so with a clear understanding of the ultimatum he'd given her. That if she made the decision to pursue him for the photos she wanted, not only was she going to have to spend the weekend alone with him, but there would be a heck of a lot more going on between them than picture taking.

A shiver stole through her, puckering her nipples against her ribbed tank top and eliciting a tumble of excitement in the pit of her belly. Oh yeah, she knew and accepted his terms, and she was perfectly aware that her unexpected presence was the equivalent of handing herself over to him on a silver platter—naked and his for the taking. Willingly so.

She hadn't had sex in a good long time, and if the chemistry that had ignited between them last night was any indication, she was in for one heck of a wild, satisfying weekend. And in the end, they'd both leave this cabin having gotten exactly what they wanted from each other—a win-win situation in her estimation.

The thought put a smile on her face, and with the push of her sandaled toe against the porch railing, she set the hammock into a slow, relaxing swing. She sighed and closed her eyes, saturating her senses with the sounds of chirping birds and the rush of water flowing through the creek that ran alongside the cabin. She couldn't help but envy Adrian for having such a peaceful place to escape to, a hideaway retreat tucked away just outside of the Kankakee River State Park and surrounded by trails and trees and craggy rocks. She appreciated Mia giving her the directions she'd needed to get here and surprise Adrian.

The rumbling sound of a vehicle driving up the dirt road leading to the cabin interrupted her peaceful interlude, and she opened her eyes to see Adrian's red Jeep appearing around a bend in the road. He came to a long, skidding stop in front of the cabin, creating a billow of dust that settled over her just washed Honda Accord. With his fingers wrapped tight around the steering wheel, he remained perfectly still and stared up at her in shock, as if he couldn't quite bring himself to believe she was for real. She grinned and waggled her fingers in greeting, making sure he realized she was no figment of his imagination.

She saw him close his eyes, take a deep breath, then slide from the driver's side of the Jeep. He walked to the back of the vehicle and grabbed a duffel bag with one hand, and two plastic sacks of groceries with the other. Then he headed toward the cabin.

That he wasn't happy to see her was an understatement. The man was downright furious, and he didn't have to say a word to express his simmering anger. The tense set of his body, his clenched jaw, and his fuming silence said it all.

Despite the sudden rapid beat of her heart, she remained right where she was—on the hammock, waiting to take her cue from him. He climbed the steps, and without so much as looking her way or acknowledging her, he unlocked the door and entered the cabin with the screen door slapping shut behind him like a gunshot. The loud sound made her jump and question the wisdom of infringing upon his male domain.

She immediately pushed that thought out of her head. She would *not* let him intimidate her this time.

A moment later he came back out; still ignoring her, he returned to his Jeep to retrieve more bags of groceries. Once again, he entered the cabin without so much as eye contact, treating her as if she didn't exist. That if maybe he didn't acknowledge her, she'd go away.

Nope, not a chance.

She'd expected him to verbally vent his displeasure, but his silent treatment and his barely restrained temper were almost worse than him just getting pissed at her and letting it out of his system. And sooner or later, she had no doubt his control would snap and he'd vent all that resentment shimmering off him in waves.

Hearing him moving around inside, making no attempt to deal with the woman waiting for him on the porch, she realized she had two choices—to leave and forget about Adrian, or face the gorgeous, moody Adonis inside and let him know she was here to stay. Since going home wasn't an option, she headed down to her car to retrieve her overnight bag and camera equipment, and prepared herself for a confrontation.

It took her two trips to bring everything inside, and she set her belongings in the living room. The cabin was small, but well kept and nicely furnished in oak, beige tones, and hunter green accents. In a sweeping glance, she was able to see the entire layout of the place. Two doors led to two separate bedrooms, one that looked slightly larger than the other. There was a bathroom, and a cozy dining area that adjoined the kitchen.

Knowing Adrian was putting away his groceries, she headed in that direction. Her sandals clicked on the polished wood floor, announcing her presence, but he didn't turn around and kept stocking the shelves with canned goods.

That was okay by her for the moment, since his backside was especially fine to look at. Leaning against the door frame, she eyed him from a professional standpoint, as a subject she'd be photographing. But it didn't take long for feminine instincts to take over, and soon she was studying him as a man in his prime, physically and sexually.

He had an amazing body, athletic and honed to perfection from his business that catered to extreme sports and outdoor adventures, and his obvious hands-on dedication to rock climbing, water rafting, and skiing in the winter. He was tall, with wide shoulders that tapered to a lean waist. Faded, well-worn jeans hugged his tight ass and strong-looking thighs. There wasn't an ounce of excess fat on his lean, muscled frame from what she could see.

He wore his pitch black hair longer than was stylish. The thick, glossy strands were tousled around his head from his drive in his open-air Jeep, adding to his bad-boy appeal. The man was outdoor rugged and a little rough around the edges, pure sex and sin in one breath-stealing package. An untamable rebel who tempted her to take a walk on the wild side with him.

If only he'd acknowledge her.

Tired of his silence, she opted to lighten the atmosphere. "The hospitality around here sure is lacking."

"If you want to be waited on, I suggest you go stay at the St. Claire." Finished stashing the perishables in the refrigerator, he twisted the top off a bottle of orange juice and chugged half the contents.

The St. Claire was one of Chicago's finest hotels, and far beyond what her budget could afford. "Okay, so there's no bellman to help bring in my bags or room service to make my meals. I can live with that. I swear I'm not high maintenance at all. In fact, I don't need much—"

He spun around so quickly, she lost her train of thought and her ability to speak. His intense blue eyes bore into her, searing her with that burning look. *"What* are you doing here?"

She thought that would have been obvious, but it was clear that he'd never anticipated that she'd actually take him up on his offer. It was nice to see *him* off balance for a change. "If I remember correctly, you invited me here."

He set the bottle of orange juice on the counter with a loud *thunk.* "If I remember correctly, you said *no.*"

"I changed my mind." She shrugged her shoulder, and felt her breasts rise and fall with the movement. "A woman's prerogative and all that."

High color slashed across his cheekbones, and his lips flattened into a grim line. His gaze raked down the length of her body, taking in her tank top and drawstring shorts in that one scathing glance, making her feel as though he'd stripped her naked. His eyes lingered on her chest, and in response her breasts swelled and her nipples tightened. She wasn't wearing a bra. She wasn't so huge that she needed one all the time, and since she'd never liked the feeling of being confined, she went without a bra whenever she could get away with it.

She refused to cross her arms over her chest like a timid virgin, and he made no attempt to conceal his hot, hungry gaze, or the impressive erection making itself known behind the fly of his jeans. He'd made it abundantly clear last night that he wanted her body, and obviously a night's sleep hadn't changed his mind.

"How did you find this place?" he demanded gruffly.

She figured she owed him that much of an explanation. "I called Mia, and since she didn't know how to get here, she called your brother Steve and he was nice enough to give her directions, which she passed on to me."

He scrubbed a hand along his taut jaw. "I'm going to kick his ass when I get home," he muttered.

"He was only being helpful."

"He's overstepping boundaries when this is none of his business." He pointed a finger at her, his defenses flaring again. "As for you, you wasted a trip, so you might as well take that sweet little ass of yours back to Chicago before I decide you're fair game."

A tiny thrill shot through her, bolstering not only her desire for this man, but her fortitude, as well. She was beginning to understand Adrian well enough to realize he was trying to instill a bit of fear in her with his words, and eventually, his actions. But she was ready to take whatever he dished out and give back as good as he delivered.

"I don't consider my trip here wasted. Not according to the ultimatum you issued me last night." She smiled confidently. "I believe you told me that if I wanted the pictures, I was going to have to spend the weekend alone with you here at your cabin to get them. Well, here I am. I'll honor my end of the bargain if you honor yours."

"God, you are the most thickheaded woman I've ever met!" He slashed a hand between them. "You just don't get it, do you?"

"No, I don't get your resistance at all." And she desperately wanted to understand his reasons.

He stalked toward her, slow and predatory, his expression as dark as a summer storm. "You don't want me for your calendar."

She released an exasperated breath. "I wouldn't have come this far if I didn't." She shook her head, and the swish of her hair tickled her neck. "Mia told me you're one of the kindest, most caring and giving guys she knows, and even she can't understand why this is such a problem for you."

He stopped less than a foot away, the heat and male scent of him overwhelming her thoughts, arousing her body, and creating a heavy, tingling sensation between her thighs. The man's ability to turn her on, even during a confrontation, was nothing short of amazing. Then again, Adrian was an amazingly sexy guy who'd been a part of her most erotic fantasies for months now.

He didn't reply, just glared and remained quiet, emanating a sexual kind of tension that seemed to increase with each passing second between them.

"Give me a solid reason why you can't do this calendar project for me," she said, pushing him for an answer, even while she resisted the urge to reach out and touch him, to see if she could shatter that control of his. Instead, she provoked him with the only arsenal she had at hand—her words. "Quit skirting whatever it is that has you so bent out of shape, and convince me that I need to find someone else."

"You want a solid reason?" He was literally in her face, his tone low and furious as he yanked the hem of his gray T-shirt from his jeans. "I'll give you *three* reasons why you need to turn tail and get the hell out of here and find yourself another *willing* guy."

In one smooth move, he turned around and ripped his shirt over his head and tossed it onto the counter. For a moment she was confused, and then she gasped in startled surprise when she noticed that his beautiful back, sculpted from outdoor sports and physical labor, was marred by two long, thick, healed scars that slashed from his left shoulder down to the middle of his back.

"That's two reasons," he bit out, and faced her again, his hands quickly unbuckling his belt, unfastening the button to his jeans, and easing down his zipper just low enough for him to tug down the waistband of his pants and briefs to show her yet another imperfection. "And here's your third reason."

She swallowed hard and glanced down, following the black line of hair that bisected his abdomen, swirled around his navel, and arrowed down to his groin. Somehow, despite the raging arousal straining against the confines of his underwear, he managed to remain decent. But at the moment, it wasn't his erection that captured her attention; instead her gaze was riveted to yet another line of red, puckered skin that started just above his hipbone, traveled inward, and ended only inches away from the most masculine part of him.

"Satisfied?" he drawled in a mocking tone.

She lifted her gaze back to his face just in time to see

a glimpse of guarded emotions before they were chased away with a scowl. There was a story behind those scars, she was sure. One that encompassed a whole lot more than sustaining a physical injury. Those wounds might have healed, but she was betting there were other memories that were still fresh and raw, which was the cause of those barriers he'd erected between them, along with his defiant anger. She ached to know what happened, but knew now wasn't the time to press that particular issue.

"Adrian," she breathed, not sure what to say for pushing him to this extreme, but unable to regret finding out the truth. "I'm sorry."

"I don't want your pity or sympathy." He paced away from her, not bothering to zip up his jeans, and those scars on his back shifted and bunched with every move he made. "I just want you to leave me the hell alone."

She just bet he did, but he'd done nothing to convince her to find another guy for her project. She still wanted Adrian, and all he represented. Strength, athleticism, along with an untamable wildness that would prompt a whole lot of women to purchase the calendar.

She followed behind him, uncaring that she was crowding his personal space. "I don't pity you. You wanted to shock me, and you did, because that was the last thing I'd expected. But those scars don't change my mind. In fact, they make you human and give you a sexy edge that makes you all the more appealing."

He turned back around, his expression a mixture of incredulity and anger. Her traitorous gaze was once again drawn to the scar on his hip that now disappeared into the waistband of his briefs. His entire body vibrated with aggression, like a high voltage wire just waiting to snap.

Slowly, she reached out and glided the pad of her

finger along the beginning of the scar. He flinched, and before she could trace the length, he grabbed her wrist and yanked her hand away, but didn't let her go.

*"Don't."* A muscle in his cheek ticked, and he pressed his thumb against the rapid beat of the pulse in her wrist.

She frowned, wondering if the injury still caused him pain. "Does it still hurt?"

*"You* make me hurt," he said huskily, and released her hand. "And if you touch me again, if you stay, then consider yourself touched in return."

The threat was inherently sexual, and wholly exciting. This time, Chayse knew exactly what was in store for her and was prepared to accept the consequences of her actions. Holding his gaze, she brazenly stroked her fingers along the scar, blatantly touching him. Daring him. "Then do it, because I'm not leaving until I get what I came here for."

In a lightning quick move, he lunged at her, buried his fingers in her hair, and pressed her up against the refrigerator with his hard, undeniably aroused body. With a low growl encompassing both frustration and urgent need, he slanted his mouth across hers and sank his tongue deep, kissing her just as recklessly as he had the night before. His mouth promised sin and unrestrained, carnal pleasure, and she matched him stroke for stroke, chasing his tongue with her own, letting him know that she was with him all the way.

The feverish intensity between them was sizzling hot, the strength and immediacy of her arousal making her knees weak. She slid her arms around his waist and skimmed her hands down to cup his buttocks through soft, worn denim. The muscles tightened under her palms, and the long, hard length of him pushed insistently against the crux of her thighs. She felt the bite of his belt buckle against her hip, but she was too swamped with the desire and need coiling tighter and tighter within her to care about the minor discomfort.

With his lips still devouring her mouth with aggressive, utterly devastating kisses, he shoved the hem of her tank top up impatiently, baring her naked breasts to the cool air in the cabin. She shivered and moaned as his big, warm hands closed over her breasts, rubbing and massaging the small mounds of flesh, then rolled her hard, sensitive nipples between his fingers.

He broke their kiss, lowered his head, and closed his mouth over her taut, aching breast. He laved her nipple with his tongue before nipping with his teeth, then sucked her strong and deep, until she felt that same seductive, pulling sensation in the pit of her belly. An electric jolt zapped through her, exploding in heated ripples that thrummed across her nerve endings.

Her skin tingled everywhere, hot and alive with sensation. She twined her fingers in his soft, thick hair, feeling breathless and dizzy and unable to do anything but hold on, let him have his way with her body, and give in to the four months of wild, pent-up passion between them.

He wedged his foot between hers, widening her stance. One hand left her breast and slid down her ribs to her belly. Reaching the waistband of her shorts, he unraveled the tie with a quick yank, loosened the drawstring, and let her shorts drop to the floor.

She sucked in a quick breath, and her heart raced in anticipation as his hand slid between her thighs and his mouth returned to hers, hot and hungry and demanding, allowing her no escape. His fingers skimmed along the leg opening of her panties, and then they were edging under it, delving through damp curls and gliding along the soft, swollen lips of her sex. A blunt finger slipped easily into her, followed by a second that seemed too much to take all at once. She whimpered into his mouth and stiffened, but then his thumb pressed against her cleft, right where she needed his touch the most, both soothing and arousing her at the same time.

As soon as she relaxed, he pushed deeper, filling her, and her inner muscles clamped tight around his fingers, resisting the invasion. Her head rolled back against the wall, and she panted for air, wondering how she was going to be able to take all of him when the time came.

His big body shuddered, and he buried his face against her neck, his ragged breath hot and damp against her skin. "You are so fucking tight, so hot and wet," he rasped in her ear. "I want inside you."

Wanting that just as much, she gave him her answer. "Yes."

He withdrew his fingers, and she actually mourned the loss until he slid his hands beneath her bottom and lifted her off her feet. As if they'd done this a dozen times before, she automatically entwined her arms around his neck, locked her ankles at the base of his spine, and held on tight as he carried her toward the bedroom.

Once inside, he dropped her on the soft comforter covering the bed, the light in his eyes possessive and bright with lust as he dragged her panties off, nearly ripping them in his haste to get her naked. He left her tank top bunched above her bared breasts, and with quick, urgent movements he shoved his own briefs and jeans down to his thighs, freeing his full, thick erection. Before she could look her fill, he was pushing her legs wide apart, and his dark head dipped down. The feel of his hot, damp mouth on her inner thigh shocked her, along with the scrape of his teeth and the swirl of his tongue as he burned a sensuous path up to the pulsing, aching core of her.

She moaned as he licked her clit in a hot, searing stroke. Seemingly ruthless in his quest to make her come, he closed his warm, wet mouth over her and plunged his tongue deep. The pleasure was sharp and riveting and stole her breath. A low throbbing began in her belly, then spiraled down to her sex, and she grabbed handfuls of his hair, wanting more, needing more . . .

The sleek, gliding pressure of his thumbs caressing her soft lips and stroking her rhythmically, combined with his wicked tongue working its own seductive magic, was the most erotic sensation she'd ever experienced. Unable to hold back, she let out a cry and arched sinuously against his mouth as she came in a burning wave that shook her entire body.

Without giving her a chance to fully recover from her orgasm, he moved up over her, the slide of his muscled body against hers making her pulse leap higher and faster. She reached down to touch him, and when her fingers fluttered over the broad velvet head of his shaft, he sucked in a hissing breath. Grasping both of her wrists, he pulled her arms up and pinned them above her head, giving him complete control of the situation.

He settled more fully on top of her, his thighs forcing hers farther apart, and then he was pressing his erection intimately against her, nudging his way in, stretching her, setting her body on fire. She caught a glimpse of his dark, fierce expression before he crushed his mouth to hers and kissed her deeply, passionately. She tasted herself on his lips, on his tongue, just as he buried his shaft to the hilt in her slick heat, possessing her completely.

Their moans mingled, and once he began to move, there was no stopping him, and she instinctively knew there wasn't going to be anything slow or gentle about this first joining. No, judging by the sexual energy and potent heat radiating off him, she prepared herself for a fast, hard, unrestrained ride.

And that was exactly what he gave her. He plunged

into her, fast and deep and strong, a rich, seductive rhythm that pulsed as vitally as her heartbeat. His hips ground against hers with each driving, impaling thrust until she felt him go rigid and his lower body arched into her high and hard, pushing her up and over yet another crest. She came again in a blinding climax of intoxicating speed and delirious sensation.

This time, so did he. A low growl erupted from his chest and vibrated against her lips as his body jerked violently against hers and he finally succumbed to his own blistering orgasm.

More reluctantly that he cared to acknowledge, Adrian withdrew from Chayse's warm, soft body, rolled to his back beside her, and slung his forearm over his eyes, wondering if he'd ever be the same again. His lungs felt tight, his breathing choppy, as though he'd run a marathon. Blood pounded in his temples and his heart raced a mile a minute. He felt completely drained and totally wasted—four months of frustration and desire and lust finally spent on the one woman he'd craved for just as long.

What the hell had he been thinking to carry her into the bedroom, pin her to the mattress, and take her like some wild man? Problem was, he hadn't been thinking, at least not with the head on his shoulders. No, he'd been so caught up in Chayse, the scent that was uniquely hers, the softness of her skin beneath his hands, the taste of her on his tongue, and the gripping need to drive inside her and make her his. At that moment, nothing else had mattered.

Never had a woman affected him on such a primitive, I-need-to-get-inside-you-now level, but Chayse had that effect on him since day one, and he'd supposed it was just a matter of the right time and opportunity before they acted on their mutual attraction. Their confrontation in the kitchen had provided such an opportunity, and when she'd made the mistake of challenging him, then boldly caressed the scars he'd bared to make her back off and leave, that was all it had taken for him to unleash the fiery hunger smoldering beneath the surface of his anger.

As the cool air in the cabin rushed over his heated skin and half-naked body, a stunning realization hit him like a sucker punch to the stomach. *Holy shit.* He'd taken Chayse without protection, which said a helluva lot for his state of mind since wearing a condom during sex was a hard-and-fast rule for him. There had even been times he'd refused because he hadn't had one on hand.

Not so today. And it was an issue he couldn't ignore, for either of their sakes.

He came up on his side and gazed down at her, still lying where he'd left her minutes before, looking just as wiped out as he'd been. Her eyes were closed, and her hands were still above her head where he'd anchored them, her shirt still bunched high on her chest. Her breasts rose and fell with each deep breath, her nipples tight and just as flushed as the rest of her naked body.

She looked . . . *beautiful*, and he wanted to touch her, caress her soft, warm cheek with the back of his knuckles and smooth her disheveled hair away from her face. That bit of tenderness weaving through his system startled him, and he dismissed the thoughts filtering in his mind before he followed through on them.

He wondered if she was sleeping, or if maybe he'd been too rough with her, too demanding, and she was trying to recover. Lord knew he'd taken her with little finesse and a whole lot of sexual aggression, and that knowledge sparked a bit of worry.

"Chayse?" He murmured it gently, and did what he'd

sworn he wouldn't do again—he touched her, trailing his fingers over the slope of her shoulder and down her arm. "You okay?"

She turned her head his way, and her lashes fluttered open. And when a sated, sexy smile curved her lips, it was all he could do not to pull her beneath him again for another round.

"I'm okay," she said huskily, and finally pulled her tank top back down over her pert breasts—not out of modesty, but because he suspected she was chilled without his body heat to warm her.

"Look . . ." He drew a deep breath before saying, "I didn't use protection."

As if moving in slow motion, she sat up, reached for her panties, and pulled them up her legs and over her bottom. "Don't worry," she reassured him. "I'm on the Pill."

He nodded, extremely grateful for small favors. "Oh, good."

She glanced at him and combed her hair away from her face with her fingers. "My doctor put me on it almost a year ago for medical reasons . . . and you're the first person I've been with since then."

She obviously wanted him to know that she didn't do this kind of thing often, and that notion pleased him more than he wanted to admit. Moving to his side of the bed, he stood up and pulled his briefs and jeans back up, feeling compelled to reassure her, too. "I want you to know I'm clean, so no worries there, either."

"Me, too."

He nodded curtly, suddenly feeling awkward and uncertain with her—another first that confounded him when he was so used to emotionless encounters. And damn if he hadn't felt *something* when he'd been deep inside of her. More than sex and pleasure, she'd not only touched his scars, but managed to touch his soul, as well. And it had been a very long time since he'd let any woman that close.

"You can use the bathroom in here," he said, pointing to the adjoining door, desperate to escape to the great outdoors and breathe clear, clean air into his lungs instead of the mingled scents of sex and Chayse. "I'll use the one in the other room."

With that, he left her alone, certain after the way he'd treated her she'd get dressed and hightail it out of there and head back to the city where she belonged. The thought should have relieved him, but instead left him with a hollow feeling in his chest.

# Chapter Three

Chayse gave Adrian a half hour on his own before deciding it was time for her to fight for her cause yet again. She refused to let him withdraw from her, and she still wasn't taking no for an answer. Nor would she allow him to berate himself for what had just transpired between them. It had been a long time in coming, and so worth the wait.

She harbored no regrets, except for the fact that he'd bolted so quickly afterward, leaving her feeling much too alone. And that realization startled her, because she'd been on her own for a long time now and was *used* to being alone.

Having changed into a pair of jeans, a baby doll T-shirt sans a bra, and sneakers, she stuffed her shorts, tank top, and sandals into her duffle, her insides still recovering from their very tempestuous joining. And her outsides, for that matter, as well, she thought with a private smile. Her skin felt hypersensitive, her breasts swollen and tender, and her sex still tingled from two of the most incredible, earth-shattering climaxes she'd ever had the pleasure of enjoying. The man had easily discovered her sweetest spots, and had used that intimacy to his advantage, and hers.

Grabbing her camera and making sure it was loaded with a full roll of film, she headed outside and followed the steady and loud *thwack, thwack, thwack* sound coming from the side of the cabin. She rounded the corner and stopped in her tracks, momentarily mesmerized at the breathtaking sight that greeted her.

Adrian was chopping wood, his back facing her as he set a thick log on the base of a large tree stump, and with a very accurate, downward swing of his axe he split the limb in two. He tossed the chunks of wood into a growing pile next to the cabin, then he repeated the process all over again.

He was still shirtless, and the sun glinted off his tanned, muscled shoulders and back, and made the fine sheen of perspiration on his upper body shimmer with every move he made. His rakishly long hair was mussed from their earlier romp, and the ends curled damply around the nape of his neck. He was sex and sin personified, the complete embodiment of a gorgeous, earthy male in his element.

She couldn't have set him up with better props if she tried, or a more perfect backdrop than the craggy rocks, trees, and trails behind him. Lifting the camera, she began taking pictures. This was the real outdoor man she wanted to capture on film—no pretenses, no stiff pose or fabricated smile for the camera. Just a man at one with nature, a man who enjoyed the sun and the earth and hard, physical labor.

He didn't acknowledge her, even though she knew he must have heard her behind him, gliding closer, the click of her camera, the whir of film advancing. She moved to the side, focusing on a profile shot which would eliminate the red, puckered scars on his back that seemed to make him so self-conscious. Instead, she concentrated on his muscled arms, his defined chest and lean belly, and the way those jeans of his rode low on his hips.

She took in his dark hair that fell over his brow, the chiseled cut of his jaw, and the beautiful mouth that had given her such incredible pleasure. In time, she hoped those lips would curve into one of his trademark Wilde grins, which she'd been lucky enough to glimpse the first time she'd met him. Before he'd realized she wanted him for her calendar project.

She hadn't seen that sexy smile since.

As she continued taking pictures, she read his body language and those subtle nuances she picked up behind the camera, and knew there wasn't much anger left in him. He was releasing a whole lot of frustrated energy, yes, but there was a resignation about him that bolstered her confidence and gave her hope that she had his cooperation from here on.

He stopped chopping wood and finally glanced her way as she snapped another picture. He said nothing, another good indication that he wasn't going to order her away yet again. Not that she'd go. He watched her, his seductive blue eyes intense and searching, as if he was trying to figure her out, who she was beyond the woman with the camera, what drove her . . . *and what was she hiding from?*

In that moment, she felt a sudden shift between them. Her pulse leapt, and she realized she didn't like being on the receiving end of such an analytic stare. For as much as she liked observing and scrutinizing a person's personality and actions from behind her camera, she'd also used that same camera as a shield to her own emotions and soul-deep pain.

She'd always felt safe behind her lens, always peeking in on other people's lives and feelings, but keeping her own hidden away. She'd never felt threatened that someone might realize her ploy, and that Adrian might have that ability made her feel too vulnerable. Because while his scars were on the outside in plain sight, hers were inside, buried deep, and she had no desire to allow anyone close enough to unearth them. As a result, her relationships had always been short-lived, with her ending things before they got too serious. Before she gave her heart and opened herself up to the possible loss and rejection she swore she'd never again subject herself to.

She realized Adrian had that power, and it was a realization that shook her to the very core of her being.

Finally, he spoke, and she was grateful for the reprieve from her unsettling thoughts. "I'm sorry for what happened in there," he said, his tone low and sincere, his gaze still watching her.

"I'm not sorry, so don't go and heap guilt on your conscience for my sake." Not quite ready to lower her camera, she took another picture of him, then another. While she wasn't ready to let him look her in the eyes, she had no problem being honest on this particular issue. "I was a willing participant every step of the way, and that was the best sex I've had in a long time."

"Yeah, me too." The corner of his mouth quirked, the closest she'd gotten to a smile from him in months, and she caught it on film.

He tipped his head, and for as much as he'd previously protested her taking his picture, he didn't so much as object to her enthusiasm now. "Are you still planning on staying the entire weekend?" he asked directly.

He wasn't ordering her to leave, and she took that as a very positive sign. "Yep," she replied with absolute certainty, and took an upper body shot of him before finally lowering her camera.

His gaze slowly flickered down the length of her, then traversed its way back up to her mouth. "Good, because it's going to take me at least that long to get you out of my system."

Shivers of delight rippled through her at the thought of being Adrian's for the weekend, of letting him have his way with her and being able to fulfill a fantasy or two of her own. "I take it we have ourselves a deal?"

The wicked gleam in his blue eyes spoke volumes. "I believe we do."

She breathed a sigh of relief, and felt compelled to let him know she understood his reservations, that she wouldn't exploit him in a way that made him uncomfortable. "Adrian . . . while a great body is essential for this calendar to draw buyers, it isn't all just about hard bodies. It's also about a certain smoldering look, which you have, a come-hither glance, a tempting smile. Those are the things that cause a woman's stomach to flutter and make her weak in the knees when she looks at a picture of you." He definitely had that seductive effect on her. "I also want you to know that I respect the way you feel about those scars, and I'll take the pictures in a way that won't blatantly display them. I'll even let you have final approval of what shots go into the calendar."

He nodded, his expression one of gratitude. "Fair enough."

Luckily, he looked good from any angle. She nodded toward the pile of wood, and strove to lighten the last bit of tension between them. "So, are you done taking out your frustration on those logs?"

He actually laughed, the sound rich and warm, like a fine cognac. "Yeah, I'm done," he said, and buried the blade end of the axe into the tree stump.

Oh wow, an amused, agreeable Adrian was far more potent than the stubborn man she'd been pursuing for months now. Mia had told her that under normal circumstances Adrian was charming, carefree, and flirtatious, and it pleased Chayse to see this side of him. To be the recipient of more than just his scowls and resistance.

"I was hoping we could go hiking through some of

these trails and I could take more shots of you outdoors, while the sun is still high in the sky," she said.

Hands propped on his hips, he glanced up at the
rugged hills surrounding the cabin, then back to her, a
glimmer of doubt in his gaze. "You sure you can handle
these mountains?"

It seemed he'd already learned how best to provoke
her, and that she wasn't one to resist a challenge. "Of
course I can handle it!"

"Alright," he drawled lazily. "Then let's do it."

Two and a half hours later they returned from their
jaunt through the hills behind the cabin. Adrian was
running on pure physical adrenaline, the kind that rushed
through his blood after a good, long, hard workout.
And navigating the uneven terrain and steep slopes that
made up the trails he liked to hike definitely qualified
as strenuous exercise.

He cast an amused glance at the woman who'd accompanied him on the hike. While she was panting for
breath, her skin flushed and glowing with perspiration,
he felt invigorated and ready to do it all over again.

"Good Lord," Chayse said as she dragged herself up
the front steps of the cabin to the porch. "Why didn't
you tell me we'd be climbing Mount Everest?"

He chuckled, glad to see she'd found some humor in
the situation when most women would have whined and
complained once they'd grown tired. Chayse had been
a trooper, sucking it up even when he'd noticed how exhausted she was. And that's when he'd headed back
home, knowing she'd had enough.

"That was nothing, sweetheart," he said, and jogged
effortlessly up the steps behind her. "You ought to join
me on a rock climbing expedition sometime."

"Thanks, but no thanks." She collapsed in the hammock, her body sprawled on the netting and one leg hanging over the side. "God, I'm so out of shape," she muttered in disgust. "My legs and thighs feel like Jell-O."

"But you have to admit you got some great shots out there."

Her lashes drifted shut and she grunted. "Yeah, when you stopped long enough to let me take a few pictures here and there."

"It was purely an incentive to keep you going and make sure you didn't pass out halfway through the hike," he teased, and realized that he was smiling. Again. "It was one thing to carry your backpack of photography paraphernalia for you, but no way was I going to heft you all the way back here as dead weight."

Another grunt, which didn't sound all that complimentary.

His grin slid into a frown as he stared at her limp form. He'd meant to give her a workout, yes, but maybe he'd pushed her too hard, and that thought prompted a smidgeon of guilt. "You stay put and I'll go get you something to drink."

"Trust me, I'm not going anywhere," she murmured.

He went inside and dropped her backpack off in the living room before heading to the kitchen for a bottled water for her, and a cold beer for him. By the time he returned to the porch, she'd drifted off to sleep and was snoring softly.

Shaking his head at how quickly she'd dropped off, he perched his backside on the porch railing in front of her, twisted off the cap of his beer, and took a long drink of the malt liquor that quenched his thirst and cooled his body. Unerringly, his gaze drifted to Chayse, at the softly parted lips he'd kissed earlier and ached to kiss again, and the disheveled, chin-length, honey blond curls falling haphazardly around her face. His eyes lowered to her chest, taking in her braless breasts beneath her T-shirt, and the way the small mounds rose and fell from her even, steady breathing. It was hard not to notice her erect nipples, too, which pressed against the cotton material and made him remember how those crests felt in his mouth, against his tongue.

Ignoring the heat settling in his groin, he took another swallow of his beer, and was forced to admit that he'd actually enjoyed being with Chayse during their hike. He'd teased her, and she'd laughed and even provoked him a time or two herself. She was definitely a woman who could hold her own with words and comebacks, and he'd had a great time sparring with her. And yes, even flirting with her.

With his anger and grudge toward her dissipated, and an amenable compromise agreed upon, he'd allowed a few guarded walls to crumble. A smart move, or a stupid one, he wasn't sure yet, but he believed Chayse when she said she respected him and his feelings regarding his scars, and instinctively knew she wouldn't publish any photos without his permission or approval.

With that understanding between them, he'd decided that he wasn't going to fight whatever was between him and Chayse. His attraction to her was too strong to deprive himself of the pleasure of being with her sexually, and she'd made it perfectly clear she wanted the same thing. And he'd discovered during their hike that he flat-out *liked* her. She had a good sense of humor, and enough spunk to keep him on his toes. He admired her determination and grit, and she was completely dedicated to the calendar project he was beginning to suspect she was doing for very personal reasons that she'd yet to share with him. Then again, he'd never asked her why this project was so important, and he was suddenly very curious to know the answer.

He polished off his beer and decided to go and take

a shower, then start fixing dinner. He was just finishing up the steaks on the small outdoor grill he'd set up when Chayse finally woke up from her nap. She sat up in the hammock, combed her hair away from her face with her fingers, and rubbed at her eyes. She slowly stood up and straightened, then grimaced and placed a hand at the small of her back, and he could only assume her muscles had tightened up while she slept.

Transferring the meat to a plate, he turned off the propane tank and climbed the steps up to the porch. "Hey, sleepyhead, you planned that perfectly. The steak and side dishes are done, the table is set, and all you have to do is wash up for dinner."

"Wow, impress me with the service around here, why don't you." A sleepy smile curved the corners of her mouth, and her still hazy violet eyes met his. "The St. Claire has nothing on you."

He pointed the tongs at her, fighting another smile. "And don't you forget it, sweetheart." He held open the screen door for her, then followed her inside.

She washed her hands at the kitchen sink, then met up with him at the small dining table and sat in the seat next to his, her movements stiff and not at all relaxed. She took in the two rib eye steaks, the rice pilaf, and bowl of salad, then eyed him with mock suspicion. "You have enough here to feed *two* people. Are you sure you weren't expecting company?"

"The last thing I was expecting was company of any sort," he drawled wryly, and forked a steak onto her plate. "Everyone in my family who uses the cabin tries to keep the place well stocked. There were extra rib eyes in the freezer, and I defrosted them in the microwave before throwing them on the grill. The rice was from a box in the cupboard, and I bought enough lettuce and fixings at the grocery store on my way up here to make a salad."

She helped herself to the rice pilaf and slanted him a wide-eyed, hopeful look. "Do I get crème brûlée for dessert?"

"Don't push your luck," he said, and passed her the salad. "I bought some chocolate fudge brownie ice cream, and *maybe* I'll share it with you."

"Now there's an incentive to be good." She stretched her arm to set the bowl down on a cleared spot on the table, and winced and rubbed at her shoulder. "Wow, I can't believe how much I ache all over. You're a hard man to keep up with out there."

"You did good," he said, and meant it.

"Thanks." She poured dressing over her salad and added some croutons. "I wasn't about to admit defeat."

He laughed, not at all surprised to find out that she had a competitive nature to go along with all that determination.

A comfortable silence descended between them as they started in on their meals, and he was amazed how they'd gone from adversaries to friends in such a short time. Not to mention lovers, too. And there was no denying that he preferred their amicable rapport and the draw of sexual awareness between them much more than the contention of the past four months.

He cut a piece of steak and chewed on the juicy chunk of meat. "So, what's your vested interest in this calendar project, other than being the photographer, that is."

She raised a brow, seemingly surprised by his question, and possibly his insight. She took a long drink of the milk he'd poured for her, then asked right back, "What makes you think I have any ulterior motives other than being the photographer?"

There was enough caution in her expression to confirm his hunch, that there was much more to Chayse Douglas than met the eye. Now that they'd established a truce, he wanted to know what drove this woman, personally and professionally. "Because you're very passionate about the project, and how it's being developed. Is it all for the kids at the Children's Hospital, or is there a more personal reason involved?"

"Both," she admitted, and pushed her fork through her rice pilaf. After a moment of silence, as if contemplating whether or not to elaborate, she finally continued. "My brother Kevin died from a brain tumor when he was ten. I was fourteen at the time, and I spent most of my spare time at the hospital visiting him. I also met a lot of the other kids who were in there for other illnesses, some terminal, like Kevin's." Her gaze held a wealth of sadness. "I've been involved in other charity events to raise money for the children's ward, but yes, this calendar project is my personal baby."

He placed his hand over hers on the table and gave it a squeeze. "I'm sorry about your brother." He couldn't imagine losing one of his brothers, or any of his cousins, for that matter. They were a tight-knit group, and something like that would have devastated all of them—just as her brother's death had obviously devastated Chayse.

"He was a great kid. Always happy and optimistic, right up to the very end." She ate another bite of her steak, and went on. "But I still miss him, and often wonder what my life would be like if he were still around, if my parents would still be together . . ." Her voice trailed off and she grew quiet, as if she'd revealed more than she'd intended.

"They divorced?"

She nodded, then hesitated for a moment before trusting him enough to divulge more. "After my brother's death, my mother completely shut down emotionally, and she fell into a deep depression and refused to get treatment. My father couldn't handle the situation, so he filed for divorce, went on his way, and ended up marrying another woman."

The hurt in her voice was near tangible, wrapping around Adrian's chest and squeezing tight. For months now all he'd known was the stubborn woman with the smart mouth and spitfire attitude, and he found himself poleaxed by the vulnerable, lost little girl she'd been, and apparently still was deep inside.

"Where are your parents now?" he asked, curious to know the end to this particular story.

"My mother passed away two years ago, and my father is living in Arizona with his wife and new family." She drained the rest of her milk, and tried for a nonchalant shrug. "I don't talk to him much, maybe twice a year."

So, she truly was alone. The thought compounded the ache in his chest and made him want to reach out and pull her into his arms and do his best to chase away those unpleasant memories.

She ducked her head, looking stunned and a little embarrassed that she'd spilled so much—to him, no less. "I've never told anyone all that, except for my best friend, Faith."

He wondered if anyone had ever cared enough to ask, which said too much for his own interest in her life and past. "I promise your secret is safe with me." And what a painful one it was, which made his own private past pale in comparison.

They finished dinner, and when she stood to help clear the table, she winced again as her tendons protested the extraneous movement.

Taking the plate from her hand, he stacked it on top of his. "Go and take a long, hot shower to help loosen up those overworked muscles. I'll do the dishes."

"Now there's an offer I'm not about to refuse." A

playful smile curved the corners of her mouth. "I *hate* doing dishes."

He chuckled and watched her go, refraining from the urge to join her in the shower and help ease those achy muscles and joints in a more hands-on manner. But after their too serious discussion, he suspected she needed a bit of time by herself to regroup.

Besides, he had the rest of the night to seduce her.

Chayse stepped out of the shower and grabbed a dry towel, feeling refreshed and somewhat relaxed, if not a little off balance for how easily she'd opened up to Adrian about her past and family situation. It was true she'd never discussed those details with anyone other than Faith, and while she was shocked that she'd revealed so much to Adrian, she had to admit that his genuine interest and undivided attention had prompted her to share. Undoubtedly, those caring traits of his were dangerous to her heart, and she'd do well to keep her emotions out of this weekend's equation. They had a deal, one that encompassed pictures for her calendar and great sex, nothing more, and she'd do well to remember that.

She toweled off her body, ran a brush through her damp hair to let the strands air dry, and changed into the cotton boxer pajama set she wore at night. She headed out of the bedroom, which adjoined directly to the living room, and came to an abrupt stop when she saw how busy Adrian had been in her absence.

An air mattress had been blown up and was situated in between the couch and love seat, and was covered with blankets and pillows, making up their own little den of iniquity. Adrian himself was squatting in front of the brick hearth, tending to the crackling fire on the grate. He was shirtless, the way she liked him best, and had changed into a pair of gray cotton sweatpants. He stabbed at a burning log with a poker, and she watched the play of muscles across his broad back, toned and smooth except for those two long scars she'd yet to ask him about. And he owed her the story, after everything she'd divulged earlier.

"Hey," she said, announcing her presence as she moved deeper into the room, drawn to the man and the warmth from the fireplace. "What's all this?"

He tossed another log on the grate, adjusted the screen in front of the fire to protect them from popping embers, and straightened. He turned to face her, his gaze taking in her nighttime attire in a quick glance before returning to her freshly scrubbed face. "I thought you might like to relax by the fire. I'll give you a back rub to help soothe your abused body."

Her aching muscles rejoiced at his offer, and the rest of her body was equally thrilled at the thought of having his hands all over her. "That sounds wonderful."

"Consider me your personal masseur for the evening." A boyish smile eased up the corners of his mouth, and her stomach tumbled and her knees went weak. "It's the least I can do since I'm the one who pushed you out there on the trails today."

"So you were," she murmured, realizing just how dangerous a playful, wholly seductive Adrian could be to more than just her senses. The mattress separated them, and uncertain what he wanted her to do, she asked, "Where do you want me?"

"Now there's a loaded question." His voice was a sexy, teasing rumble, and he crooked his finger at her in a very tempting way. "Come over here, take off your top, and lay facedown on the air mattress."

She came around to where he stood, peeled off her cotton pajama top in one quick movement, and lay down in the center of the soft, fire-warmed blankets.

Cradling her head in her arms, she waited for the glorious feel of Adrian's strong, capable hands kneading away her physical aches and pains.

The mattress dipped by her side, and he sat astride her thighs from behind. He was still wearing his sweatpants, but the cotton material did nothing to conceal the hard ridge of his erection nestling intimately against her bottom as he leaned forward and splayed his big hand on her narrow back, then kneaded his fingers down the tight muscles bisecting her spine.

She groaned low in her throat, sank into the mattress like a limp doll, and melted beneath his firm, knowing touch. "That . . . feels . . . *sooo* good. By the time you're done with me, I'm gonna be putty in your hands."

"God, I hope so," he said huskily, and pressed his thumbs against a tight knot right below her shoulder blade. "So tell me, how did you get into photography?"

She buried her face in her arms, which also helped to hide her smile. "Back to me again, huh?"

"What can I say? You intrigue me."

The feeling on that was mutual, much more than was wise. "You do realize, don't you, that turnabout on all this questioning is fair play?"

"Mmmm," he replied noncommittally as his hands continued to work their magic. "I'll deal with that when the time comes."

She just bet he would, and wondered if he'd willingly tell her all about those scars of his if she asked, or evade the subject for the weekend. She planned to eventually find out.

As for the question he'd just asked her, he'd picked a safe topic, one she was comfortable with and didn't mind discussing. "When I was a junior in high school, I took a photography class. By the end of the first semester, the teacher proclaimed me a natural, took me under her wing, and taught me everything I could ever want to know about photography, like lighting and special effects, and how to develop the film on my own."

She thought back on that teacher's enthusiasm and encouragement, and how it had shaped her future. "Photography opened a whole new world for me and gave me something to focus on when everything at home was falling apart." Painful memories tried to crowd their way in, and she inhaled a deep breath, refusing to travel down that emotional road again. "After high school, I took some courses at a junior college while waitressing in the evenings. From there, I went to work at a portrait studio, but after a few months I grew bored doing the same thing day after day."

"You like to be mentally stimulated," he guessed, and ran his thumbs up the shallow indentation of her spine, all the way up to the nape of her neck, where he rubbed more taut muscles.

She shivered at the sexual connotation to his words. "That, and I like new challenges. Now I do a lot of freelance work for a couple of advertising firms who commission me for brochures and magazine ads and that kind of thing. It pays the bills and keeps me busy *and* stimulated, but someday I'd love to open up my own photography shop and offer a little bit of everything."

He skimmed his palms down her sides, his fingers brushing the plumped swells of her breasts, causing desire and liquid heat to spiral low. "I have no doubt you'll attain that goal."

Her body turned fluid under his hands, and very aroused. "And why is that?" she asked curiously, and stared at the fire burning and crackling in the grate.

"Oh, I don't know," he said in a low, mellow baritone. "It might be that stubborn, determined, persistent streak of yours that makes me believe you'll achieve anything you set your mind to. Like convincing me to do this calendar for you."

He moved off her, but before she could protest the loss, he slipped his fingers beneath the waistband of her pajama bottoms and panties, and pulled them down her long legs and off. She came up on her elbows and attempted to turn over, but before she could execute the move he was back, his thighs straddling hers once again to keep her pinned to the air mattress.

This time, he was completely naked, too, his thick erection nestling between the crease of her buttocks as he covered her from behind and aligned his chest and belly against her backside and pressed her back down onto the mattress. He twined his arms around hers, stretched her hands above her head, and wove their fingers together.

She moaned, and her pulse tripped all over itself, the delicious weight and heat of his body against hers instigating a hungry ache through her veins, as slow and lazy as warmed molasses. The man definitely had a thing for being in control, a dominant male who obviously enjoyed being sexually assertive. Not that she minded, since she knew she'd reap the pleasure of all that confident, exciting masculinity.

"Okay, your turn," he whispered, just as his soft, warm lips touched down on her shoulder, then moved to the side of her neck, making her shiver as his damp mouth and hot breath rushed over her skin and teased the shell of her ear. "Ask me something, anything at all."

He'd just given her the opportunity to turn the tables on him, to inquire about those scars of his, but how was she supposed to focus on anything remotely serious when all she could think about was having him inside her again?

A smile curved her lips, and she decided to play along with this seductive game of his. "Tell me a fantasy of yours."

"God, where do I start?" he murmured hotly in her ear, and arched his hips against her bottom, the heat and pressure of his shaft along her buttocks a maddening, arousing sensation. "You've inspired my most erotic fantasies for months now, and in my dreams I've taken you a dozen different ways. I've imagined taking you from behind like this, your tight little body clutching mine greedily, until you scream from the overwhelming pleasure of me stroking deep inside you."

A shudder rippled through her, drugging her mind, her limbs. She wanted that, too. Her sex felt swollen and achy, and she tried to open her legs for him to slip between, but he kept his knees locked tight against her thighs. Frustration mingled with her rising excitement. "Adrian, please . . ."

"Shhh, I'm not done telling you my fantasies." Releasing one of her hands, he pushed her damp hair away from her face. He nibbled her earlobe, then swirled his tongue along her neck while his fingers strummed across the plump outer swell of her breast. "I've imagined you sucking me with that soft, sexy mouth of yours, then climbing on top of me and riding my cock while I watch you caress your breasts and make yourself come. That one's a particular favorite of mine."

He was slowly driving her insane, her body strung tight and throbbing for release. And she'd do anything at all to claim the orgasm tingling just out of her reach, fulfill every erotic fantasy he desired if that's what it took to give her body what it craved. "Then let me do it."

"Mmmm, maybe I will . . . in a minute or two."

Obviously, he wasn't done tormenting her, and since she was pinned beneath him, all she could do was let him have his way with her. His flattened hand slid between the mattress and her belly and moved downward, and she almost wept in relief when his long, warm fingers burrowed between her nether lips.

He stroked her sensuously, expertly. "I love how soft you are right here, so wet and sleek. And now that I know you taste like the sweetest nectar, I just want to lap you up."

She moaned as his tongue dipped into her ear, matching the slow, intimate swirl of his fingers. Her breathing quickened as he continued to share darker, more forbidden fantasies in a low, wicked tone, until her mind and body couldn't take any more stimulation and she came on a long, intense orgasm that ripped a hoarse cry from her chest.

He withdrew his hand and moved off her, and she immediately missed his warmth and weight. She heard him throwing a few more logs in the fireplace, then silence descended, except for the crackle and pop from the wood on the grate. It took her a few moments to recover enough to turn over to see where he'd gone. He wasn't far away, and that was a good thing, because she wasn't done with *him* yet. He sat with his back against the sofa, his legs drawn up slightly, his own body far from sated.

He gazed at her through hooded blue eyes, and crooked a finger at her. "C'mere and ride me, Chayse."

It was an order she wasn't about to refuse. Licking her lips in anticipation, she crawled over to him, but instead of immediately climbing on top of his lap, she decided to put her mouth to good use and make him suffer a little bit before she put him out of his misery.

Leaning forward, she captured one of his rigid nipples between her lips, laved the erect nub of flesh with her tongue, and grazed the tip with the edge of her teeth. A groan rumbled up from his chest as she traversed her way lower, spreading hot, wet kisses on his taut, flat belly. The scar on his hip caught her attention, and she caressed the puckered skin with her tongue, and heard him suck in a surprised breath in response to her tender ministration. Finally, she came to his thick, straining erection, and even that part of him was as gorgeous and magnificent as the man himself.

She wrapped her fingers around the hard, velvet-textured length of him, and felt him pulse in her tight grip. A drop of pre-come appeared, and she smeared the silky moisture over the big, plum-shaped head of his cock.

*She had to taste him.*

She took him in her wet mouth, his skin hot and salty against the stroke of her tongue. He shuddered and tangled his hands in her damp hair, and she sucked him, taking him as deep as she could, making the fantasy he'd whispered into her ear a hard-core reality. She pleasured him with her mouth, teased him with her tongue, and aroused him to a fever pitch of need that made his entire body shake with the restraint of trying to hold back.

"Oh Christ," he breathed, and frantically tried to tug her back up. "If you don't stop now, I'm gonna come."

Since she still had more lascivious intent in mind before she let him climax, she heeded his warning. With one last irresistible lick along his shaft, she kissed her way back up his body and crawled into his lap. She straddled his hips with her knees, and directed his shaft upward. She was very wet from all their foreplay, and with deliberate slowness she sank inch by inch on top of him, until he filled her completely and her sex stretched tight around his width.

His nostrils flared, and stark male desire heated his eyes. He clutched her waist with his hands and rocked her tighter against his straining body, setting a rhythm she knew would take him quickly to his own orgasm.

Feeling naughty, and a bit wicked, she grasped his

wrists and pulled his hands away. "If I remember your fantasy correctly, you wanted to watch me come like this."

He groaned like a dying man. "I don't know if I can last that long."

Smiling, she pushed his arms to his sides. "I'll make sure you do."

What he obviously didn't realize was that in this favored position of his, he'd given her complete control of his pleasure, of his release, and she reveled in the feminine power that was hers. With him still impaled deep within her body, she cupped her breasts in her hands, fondled the small mounds, and rolled her nipples between her fingers before sliding her flattened palms down her stomach and between her splayed thighs.

She made a soft purring sound of pleasure as her fingers slipped between her soft, lush folds, then strummed across her clit. His chest rose and fell heavily, his expression fierce and hungry as he watched her caress herself and perform an erotic lap dance for his eyes only.

She felt the hot, spiraling sensation of an approaching orgasm, and she rocked into Adrian, just enough to increase the friction inside of her and against her sex. She pressed down on his erection, hard and deep, and came on a soft, shivery moan before collapsing against his chest.

"Nice fantasy," she murmured, a smile on her lips.

He laughed, the sound strained as he trailed his fingertips down her spine. "For you, maybe. I'm still hard as a spike."

"Mmmm, so you are." She'd left him that way, deliberately so, and wriggled her bottom against his groin, which prompted a low growl from him.

She lifted her head and stared into his blue eyes, bright with firelight and a burning passion she'd never seen in another man's eyes before. It was passion for her, and the knowledge was like an aphrodisiac to her body and soul.

"In the fantasy you told me, you never said anything about *you* coming," she murmured. "But if you ask real nice, I think I might be able to oblige you."

An amused smile made an appearance as he played the game her way. "Make me come, Chayse," he said, and nipped her chin, then her jaw, all the way up to her ear. "I need you *real* bad."

She liked the sound of that. "How do you want it?"

"As wild as you can be," he urged.

More than eager to give this man anything he desired, she wrapped her arms around his neck, locked their bodies so that they were meshed from chest to thigh, and let her inner vixen take over. Lowering her mouth to his, she sucked and nibbled his lower lip, and when he opened for her, she slipped her tongue inside in a smooth stroke that matched the roll and glide of her hips against his.

This time when he gripped her hips, she let him, but he allowed her to set the pace, and she moved on him, enthusiastic and shamelessly uninhibited. She felt his thighs tense beneath hers, felt his stomach muscles ripple, and knew he was nearing the peak of his orgasm.

Twining her fingers in his silky, rebel-long hair, she pulled his head back and dragged her damp, open mouth along his throat, then gently sank her teeth into the taut tendons where neck met shoulder, and put her mark on him.

He bucked upward one last time, hard and strong, and his groan of surrender in her ear was the sexiest sound she'd ever heard.

Once his tremors subsided, he tipped her back against the mattress so that he was lying on top of her, and stared down at her with a crooked but satisfied grin on his face. "I hearby bequeath my nickname of the Wilde One to you. You've earned it."

She laughed, happy that she'd pleased him. "I'm so honored," she replied, and ignoring the glimmer of adoration in his eyes, along with the emotional tug on her heart that warned her she was falling for this man, she pulled him down for another wanton kiss.

# Chapter Four

The early morning sunlight filtering through the living room window didn't provide adequate lighting, which Chayse would have liked, but she wasn't about to pass up the opportunity to photograph Adrian in all his glorious, morning-after sexiness.

She moved silently to the air mattress with her camera in hand, and knelt down so she was more on Adrian's level where he lay sprawled facedown amidst the pillows and rumpled blankets. She probably didn't need to be so quiet, considering the man slept like a rock, and even now his breathing was deep and measured. No doubt he was exhausted after their night together, and his body was recovering. She, too, had slept soundlessly, once Adrian had allowed her to drift off to sleep, that was. The man had been utterly insatiable, she thought with a reminiscent smile.

Her stomach did a free-fall tumble that had nothing to do with being hungry for breakfast, and everything to do with her intense attraction to Adrian. God, the man was so sinfully gorgeous, he ought to be deemed illegal. Even asleep and completely mussed, he managed to exude an earthy, sexual magnetism, one she was finding dangerous on so many levels—physically, emotionally, and mentally. The fact that this man had the ability to affect her so completely was a scary prospect she wasn't prepared to face or deal with.

She adjusted the settings on her camera to compensate for the lack of lighting, then glanced back at her subject, taking in his natural pose and the naked slope of his beautifully muscled back, all the way down to where the blanket was wrapped low around his hips. She'd also discovered that Adrian was extremely hot-blooded and didn't require much to keep him warm, whereas she liked to burrow beneath a mound of covers.

Yet their different levels of sleeping comfort hadn't stopped him from reaching for her during the night and tucking her tight against his body. And she'd gone to him willingly, letting his presence fill that vast loneliness that had been such a part of her life for so long. She'd allow herself that luxury, if only for a night or two, before the real world intruded on their weekend affair. And before they parted ways, she wanted to remember him just like this; these photos would be her private souvenir of their time together.

Lifting the camera and bringing Adrian into crisp, clear focus, she began taking her pictures. Surprisingly, it didn't take long for the clicking sound to rouse him from slumber. Through her lens, she watched him stir, and caught his gradual awakening on film. One eye slowly opened, then the other. A dark brow lifted lazily, as did one corner of his sensual mouth.

"Smile, you're on *Candid Camera,*" she greeted softly.

He chuckled, a low, rumbling sound that tickled the pit of her belly. Then he rolled over to his back and stretched the kinks from his long, lean body, and she took advantage of all that naked flesh and rippling muscles. His glossy hair was tousled in a messy disarray around his head, and dark stubble lined his jaw, making his eyes stand out like twin sapphires. Even the hair in his armpits was silky and sexy looking.

As he flexed his legs, the blanket around his hips slipped lower on his abdomen, revealing not only his scar, but the fascinating trail of hair that led to more delightful treasures. "You better put the camera down before you get some indecent shots," he warned, his tone low and wicked.

"Don't worry, you can get as indecent as you want. I develop all my own film." It was then that she noticed the impressive tent his erection had made beneath the covers, and she glanced at him from above her camera in mock reproach. "Why Adrian, is this photo session turning you on?"

He gazed at her through lashes that had fallen to half-mast. "No, *you* turn me on. I can see your nipples through that T-shirt you're wearing, and I vividly remember what those panties are covering."

She shivered, but not from the cool morning air in the cabin. The man had a way with words that made her melt, along with a natural ability to seduce the camera, and her. "Ever thought of posing for *Playgirl?*"

"Not on your life." He looked completely stricken by the very idea. "This beefcake calendar is as far as I go."

She laughed, feeling carefree and flirtatious, and enjoying the private, intimate moment between them. One that would always be theirs alone. "You'd make a lot of women really happy."

"I'm not interested in making anyone happy but you."

Her heart stuttered, then resumed at a frantic pace. She told herself she was reading too much into his words, that she'd most definitely misinterpreted the deeper meaning she'd seen in his eyes. "Then you'll be satisfied to know that you made me deliriously happy last night."

"And I can do so again this morning," he drawled, all arrogant, presumptuous male.

And because Chayse had firsthand knowledge that he was a man who more than lived up to his provocative claims, she couldn't find fault with his very confident assumption.

An irresistible smile tipped up the corners of his mouth. "Put down the camera, come here, and let me show you how happy I can make you."

Unable to refuse him anything—or herself, for that matter—she set her camera safely aside and crawled across the mattress to him. "Think you can top delirious, do you?" she taunted playfully.

"Sweetheart, I *know* I can."

He tumbled her onto her back, and before her peal of laughter could subside, he had her shirt skimmed over her head and tossed to the floor, and her panties a distant memory, as well.

He pushed her legs apart, moved in between, and slowly stroked his warm, callused palms up her thighs until his thumbs caressed her intimately. "I think the real question here is, can you survive just how happy I'm going to make you?"

Already, she was trembling in anticipation, and the rogue knew it, too. "There's only one way to find out, now isn't there?"

"Oh, yeah," he agreed huskily, and she caught a quick glimpse of his I'm-gonna-lap-you-up-until-you-scream grin as he settled himself more comfortably between her legs. He nuzzled her thigh and applied wet suction to a patch of flesh that made her gasp and would no doubt leave a hickey behind.

"Forget delirious," he rasped, once he was done branding her, his tongue now swirling a path to where she ached for his attention the most. "We're going for blissful, ecstatic, and rapturous."

The man was as good as his promise, and delivered on all three.

Adrian took Chayse on another long hike, though this one was not as strenuous as yesterday's trek. They followed a trail alongside the creek by the cabin that led upstream, which provided plenty of clearings and backdrops for her photos. Today he'd worn a white T-shirt, jean shorts, and hiking boots, and while she'd gotten a couple of shots with his shirt on, it didn't take her long to ask him to strip it off for another round of photographs.

Once she was done with their two-hour session and declared herself starved for the lunch he'd packed, he didn't bother putting his shirt back on. The day was cool, but the sun on his skin felt warm, soothing even. And he was beginning to learn how impetuous Chayse could be when it came to taking pictures, and he figured he might as well be ready for her spontaneous snapshots.

She helped him spread a blanket in a clearing and out in the sun, and sure enough she insisted on getting a few pictures of him stretched out on the blanket, arms behind his head, and chewing on a long piece of grass. All he had to do was think about this morning's tryst with Chayse, the hickey he'd put on her thigh, and how many times he made her come before he'd taken his own pleasure, and the sexy smile she asked for appeared on his lips.

She took shots from a dozen different angles, and he watched her while she worked, his eyes following the camera as she directed. The woman had so much passion and enthusiasm, and applied it to everything she did—from standing up to him and following him to the cabin to get what she wanted, to taking her pictures, and even making love. It amazed him that no other man had appreciated all her qualities and snatched her up for his own.

Then again, he guessed that just like himself, she'd kept the opposite sex at arm's length to protect her emotions, and he understood that safety net she was clinging to because he'd been using one himself for the past four years. Everyone saw him as a carefree, footloose bachelor who loved adventure and thrills. But few knew the man beneath, the one who'd grown cautious and guarded after being burned by another woman.

And now, he was prepared to share that private side with Chayse, because he wanted whatever was between them to last a helluva lot longer than just the weekend. Not just the hot chemistry and great sex, but the friendship and emotional connection he felt with her that he'd never, ever experienced with another woman before. She was his match in so many ways, and after months of denying his feelings for her, he wasn't about to let her go without giving them a chance. And that meant opening up and trusting her with his past.

"Oh, damn, I'm out of film. I left the extra rolls at the cabin."

She sounded so disappointed, but a part of him was relieved. Between yesterday and today she must have taken ten rolls, and while he was cooperating in the name of charity, he so wasn't cut out to be a model. "Good, now we can eat." He reached out to where she stood less than two feet away and cupped his hand over her smooth calf, then moved closer and nibbled on her leg with a low, rumbling growl. "I'm so hungry I'm about ready to take a big ol' bite out of you."

She laughed, sidestepping him before he could sink his teeth into that tempting bit of flesh, and sent him a chastising look. "You know, so much sugar really isn't good for your system."

*Sugar and spice and everything nice.* Oh yes, she was especially sweet, in every way. "Okay. Lunch first, then dessert." He waggled his brows at her, making sure she knew he considered *her* his dessert.

While she put away her camera, he sat up and reached for the extra backpack with the lunch he'd made for the two of them. He pulled out three ham and cheese sandwiches—one for her and two for him—a bag of chips, and two cans of soda. She settled in beside him, and he was done with his first sandwich before Chayse finally broke the compatible silence between them.

"Okay, Mr. Wilde," she said, slanting him a speculative glance. "You owe me."

He raised a teasing brow. "What, *another* orgasm?"

She actually ducked her head and blushed, and he found the gesture very endearing, showing him a softer side to the woman that touched him in long forgotten places. She'd stood toe-to-toe with him during numerous heated arguments since they'd met, had let go of every inhibition with him sexually, and now she'd been struck by a moment of modesty. This sexy yet vulnerable woman never ceased to intrigue him.

"You've more than made up for that, especially this morning." She took a long drink of her soda, then reached for a potato chip. "Remember turnabout being fair play and all that? It's time for you to pay the piper and answer a few of *my* questions."

He took a big bite of his second sandwich and glanced out at the blue, cloudless sky. He'd known this interrogation was coming, knew in his gut what she was going to ask, and had no intentions of skirting the issue as he had for the past four months with her. It was time to get everything out in the open, to let go of the bad memories and start out fresh and new.

"I'm an open book, sweetheart," he said with an engaging smile. Done with his sandwich, he shoved his empty baggie and napkin into the backpack. "What would you like to know?"

Her gaze flickered from the puckered skin on his bare abdomen to his face. "Those scars . . . how did it happen?"

It wasn't often he thought back to the skiing accident that had nearly killed him, and made him realize that not many women were equipped to understand and accept his need for thrills and extreme adventures. "It happened four years ago. Me, a few friends, and our girlfriends took off for a winter vacation in Jackson Hole, and while the women were out shopping for the day, the four of us guys decided to go heli-skiing."

He saw her confused expression and explained. "That's where a helicopter takes you to the top of a mountain peak in a remote area with virgin snow and untouched terrain. They let you out with a guide, and off you go, down five thousand vertical feet of pure adrenaline rush."

Her eyes widened in shock. "That's absolutely *insane.*"

"That's the whole point of extreme sports," he agreed with a laugh. He'd always loved the challenge and risks involved, which made each adventure all the more exciting. "I've been heli-skiing before, and there's nothing like all that fresh powder, steep slopes, and speed to get your heart pumping and your blood flowing in your veins. Of course, navigating all those jagged peaks, glaciers, and Alpine bowls can be very dangerous if you're not a skilled skier."

Unfortunately, not even his experience, expertise, and normally quick reflexes had been enough to save his sorry ass that fateful day. "Everything was going great until I skirted too close to the edge of a rocky peak. I dislodged a boulder and I went down with it. I plunged over the edge of the cliff, right into a ravine, and tumbled a good five hundred feet while being ripped apart and impaled by razor-sharp rocks."

She sucked in a breath and pressed her hand to her heart. "Ohmigod, Adrian . . ."

He knew the horrifying images his words must have put into her mind, but there was no way around the truth of the matter, so he met her concerned gaze and finished his tale. "Unfortunately, there aren't any safety brakes on this kind of thrill ride," he said wryly. "You just have to hang on and ride it out until the very end. By the time the rough terrain spit me out at the bottom of the mountain, I'd sustained a concussion, four broken ribs, and three deep gouges from the jagged rocks that had ripped through my jacket and clothes, which accounts for the scars on my back and lower stomach."

She shook her head in wonder, and her silky hair grazed her chin with the swift movement. "You're lucky to be alive."

"Wearing a helmet saved my life, I'm sure. Without it, I would have ended up with more than just a concussion." He didn't go into the unpleasant details of that particular scenario, but it was obvious by her grimace that she'd come to her own gory conclusion. "It also helped that the helicopter was right there to airlift me off the mountain and take me to the nearest hospital. My girlfriend at the time, Felice, was the first person I saw once I woke up."

A long breath unraveled out of Chayse. "She must have been frantic with worry."

"Yes, she was." He drew up his knees, crossed his ankles, and wrapped his arms loosely around his legs. "The accident gave everyone a good scare, myself included, but I wasn't expecting to deal with an immediate ultimatum the moment I opened my eyes. I remembered trying to smile at Felice, which hurt like hell, and the first words out of her mouth were a demand for me to choose either her, or extreme sports and my business, because she wasn't going to stick around if I continued to put my life at risk. Needless to say, she flew back home alone before I was even discharged from the hospital."

"That would be like someone forcing me to give up photography. I could never, ever do that." Her tone was just as vehement as the violet fire flashing in her eyes—all on his behalf. "You made the right choice."

He should have known that Chayse would understand, and experienced a huge amount of relief that she'd jumped to his defense. "Without a doubt." At the time, it had been difficult to watch Felice walk out of his life, especially when he'd needed her the most. But in the end, she'd done him a huge favor by ending their relationship before he'd grown to resent her constant demands to give up something that was such a huge part of his life.

Chayse reached out and trailed the tips of her cool fingers along the two long slashes on his back, her gentle, intimate touch a balm to his soul. "These scars . . . they give you character, Adrian. They're a part of who you are and what you do, and always will be."

She understood so much about him, and her acceptance mattered more than he'd realized.

Since his accident, he'd never allowed himself to care what another woman thought of his scars or the extreme adventure business he ran for a living, and it was a huge, shocking revelation to realize that Chayse's opinion mattered the most. With sudden clarity, he knew that was part of the reason why he'd avoided her for four long months, because his subconscious had obviously known what his emotions hadn't been ready to face or accept—that this woman who challenged him at every turn, who pursued him despite every attempt he'd made to reject her, and who gave of herself so openly and generously when they made love, could very well be the one for him.

He felt lighter and freer than he had in years, and Chayse was the reason. He glanced at her, met her soft violet gaze, and wanted to tell her everything he'd just discovered himself and how much he wanted her to be a part of his life, but was fairly certain she wasn't ready to hear something so life-changing. If he'd learned anything about Chayse this weekend, it was that she had her own personal issues to work through, and her own past to come to terms with. That despite her outward show of determination and impetuousness, inside she was a woman who was as vulnerable and fragile as fine crystal. And he had to treat those emotions accordingly.

When she leaned toward him and her lips drifted over his shoulder and along those scars of his, arousing and distracting him, he figured he had the rest of tonight and tomorrow to help her work through those issues and state his intentions.

"You know, I'm suddenly ravenous for dessert, and I want to eat it right out here in the great outdoors," he announced, and burying his fingers in her hair, he brought her mouth to his and kissed her, long and slow and deep.

Between wet, leisurely, tongue-tangling kisses, they undressed one another, until they were both naked and the sun dappled their skin with warmth. He pressed her down on the soft blanket, proceeded to feast on every sweet inch of her, and took his time doing so. He lapped in her honeyed essence, and touched and stroked her in all the places he knew she liked to be caressed the most, until she was breathless and trembling and begging him to end the sensual torment.

Only then did he drive into her soft, welcoming body, and she automatically arched to take all of him. In this, she held nothing back, and it gave him hope that he'd be able to breach other barriers with her, as well. He reveled in her uninhibited response to him, and the way she wrapped her legs around his waist and urged him to a stronger, harder rhythm that sent her soaring.

She came with a soft moan, and only then did Adrian allow himself to let go of his own orgasm and lose himself in everything that was Chayse Douglas.

Chayse curled her feet beneath her on the couch and watched as Adrian tossed a few more logs on the grate and stoked the fire to life. A smile touched her lips as she enjoyed the play of his muscles across his bare back and the way his sweatpants rode low on his lean hips. Her fingers itched to grab her camera to add this sexy pose to her own personal collection of candid shots of Adrian, but she managed, just barely, to restrain the urge.

She stifled a sleepy yawn, and even though it was nearing midnight, she wasn't ready to call it an evening just yet. Nor did she want this fun, relaxing weekend with Adrian to end, but she knew that was as inevitable as the sun rising in the morning.

This afternoon and their conversation about his scars had triggered feelings she hadn't expected. She'd meant it when she'd told him she understood his love for his job, for taking risks with extreme sports, but her emotional reaction to his story underscored her fears of getting too close to Adrian and caring whether or not he left her like everyone else she opened up her heart to. And that knowledge scared her enough to cement her decision to make a clean break tomorrow.

As for today, the afternoon had passed much too quickly for her liking, but the memories dancing in her head were ones she'd cherish for a long time to come. They'd returned from their photo session after making love outdoors not once, but twice, and shared a nice, long hot shower together. Then, with a blanket tucked around the two of them, she'd snuggled up to his side and they'd taken a nap in the hammock. He'd made spaghetti and garlic bread for dinner, then afterward fed her his chocolate fudge brownie ice cream. They played a few games of cards, drank hot cocoa with marshmallows, and discussed recent movies, books, and other personal favorites. And then he'd regaled her with amusing tales of his brothers and cousins, and his large, happy family that made her laugh, but also made her all too aware of the fact that she had no light-hearted stories of her own to share in return.

No, her own childhood had been emotionally painful and unstable, and there weren't a whole lot of cheerful moments to recall. From the loss of her brother, to her mother's withdrawal and depression, to the father who hadn't been there for her when she'd needed him the most. She'd been forced to grow up much faster than any teenager should have to, and had learned to guard herself from any more pain and loss by keeping people, and men, at a distance. And so far, those barriers had served her well and had kept her heart protected.

She envied Adrian his close-knit family, the stability and unconditional love and support he'd grown up with. It was something she'd always dreamed of, wished for, but her past was unchangeable and she accepted that. She'd made the best of the hand she'd been dealt, and she was proud of her accomplishments. She had a thriving photography business, her best friend Faith, and all the kids that became a part of her life during their stay at the Children's Hospital.

*And now there was Adrian, a man who had an effortless way of filling the vast emptiness inside her with laughter and fun and incredible, vibrant feeling.*

"Hey, you ready to call it a night?"

Startled from her thoughts, she met Adrian's caring gaze, and knew how easy it would be to drown herself and her painful past in those velvet blue depths. But not yet, she told herself. This man had let her into his life in so many ways, and had shared his family with her in those humorous, uplifting stories that had given her such a deeper insight into him as a man, a brother, and a son. And while she might not have fun, amusing childhood tales to entertain him with, there was a private part of her life she wanted to share with Adrian in return. A piece of herself she'd never allowed another man close enough to see or be a part of.

"I want to show you something," she said, and before she lost the nerve, she moved off the couch and retrieved a pocket folder from her backpack. Then she joined Adrian on the mattress, crossed her legs, and opened the portfolio.

She spread out a few dozen different snapshots that encompassed people of all ages, genders, and ethnicities, most of which had been taken candidly or with a telephoto lens so as to keep her hobby discreet, and without rudely intruding on a stranger's life. There were photographs of people at Lincoln Park, others at Navy Pier, and many she'd taken while strolling through the city on a Saturday afternoon. She rarely left home without her camera, and she'd learned that anything could become a photo opportunity at any given moment.

"Did you take these pictures for clients?" he asked curiously.

"No, I took these photographs for my own personal collection." He appeared confused as to why she'd take pictures of virtual strangers, and she explained. "When

I first started taking photography classes in high school, I'd spend my afternoons and weekends practicing by taking pictures of everything, but I was mostly fascinated by people, because their pictures always seemed to show so much emotion. Taking candid shots turned into a hobby for me, a way to escape the world in which I lived and wonder about the other person's life."

Adrian picked up a photograph she'd taken at a Little League game she'd happened by one morning. "How about this little guy? Is he someone you know?"

"Nope. Another casualty of my trigger finger, I'm afraid," she said jokingly. "I was out one Saturday morning and came across this ball game in progress, so I stopped to watch the kids play. This young boy was up at bat, bottom of the ninth with the bases loaded. He was so disheartened after two consecutive strikes, and you could tell he didn't want to disappoint his teammates by striking out and losing the game. No matter the outcome, I knew this was a picture I wanted for my collection."

She smiled, remembering how the boy's expression and attitude had changed to determination and what she'd ultimately captured on film. "On the next pitch, he smacked the ball over the fence, and here he was, still standing at home plate, the bat in his hand, his eyes wide with awe and disbelief as he watched the ball soar through the air. The crowd behind him was standing and cheering, and in a split second, he became the hero who saved the game." She cast Adrian a sidelong glance to gauge his response. "It's one of the neatest photographs I've ever taken."

"It's pretty amazing, actually." He met her gaze, the bright firelight causing his irises to glimmer with blue heat. "I can actually *feel* that kid's excitement."

"Exactly." Elated that his own emotions had been touched by a snapshot *she'd* taken, she sought out another picture to show him. "I was at the mall one day, strolling along the upper level, and I happened to glance down and saw this mother and daughter standing outside an accessory store. As you can see, the girl is showing her mother her new belly button piercing and trying to convince her that it's the 'in thing' right now, but mom's not going for it."

Adrian chuckled in amusement. "Oh boy, her mother has that wait-until-your-father-finds-out-about-this look on her face."

Chayse lifted a brow. "And how would you know that look?"

"Because it's a universal look among mothers, my own included," he said with a shrug that made the firelight play along the muscles in his back and arms. "Anytime my mother shot any of us boys 'that look,' we knew we were in *big* trouble when Dad got home."

She sorted through more photographs, wishing her mother had cared enough to snap out of her depression long enough to take an interest in whatever her daughter was doing—good, bad, or otherwise. Luckily, Chayse's photography hobby had kept her from turning into an outright rebel with a cause. And Lord knew she'd had *plenty* of cause.

As the fire crackled warmly in the hearth, and with Adrian enjoying her pictures, Chayse continued to entertain him with the stories she saw within the photographs. On some of the snapshots, he even offered his own observations, most of which echoed hers. When she came across a picture she'd taken of a homeless man, her chest tightened with emotion as she remembered that day.

"This is Frank," she said, and showed Adrian the five-by-seven shot of a man sitting on a park bench, his clothes old and tattered. His hands were gnarled and dirty, his face unshaven, and he was holding a crude cardboard sign that said "Will Work For Food." "I took one look into his sad eyes and knew he'd lived a long, hard life. I bought him a hot dog and soda from a vendor in the park, and I sat down to talk to him. Despite how gruff and scruffy he looked, he was a sweet man, and when I asked if he had any family, he told me he'd lost his wife and two kids twenty-three years ago in a car accident, and that he'd been the sole survivor of the accident. It didn't take much to figure out that the loss had devastated him, to the point that he stopped caring about anything, including his own life."

She brushed her thumb along the edge of the photograph, feeling the man's pain and heartache deep in her chest. "I asked him if I could take his picture, and he gave me permission to do so. He even smiled for me," she said, pointing to the man's gap-toothed grin.

Adrian glanced from the photo to her. "I'd bet you were the bright spot of that man's day."

"I'd like to think that I was. Before I left, I gave him twenty dollars to make sure he had a few more good meals, but he gave me so much more in return." A lump rose in her throat when she thought about her memorable encounter with Frank. "This photo tells a hundred stories, and every time I look at it, I hear a different tale. Crazy, huh?"

Adrian gently tucked wayward curls behind her ear, his expression full of tenderness and understanding, as if he had a direct link to the lonely, vulnerable little girl inside the woman who sought comfort in her pictures of other people. "No, it makes perfect sense to me."

Her breath caught and held, much like her stuttering pulse and the squeeze of her heart that yearned for all the things she'd grown up without. All the things she swore she didn't need in her life, but Adrian made her believe were possible.

Fears and insecurities reared their ugly heads, and

she looked away and began picking up the pictures to put back in the portfolio folder. "Most people read books. I read pictures," she went on in a rush. "And the photos I take outside of the studio are my own personal storybook."

"I like that," he murmured, more calmly than she felt.

She knew she was babbling—anything to keep the conversation going. "Sometimes I take certain shots of people, and it's like I have a window straight into their souls." Finished putting away the snapshots, she set the folder up on the couch, but couldn't bring herself to look at Adrian again.

But she should have known that he wouldn't let her escape him so easily. His fingers curled around her arm, and he gently tugged her down onto the air mattress, then stretched out beside her, with half his body pressing against hers and a thigh resting heavily between her legs.

He stared deeply into her eyes, so intuitive and determined. "Sometimes people don't need a camera to see into another person's soul," he said, and cradled her cheek in his big, warm palm, forcing her to confront the emotional connection between them that scared the living daylights out of her. "I look into your eyes and I see a little girl who's carried a wealth of emotional burdens for too many years now, and a woman who is afraid to take chances on what most likely is a sure thing. I see a woman who hides behind her camera, even while she tries to uncover everyone else's deepest secrets."

She shook her head frantically, trying to deny the painful truth he'd so easily unearthed about her. She'd let him too close, shared things with him she should have kept to herself. "Adrian—"

He pressed his fingers against her lips, quieting her.

"You don't need to hide anything from me, Chayse. Ever. I'll always be here for you."

It was those words that she found the hardest to trust, even though her heart wanted so badly to believe in Adrian—the honorable man he was, and the promises he made. Tears gathered in her eyes and stung the back of her throat. Not wanting him to witness her weakness, her greatest fears, she plowed her fingers through his hair and brought his mouth down to hers.

She kissed him deeply, hungrily, *desperately*, striving for mindless pleasure to chase away her doubts and uncertainties. Sliding her hand down his belly, she cupped his erection in her palm and stroked him through the soft cotton of his sweatpants. She felt him grow and harden from her touch, and started to move over him to straddle his waist, needing him in ways she couldn't define. Physical need was a given, but it was all the other emotional chaos swirling within her that made her feel as though her carefully guarded life was spinning out of her control.

He caught her around the waist before she could crawl on top of him and eased her back to his side. She made a small sound of frustration, and he deliberately slowed their kiss, soothing rather than arousing her with the slide of his lips against her soft, yielding mouth. Then he grasped her wrist and rested her palm right over his rapidly beating heart, and held it there with his hand.

He ended the kiss and nuzzled her cheek, her hair. His shaft pressed against her hip, but it was obvious to her that he didn't intend to do anything about that particular discomfort. "Just let me hold you, Chayse," he whispered in her ear.

She nearly broke down right there, but after years of being strong and holding herself together, she was conditioned to keep her emotions locked away tight. And those honed instincts kicked in now, enabling her to keep her tears at bay.

Still, she couldn't ignore his tender offering. He wanted to hold her. When had anyone ever just held her, without the pretense of anything more? And how did this incredible man know exactly what she ached for, right when she needed it the most?

Tired of pretending that she could face the world alone, she sank against Adrian's side, rested her cheek on his chest, and absorbed the comfort and affection he so selflessly offered her.

She closed her eyes, and as he held her in his embrace and she let his strength take over, she knew this weekend together wasn't about sex anymore. Not for either of them.

# Chapter Five

Chayse slept better than she could ever remember and woke the following morning to the familiar sound of a camera clicking. Knowing for certain she wasn't dreaming, she opened her eyes and found Adrian standing at the edge of the mattress, her camera in hand, focusing on her.

*Click, click, click.*

She frowned, unable to believe that Adrian had been bold enough to turn the camera on her when no one ever had before. And especially after their conversation last night. "What are you doing?" she asked warily.

He flashed her a killer grin that looked positively devious combined with the dark stubble on his jaw. "Getting even."

"Oh, ugh!" She put a hand up to ward him off, but he was a man on a mission and kept taking her picture anyway. "Adrian, I look like a wreck!" And no way did she want to be a part of her own private collection.

His dark blue eyes peeked up at her from above the camera, and he waggled his brows. "A beautiful, gorgeous, sexy wreck."

She rolled her eyes at his misplaced flattery. "You can't be serious, and I've got a major case of bedhead," she complained, knowing her hair was tweaked every which way.

Undeterred, he refocused on her and snapped another shot. "The politically correct term for bedhead is tousled," he informed her, a teasing note infusing his deep morning voice. "And tousled is *very* sexy."

She laughed at his attempt at humor and forced herself to relax. To not feel so threatened by her own camera. "I'm grumpy in the morning, especially when I wake up to find someone taking my picture." She stuck her tongue out at him to prove her point.

He captured her petulant attitude and pout on film. "I can handle grumpy," he assured her, and knelt on the mattress to get a close-up of her. "In fact, I know a very good cure for the morning grumpies."

Her body warmed at the provocative, tempting insinuation in his tone. There had been no making love last night, just cuddling, and she suddenly craved him one last time before she left to return to the city. Before she left Adrian behind, which was the right thing to do, because he certainly didn't need an emotionally screwed-up woman like her in his stable life.

She smiled to cover up the heartache making itself known and stretched, causing her T-shirt to ride up on her belly and tighten across her breasts. "Tell me more about this cure of yours, Mr. Wilde One."

He paused for a moment to stare at her hard nipples before lifting his heated gaze to hers. "I promise to share my therapeutic remedy, just as soon as you cooperate a little for me. Seduce the camera, and have a little fun with this."

How many times had she told Adrian the very same thing? "I never thought those words could come back to haunt me." Even though the camera unnerved her because she knew what depths a photograph could reveal, she resigned herself to this playful, intimate moment between them.

She made it a game of seduction in her mind, her ultimate goal to make Adrian lose control and forget about taking her picture. First, keeping herself covered with the thin thermal blanket, she peeled off her T-shirt and tossed it aside. Then she wriggled out of her boxer shorts, then her panties, which she tossed at Adrian, managing to land them on his shoulder. He picked up the scrap of fabric, and grinning like the bad boy he was, he brought the silky material to his nose and inhaled deeply.

"God, you smell good," he groaned, and breathed in her scent again before dropping her panties to the floor and returning his attention to the camera, and her. "Flash me some skin, sweetheart."

She lowered the covers to the upper swells of her breasts, and slipped one leg out so she was bared to the curve of her hip. Lowering her lashes, she smiled provocatively and gave him a sultry, Marilyn Monroe-like pose that made her feel sexy despite her bedhead. Before long, she was lost in Adrian's husky praise and coaxing as he continued to capture her seduction on film, and enjoyed herself and the fact that she was turning him on, too.

Deciding to turn up the temptation a few notches, she rolled to her stomach and let the blanket slide down her back to the base of her spine, so that her bottom was still covered, just barely. Angling her knee so that her thighs were spread beneath the blanket, and using one arm to keep her upper body braced, she slid her flattened hand along her belly. She looked over her shoulder at Adrian, her disheveled hair in her face, and slowly glided her splayed palm downward, until her fingers encountered the creamy, wet warmth of her arousal.

A low, breathy moan tumbled from her lips, and she tossed her head back, the click and whirl of the camera fading from her mind as erotic pleasure took over. Biting her lower lip, she stroked her aching, swollen flesh, and clutched the pillow beneath her breasts as an explosive orgasm beckoned.

She heard a soft, explicit curse from somewhere behind her, and gasped in startled surprise when the blanket was yanked away. Before she could react, Adrian was covering her from behind, gloriously naked, his skin searing hot, his body hard all over. Especially the erection nestling so insistently between her spread thighs.

She attempted to pull her hand away so that he could take over, but he wasn't having any of that. He grasped her wrist and kept her fingers in place. "No, don't stop," he ordered gruffly in her ear. "Guide me in."

She caressed the head of his cock with her fingers, lubricating him with her moisture before poising his shaft at the core of her womanhood. His groan vibrated along her back as he slid in an excruciating inch. She arched her bottom against his hips, seeking more, just as he surged forward and filled her.

His slow, gyrating thrusts gradually gave way to deeper, heavier lunges that possessed and claimed her in an inherently primitive way. Reaching up, he entwined the fingers of the hand she'd curled into the pillow and slipped his other hand between her body and the mattress. He cupped her breast in his palm, squeezed and fondled the pliant mound, and lightly pinched her nipple between his fingers before skimming his hand lower, along her belly and down to her aching sex. His fingers joined with hers, adding to the hot, wet, slippery sensation along her clitoris, the dual erotic stimulation causing her to whimper and rock frantically against his pistoning hips.

"Come for me," he rasped, and she felt his thighs

tighten along the back of hers, felt his hot, damp, panting breaths rushing against the side of her neck, along with the arousing scrape of his unshaven jaw. "Oh God, Chayse, *now,*" he growled, and pressed both of their fingers against her cleft, as deeply and rhythmically as his wild, untamed thrusts.

Her release crested right when his did, and they both rode out the exquisite pleasure of bodies meshing, hips pushing and straining, inner muscles clenching, and an incendiary heat that consumed them both.

Long moments later, Adrian rolled to his side, cradled her back against his chest, and whispered huskily in her ear, "Are you still grumpy?"

She laughed, unable to summon a grouchy reply, even a playful one, when she felt so sated. "Not in the least. What an amazing cure you've come up with," she murmured. "Ever thought of putting it on the market?"

"Can't," he said, and dropped a warm, lingering kiss on her neck. "The remedy was designed solely for you, no one else, so I think you're stuck with me."

His meaning was clear, that he wanted to be stuck with her for a long time to come. She swallowed hard, battling more emotions, more insecurities, and feared that there was no cure or treatment for a troubling past that would always come between them.


Adrian's lungs burned and the muscles in his thighs flexed and bunched as he sprinted up the steep path weaving alongside the hill behind the cabin. He'd been out jogging nonstop for nearly an hour now, letting the clean mountain air clear his mind and using the physical exercise to pump him up for what lay ahead between himself and Chayse—a confrontation that would state his intentions and force her to finally acknowledge that there was more than just great sex between them.

The bit of solitude and mindless activity also gave him time to think, without Chayse distracting him with her luscious body and innate sensuality he couldn't seem to get enough of. Out here with nothing but nature's beauty to inspire him, he was able to finally come to terms with his own feelings for Chayse.

He was falling in love with her.

It was simple as that, and he wasn't going to fight something that felt so amazingly right to his heart and emotions. Though he had to admit that such a huge, life-altering revelation was both a scary and exhilarating prospect, like the first time he'd gone skydiving and realized how much he loved the rush he experienced as he'd jumped out of the plane and soared through the sky. That's what Chayse was to him—a source of adrenaline for his mind, heart, and soul. And he wanted to experience that exciting, pulse-pounding rush on a daily basis.

Unfortunately, he still had Chayse's resistance to deal with—those soul-deep insecurities she'd allowed him to glimpse this weekend, and those painful vulnerabilities that kept her from letting anyone too close for fear that she'd end up all alone again.

He'd learned that Chayse was all woman on the outside, tough and sexy and determined, but internally she was still a little girl, aching for the love and approval she'd never gotten from her own parents, and searching for a place where she belonged. A place stable and safe and filled with unconditional acceptance. A place where she didn't have to worry about the people whom she trusted and loved turning their backs on her when times got tough and she needed them the most.

Adrian wanted to be there for Chayse, always—as a friend, a partner, and a lover. And it wasn't a commitment he planned to take lightly. Now all he had to do was convince her just how sincere he was, that he wanted this short weekend fling to last a lifetime.

He picked up his pace, eager to be with her again. He grinned like a fool, finally understanding what his brothers had found with each of their wives. He'd given both Eric and Steve a hard time when they'd taken the plunge and admitted they'd fallen in love, and all the while he'd sworn that he had no desire to let another woman get to him on an emotional level ever again. His brothers had been emphatic that it was a matter of finding the right woman, and he distinctly remembered Eric making the comment that he'd better be careful, because love might just sneak up on him and bite him on the ass when he least expected it.

At the time, he'd scoffed at Eric's sappy analogy. Now Adrian was forced to admit that he *had* been bitten when he'd least expected it, big-time, and both of his brothers were going to have a field day when they discovered his downfall. But it was a small price to pay for all that he'd gained.

Adrian's heart pumped anxiously as he rounded the bend in the road and came in for the home stretch, until he noticed that Chayse's car was no longer parked next to his Jeep.

His stomach twisted with dread as the truth kicked him in the chest. He was too late to tell Chayse how he felt about her, to convince her to take a chance on him. She was already gone.


Oh Lord, what had she done?

Pressing her fingers to her trembling lips, Chayse stared at the photos she'd developed from her weekend with Adrian, which were spread out on the coffee table in her living room. Nearly six hours had passed since she'd left the cabin while Adrian was out on a morning jog. She hadn't heard from him since, not that she expected him to make any effort to find her after the less than admirable way she'd snuck out on him.

Her abrupt departure, along with the quick, impersonal note she'd left in the kitchen, thanking him for being a part of her calendar project, had no doubt been as effective as a slap in his face after the intimate weekend they'd shared. At the time she'd convinced herself that she was saving them both an unpleasant confrontation, that a clean break was easier on both of them, but alone in her apartment with only her conscience as company, she was coming to acknowledge her leaving for the cowardly behavior it was.

Her throat tightened with another surge of tears, and she swallowed them back as she leaned forward and fanned out a pile of pictures of Adrian looking sexier and more gorgeous than a man had a right to. There were phenomenal shots of him chopping wood, and more they'd taken during their hikes. The majority had been taken without a shirt, his chest and shoulders breathtakingly wide and strong and most definitely drool-worthy. She was proud of the shots, and what one could glimpse of his scars only served to make him appear more rugged, like a real outdoor man who lived as one with nature.

He was extremely photogenic, and there wasn't a bad picture in the bunch, which made the task of finding only four for the calendar project a daunting task— the end results of which she'd promised Adrian he could approve. Which meant she'd eventually have to contact him, and see him again in person.

She pushed aside the professional shots and reached for the candid photos she'd taken of Adrian while he'd been sleeping and had gradually awakened. A smile touched her lips as she remembered the playful, flirtatious session. Now she had her own personal storybook in front of her, and there was no ignoring what she saw in Adrian's gaze, in his expression. There was adoration, sensual hunger, and a deeper emotion that made her feel weak in the knees. A blend of trust and caring she'd been so scared to believe in.

Then there were the pictures Adrian had taken of her that morning, which told an interesting tale of their own. At first, she'd been uncomfortable being the focus of his attention, but he'd coaxed her to open up, to trust him, and she had, physically and emotionally, she realized as she picked up one of the photos of her seducing the camera, and Adrian.

Her heart pounded so hard her chest hurt. Despite every attempt she'd made to keep her emotions out of the equation of the weekend, she'd gone and fallen in love with Adrian. Her own story was right there in her eyes for her to see—the way she felt about him, along with the fact that she'd given him a piece of herself that would forever be his. Not just her body, or her heart, but her soul, as well.

His words came back to her, so accurate and sincere. *I look into your eyes and I see a little girl who's carried a wealth of emotional burdens for too many years now, and a woman who is afraid to take chances on what most likely is a sure thing. I see a woman who hides behind her camera, even while she tries to uncover everyone else's secrets.*

Adrian knew her well. And she knew without a doubt that he'd taken the pictures of her this morning because he'd wanted her to see what *he* saw in her. It was all there, insecurities and fears, the gradual sensual blossoming he'd cajoled out of her, and even the love she hadn't realized had found its way into her heart.

She felt something wet trickle down her cheek and wiped away a tear. Then another. She caught sight of a picture of Adrian, the one where he was lying on the blanket near the creek, bare-chested and chewing on a blade of grass. But it wasn't the sexy smile that drew her, or even the come-hither look in his eyes that told Chayse how much he wanted her. No, it was the scar that started a few inches above the waistband of his shorts—an injury he'd been so self-conscious of, enough to keep refusing her dozens of attempts to get him to pose for her charity calendar.

She traced the line in the photograph, remembering vividly how that puckered skin had felt beneath her fingers, her lips. She thought of the way she'd confronted Adrian about those scars when she'd arrived at the cabin, how she'd made him face them, deal with them, and not let an old injury affect his decision to do the calendar project. Those scars were a part of who and what he was, she'd told him.

She laughed around another bout of tears and knew she ought to take her own advice to heart. Adrian's scars were on the outside, hers were on the inside, but the suffering and insecurity that came with those wounds were the same. And it was time she confronted her own personal scars, and her past. Face the pain, deal with it, and not let it affect her decision to let Adrian into her life.

A brisk knock on the door startled her, and she stood, swiping at her damp eyes and cheeks as she headed toward the entryway. She looked into the peephole and saw Adrian standing on the other side with a fierce expression on his face. He looked really pissed off, and she wondered at the wisdom of letting him inside. Maybe it was better if they had this conversation in the morning, after he'd cooled off a bit.

He banged on the door with his fist, rattling the wood and the chain securing the door. "Open up, Chayse," he ordered in an uncompromising tone. "Or else your neighbors are going to hear a very personal conversation out here in the hallway."

Knowing he was a man as good as his word, and not wanting her neighbors to be privy to her personal life, she unlocked the door and opened it for him. He stormed into her apartment, his entire body fairly crackling with energy and a fury she knew he had every right to feel after the way she'd bolted on him this morning. His hair was tousled around his head, he hadn't shaved since the night before, and he looked not only exhausted but dark and dangerous, as well.

But she didn't fear him. Not at all. That he'd made the effort to figure out where she lived was a very positive thing in her estimation. If he didn't care, he wouldn't be here. And she knew that wasn't the case with Adrian. If anything, he cared too much, and she was lucky to have found a man like him.

She exhaled a deep breath and asked very calmly, "How did you find out where I lived?"

He spun around and jammed his hands on his jean-clad hips. He glared at her, which did nothing to conceal the hurt she detected in his eyes, along with a brighter determination. "It wasn't easy. First, I had to hunt down Mia, who ought to wear a tracking device because I was one step behind her most of the afternoon. Once I found her, I demanded your address, and seeing that she owed me one for giving you the directions to the cabin, she cracked."

Chayse bit her bottom lip to keep from laughing, certain that Adrian wouldn't appreciate her finding humor at his expense. At least not at the moment, while he was so angry and hurt.

An awkward silence descended between them as he continued to glare at her, and she waved a hand toward the photographs on the coffee table. "Umm, since you're here, you can take a look at the pictures I took and we can decide which ones you'd like to go into the calendar."

"At the moment, I don't give a damn about those pictures!" He stalked toward her, blue fire blazing in his eyes. "That's not why I'm here."

For every purposeful step he took forward, she took one back, until her bottom hit the edge of the small kitchen table that adjoined the living room. He closed the distance between them, and there was no mistaking the erection straining against the fly of his jeans and pressing against her mound.

His gaze held hers as he tugged on the snap of her pants and ripped open the front placket. A frisson of excitement shot through her, making her feel alive and heady with anticipation, something only this man had the ability to trigger within her.

She knew what was going to happen, knew he was going to possess her in the most elemental way possible. Stake his claim on her. Brand her as his. An aggressive, wild mating that would bend her to his will and allow him to release the fury and anger swirling inside him in a purely sexual way. It was Adrian's way. Just like the first time he'd taken her so fiercely at the cabin, when she'd provoked him beyond his restraint.

He dragged her pants and underwear down her legs and yanked them off, then quickly unbuckled his belt, unzipped his jeans, and freed his shaft. He lifted her so she was sitting on the edge of the table, and with his hands pressed against her knees, he widened her thighs and fit himself in between. She was already wet and aroused, and his erection slid along her slick flesh, the head of his cock burrowing into her weeping sex.

She braced her hands behind her on the table and shuddered, wanting this, but decided she ought to put up at least a token protest. "Adrian . . . what are you doing?"

A muscle in his cheek ticked. "Since you only seem to understand the way my body talks to you, I'm going to let it do the talking for me." He grabbed her ass and jerked her to the edge of the table at the same time he flexed his hips and thrust into her, making her gasp at the depth to which he'd plowed.

He rolled his hips, grinding himself against her sex. "Do you know what my body is saying right now?" he demanded gruffly.

She shook her head, moaning as he slowly withdrew, and quivering as he filled her again. "No."

"It's telling you that I'm falling in love with you," he said, the tight edge in his voice softening as he pulled back and surged in again. "That I'm not going to ignore what's between us, and I'm not going to let you walk away either." Out . . . and back in again in a slow, languid stroke that made her melt around him. "I need you in my life, and you sure as hell need me in yours."

Her heart rejoiced, and she slanted him an assessing glance that gave away nothing of her own emotions just yet. "That's a little arrogant, don't you think?"

Watching her expression, he withdrew, and she whimpered at the loss, then gasped sharply when he returned, burying himself to the hilt. "I'm inside your body, sweetheart. As deep as I can get. I can feel your heartbeat. I can see the emotion in your eyes. I have every right to be arrogant. And demanding."

"Yes, you do," she agreed solemnly.

And then another revelation struck her. Adrian was all about taking risks, in everything he did—in his extreme sports, when making love, and even when it came to wearing his heart on his sleeve. As for her, she'd always played it safe, but not anymore. Not if she intended to meet this man halfway in all things. And that included trusting him with her heart and emotions. Right here and now.

With him full and heavy and throbbing inside her, she slid her hands into his thick, silky hair and nipped his chin, pressed a soft, open-mouthed kiss to his lips, then looked so deeply into his eyes she thought she'd drown in the unabashed emotion she saw shining there. The adoration. The hope and need that reflected her own.

She smiled and framed his face in her hands, and without any hesitation she said, "Adrian Wilde, I love you."

With a grateful moan, he captured her mouth with his, kissing her as deeply and fiercely as he plunged into her body. So much passion. Earthy and sensual and irresistible.

The ending came fast for both of them, and when his climax rolled through him, she took his harsh groans into her mouth and gave back her own sweet sounds of release.

Amazingly enough, after that physically draining session Adrian seemed to have enough strength to carry her to her bedroom, so she hung on for the ride and gave him directions down the hall. He set her gently on the bed and stretched out beside her, and she knew they still had a few things to discuss. But this time she was ready to face the past and hopefully secure her future.

"Why did you leave the cabin today without waiting for me to return from my run?" he asked as he stroked his fingers along her arm. There was no censure in his tone, no more anger, just the need to understand.

She'd already given him her love, now she gave him her honesty. "I was scared . . . mostly of what you make me feel, and my first instinct was to run from my emotions."

"What I make you feel is supposed to be a good thing, sweetheart," he murmured gently.

She stared up at him, feeling like the luckiest girl on planet Earth to have somehow earned this man's patience and understanding. "I know that now, but at the time I wasn't ready to face my feelings, or trust in them."

"Are you ready now?"

She nodded and whispered, "Yes."

He lifted a curious brow, obviously wanting more answers, which he fully deserved. "What changed your mind?"

"It was those pictures you took of me this morning. I saw myself through your eyes, just as you'd intended. All my emotions were right there in front of me, and there was no denying how hard and fast I'd fallen for you." She reached out and touched his unshaven jaw, loving the rough, arousing texture against her fingertips. "I don't want to keep living through the pictures I take of other people. I want to make my own storybook of memories, real ones, and I don't want be alone anymore, Adrian. I want to take a chance on a sure thing. I want to take a chance on you."

"Oh yeah, I like the sound of that." He grinned, looking like the rogue of her dreams, and the man who'd stolen her heart. "But taking a chance on me means being part of my big, crazy family. Think you can handle that?"

Her heart pounded crazily in her chest, the gift he was offering more than she'd ever believed possible. "Oh, Adrian, I would *love* to be a part of your family. Do you think they can handle me snapping pictures of them when they least expect it?"

He chuckled, the sound reverberating with warmth and a bit of wickedness. "They'll get used to it."

She sighed blissfully, a huge smile on her face. "With each of us bearing our own scars, we're quite a pair, aren't we?"

"We're a perfect pair." He ran the tip of his finger down the slope of her nose, then he grew serious. "I know this has all happened so quickly, but I promise we'll work this relationship thing out, take whatever time you need to adjust to having me in your life."

"I don't need any more time, Adrian." Now that he was hers, there was no room left in her heart for uncertainties. She was risking it all. "I chased you for four months and you've just given me the best weekend of my entire life. And I really do love you, and nothing is going to change that."

"I love you, too, Chayse Douglas." He kissed her lips, softly, reverently, then pulled back and grinned down at her, his eyes bright with tenderness, and something more mischievous. "You know, it's gonna take a lot of years to tame my wild ways, but I do believe you're just the right woman for the job. How do you feel about marrying me and becoming Mrs. Wilde One?"

She forced back the lump of emotion rising in her throat with husky laughter and thought to herself in triumphant awe: *He loves me! He really, really loves me!*

The knowledge chased away every last bit of Chayse's insecurities, leaving her heart wide open for this incredible man to fill up with his presence, his love. "Yes," she managed to reply around the joyful tears threading her voice. "Yes, Adrian Wilde, I'll marry you."

Giddy with happiness, she wrapped her arms around his neck and pulled him on top of her, absorbing his declaration and wanting to preserve this precious moment forever, like a rare photograph in her mind. It was a wonderful beginning to her own personal storybook of mental snapshots, and she knew her private album would grow to reflect the best years of her life with the Wilde One.

# GOING AFTER ADAM

Nancy Warren

# Chapter One

Every time Gretchen Wiest found herself tracking yet another adulterous spouse—and it seemed some days as though her private investigation agency did little else—she was glad she was single.

She searched the faces of the passengers spilling into the arrivals lounge at San Francisco airport. Her mark was easy to spot, standing a head above most of the travelers and carrying himself with an air of calmness and command that would have caught her attention anywhere. Yep, there was the latest scumsucker now. She curled her lip even as she sank deeper into the turned-up collar of her trench coat.

She glanced down at the photo in her hand because she was a careful professional, but it wasn't necessary. The man striding into the United arrivals area was Adam Stone. He wasn't a man you could mistake once you'd seen his picture. Or forget.

Same black hair, neatly combed but for the one charcoal lock that fell onto his forehead in a Byronic fashion Gretchen decided was contrived. Same deep Irish blue eyes, same rectangular face, same domineering nose, same rugged jaw, same full lips. It was quite a package.

A general's commanding presence, a poet's eyes, a fighter's nose, and a lover's lips.

He glanced her way, almost as though he were aware of her scrutiny, or perhaps her contempt had telegraphed itself, and she hastily looked away. But in the instant their gazes connected she felt his potent sexuality.

Wow. The guy was drool-worthy all right, but Gretchen's drool ducts remained tightly puckered knowing the woman who'd be slobbering over him this weekend was not his wife.

Gretchen pretended deep interest in the arrivals and departures screen, which Stone would have to pass. As he did, she turned and *accidentally* bumped into him. He had a fancy briefcase with a discreet company logo embossed in gold in one hand and a leather backpack in the other. She was aware that his lean build was solid with muscle and that he smelled good as she slipped a tracking device smaller than a dime into his pocket. With a quickly murmured apology she headed in the opposite direction and jogged for the car park.

With his crisp navy suit he looked like dozens of other professionals in for a Friday afternoon meeting. Some would fly back home tonight, some would make a weekend of it. She already knew, thanks to Mrs. Stone's lawyer, that this man planned to make a weekend of it— she hoped he enjoyed having his picture taken while he was having sex, because unbeknownst to Mr. Stone and his lover, she and her small, high-powered camera were going to be joining the party.

When Gretchen reached her nondescript beige compact, she popped the trunk, removed her trench coat, and tossed it inside, replacing it with a black pea coat. She coiled her hair rapidly into a bun, stuck a funky black felt hat on her head, and colored over her beige lipstick with a bright red.

She slipped into her car and started the ignition. She

also activated the small computer screen on her dash where the tracking device showed as a blip. Excellent.

She drove past the cab stand, noting Stone was still three back from the front of the line, and cruised by. She pulled over on the causeway and waited, using the time to call Mrs. Stone's lawyer on her cell phone as she'd been instructed to do the minute she identified Stone.

"Yeah?" a curt male voice answered on the first ring.

She blinked and double-checked the number in her Palm Pilot. She'd expected a receptionist or personal secretary. "Mr. Fisk?"

"Speaking," the voice warmed. "Who's this?"

"It's Gretchen Wiest. You asked me to call the minute I spotted Mr. Stone." She stuck a finger in her free ear, trying to block out the roar of Friday afternoon traffic. "I'm at the airport. He just landed."

While she spoke, she watched keenly as each cab sped by. She had the tracker as backup, but she planned to play Follow That Cab to be certain she didn't lose Stone.

"The airport?"

"Yes. San Francisco. I'll collect what evidence I can for Mrs. Stone."

"Excellent. You're certain it's Mr. Stone?"

"Hundred percent. He looks exactly like his photo."

"Good work, Ms. Wiest. Call me again when he checks in to his hotel."

"If Adam Stone has meetings first, that could be hours from now." She calculated the time difference between California and Houston. Texas was two hours ahead. Probably Mr. Fisk would be starting his own weekend by the time she knew more, and she'd never leave messages on voice mail with details of an ongoing investigation. There was a short pause. Her car shook as a bus roared past. "Is there another number—?"

"No. This will reach me day or night."

Wow. That divorce lawyer was one dedicated professional—she wondered if there was an adulterous spouse in his past.

And speaking of adulterous spouses, there was Adam Stone now, cruising by in the back of a yellow cab. She said good-bye to Mrs. Stone's lawyer, let another couple of cars go by, then pulled out into the traffic.

It was easy enough to keep Stone's cab in view. The volume of vehicles on Highway 101 was Friday afternoon heavy, and therefore the going slow and congested enough that she was virtually invisible.

Together, they cruised downtown, Stone in his cab and she in her car, several lengths behind. They passed the big hotels where business travelers usually stayed and entered the older residential areas. They drove up hills and down, hit Sutter Street, and finally the cab turned into a side street and pulled up at a turn-of-the-century town house turned hotel.

She gave Stone points for stealth. The guest house was small, quiet, off the beaten track. Just the sort of place she'd stay if she were planning to drop out of sight for a while. None of his business acquaintances would be likely to bump into him here. He could break his wedding vows in peace.

Or so he thought.

She drove past, circled the block, and returned, finding, miracle of miracles, that a van was pulling out of a parking spot halfway up the block. She pulled her duffel bag from the backseat of her car and retrieved her camera, checked her watch, and typed her notes into her Palm Pilot.

"Okay, scumbag," she mumbled. "This is for your wife." It was funny, but even with no-fault divorce her casework hadn't diminished. Wives and their lawyers often hired her to track cheating husbands. And the wives almost always wanted photos of the other women. It was as though they couldn't help themselves. They had to know.

Once she'd updated her notes, and verified the time Stone had entered his guest house, she waited, either for Adam Stone to leave, or for the woman to show.

An hour passed and not a single woman entered the small hotel and Adam Stone didn't leave. In her experience, and she had a lot, cheating spouses didn't waste a minute of a dirty weekend. Certainly not an hour.

Patience was the part of her job she found the toughest. She dragged out the paper, read the news, and started on the crossword puzzle. At the end of another hour, her stomach was beginning to growl. She pulled a granola bar from her bag and munched.

Finally, Stone came out of the hotel, still in his business suit. Was he trying to impress his date with his wardrobe? She shook her head and snapped a couple of photos, but he was alone. He glanced up and down the street, then took off at a brisk walk in the opposite direction.

Gretchen waited until he'd turned the corner before she got out of her car and followed him. She took the monitor from her dash and stored it inside her trunk—she'd track him on foot. But he only went as far as a corner grocery. She walked on and pretended great interest in a storefront souvenir shop, admiring toy cable cars and tins of Ghirardelli chocolates decorated with pictures of the Golden Gate Bridge. From the corner of her eye she saw Stone emerge with a brown paper sack.

Damn. He hadn't gone to meet the woman at all. She wasn't going to get any snaps of them kissing over cappuccinos in an outdoor café or playing footsie in the corner booth of an upscale restaurant.

Where was the other woman?

The obvious answer struck her like a slap. The woman

must have been waiting for her lover in the hotel. While Gretchen had been sitting outside growing stiff with boredom, trying to come up with a ten-letter word for citrus fruit, the fling had been going full tilt.

She didn't have a team or even a partner to relieve her. She snooped the old-fashioned way. She followed, snapped pictures, kept detailed notes. Testified when required. She owned a gun, a lady's Smith & Wesson with a funky pink grip, which she'd never fired in the course of her job. She rented a small office with a shared switchboard. The low overhead helped her keep her prices extremely competitive. Besides, she liked working alone.

If she wanted to get anything good tonight, she was going to have to get a little more aggressive. She followed Stone into the hotel. With luck, he'd open his door and start kissing his lady friend while still in camera range.

People in lust did the stupidest things, luckily for her business.

She breezed into the guest house, turning her head as she passed the old reception desk and pretending to dig for her key. The young woman at reception was talking on the phone and never spared a glance for the woman currently climbing into the charmingly antiquated elevator with the sliding metal mesh doors.

Stone had already started to pull the cage-like door closed when she said, "Hold the elevator please."

He sent her a quick glance, and she forced her expression to remain blandly neutral when she wanted to plow her fist into his nose. The asshole was checking her out. She recognized the quick gleam of interest, the fast head-to-toe sweep as he sized up her body. He'd barely hauled his butt out of bed from one woman, and he was eyeing another?

"Which floor?" he asked politely.

She watched his finger hover briefly over the four. "Four, please."

With a slight nod, he pushed four and the elevator whirred and creaked alarmingly as it made its slow ascent.

She was unnervingly aware of the man riding up with her. He must be a successful philanderer, she thought. He damn near hummed with sexual attraction. And her body, not as conversant with his alley cat morals as her mind, seemed to hum to his frequency.

Or maybe the sensation running up and down her spine wasn't attraction but pure, blind fear. This elevator felt like a gilded bird cage being hauled up by a palsied old woman who might drop them at any moment.

Relief hit Gretchen on many levels when the thing finally shrieked to a shuddering halt.

Stone calmly drew back the metal door and held it, politely indicating she should precede him. Damn. *She* wanted to follow *him*.

Slowly she trailed along the red carpet, threadbare in patches. The white plaster walls sported sconces and heavy gilt mirrors. Dainty antique tables held bowls of potpourri that couldn't mask the smell of must and age.

The rooms were fitted with big old-fashioned doors that had big old-fashioned locks. She grew hot thinking she'd run out of narrow corridor soon, with that maddening presence still behind her.

But, almost as she had the thought, the man behind her paused, and she heard a chinking sound like change being jingled in a pocket. She reached into her bag for her camera.

She heard the door open behind her and turned, stepping quickly and silently to intercept it before it closed. A picture of a woman naked in his bed would be good. Them necking passionately would be even better.

She got to the open door and an arm shot out, grabbing her wrist and yanking, hard. She swallowed her cry of surprise and pain as she was jolted and spun into the room.

Strong arms grabbed her, pinning her own arms to her sides and forcing her to drop both camera and bag. The door shut behind her with an ominous click.

"What the hell do you think you're doing?" She was furious with herself for being caught so woefully inattentive and with him for making her so.

Her body was pressed so tightly against his that she felt his belt buckle press into her belly, his chest flatten hers, and his breath stir her hair.

Refusing to be intimidated by his size and strength, she glared up at him.

His face was hard, the eyes glacial, but a swift streak of humor danced across the surface before disappearing. "I was going to ask you the same question."

She flicked a quick glance around, but unless the floozy was hiding under the white chenille-covered bed or inside the mahogany wardrobe, Mr. Stone was alone.

"You're the one who grabbed me," she reminded him.

"Are you armed?" Not waiting for an answer, he held her with one hand and frisked her with the other.

His paper sack of food was on the floor where he'd dropped it and after he'd satisfied himself that she had no artillery strapped to her ankles, he reached for the bag and set it on the table, foolishly turning his back on her.

She might not be armed, but that didn't mean she wasn't dangerous. In spite of years of sporadic effort, she'd never broken the brown belt barrier, but she did have a karate kick she was rather proud of, and she let Mr. Stone have it in full force.

He grunted in surprise and pain and sprawled across the table. She grabbed her bag and ran, but even as her hand closed on the ornate brass door handle, he grabbed her wrist in a painful hold.

The hell with martial arts. She sank her teeth into his arm.

He cursed, and dropped her arm.

She aimed a fist at his chin, but he dodged it and the next thing she knew she was flying bodily through the air to land on her back on the queen-sized four-poster.

Matters became swiftly worse when Stone landed on top of her. Stone? Boulder would be a better name for him, she thought dimly as the breath was knocked out of her.

The man was far more muscular than she'd have guessed. Solid muscle, in fact. Solid. Heavy. Muscle. And all of it pressed on her from breasts to toes, flattening everything. Only her arms weren't beneath him. He solved that problem by shackling her wrists in one hand and stretching them above her head.

She was absolutely helpless, robbed of even the breath to curse him with.

There was nothing in the world she hated more than being helpless. Nothing.

She glared up at him. There was a red mark on his chin, about the shape of her fist, that looked like it might bruise, and he was breathing heavily.

She hadn't gone down without a fight, but that was feeble consolation for the fact that she had gone down.

His eyes were cold and hard, and somehow dangerous. Long gone was the polite stranger who'd held the elevator door for her moments ago.

"Who sent you?" he demanded.

Like, duh! Except she couldn't say that or anything else at the moment. She couldn't so much as draw a breath. If she didn't get some oxygen soon she was going to compound her helplessness by passing out.

"Can't breathe!" she managed to gasp with the last air in her lungs.

Those cold, angry eyes narrowed in suspicion. He didn't roll off her, but he did lift his upper body a few inches. She would have preferred to curl into a fetal ball and suck air, but he wasn't giving her that option. She managed to drag in a lungful of oxygen and stave off the dizziness. Beneath her anger, she tasted her own fear. This guy was much stronger than he looked, and obviously some kind of sex maniac.

While she gasped and panted, he said, "You were at the airport. I saw you again, driving by when I paid off the cab. You followed me from the corner store."

Her irritation skyrocketed. She was good at her job, dammit. Even a trained professional would have had trouble recognizing her. How had he nailed her all those times? "Pure coincidence. I certainly don't recall seeing you before. We must have arrived at the same time and we're staying at the same place. So what? Now, if you could get off me, I'll get back to my evening."

"You're staying here in the same hotel?"

All he'd have to do would be to call the front desk to find out she was lying. "I'm staying with a friend."

He dug into her bag with his free hand and she bucked against him, hating his strength and the power he currently enjoyed. "That's private."

He pulled her gun out and waved it in her face. "You were taking a gun to visit your friend?"

She was losing what little patience she had. "Get off me!" She bucked and twisted her body, but that only reminded her that they were pressed together as intimately as lovers. He sucked in a quick breath as she arched and twisted against him and she saw a flare of heat ignite in his eyes. It was quickly extinguished, even as she fought down her own pre-feminist response to a roused male animal.

"Who sent you?" he asked again.

"Where's the woman?" she countered.

A quick puzzled frown pulled his black brows together. "You're in no position to play games. You're not staying here. You've been following me. Why? Who sent you?"

She glared right back at him. If he was smart enough to spot a tail, he was smart enough to figure out who'd hired her. He was the game player. "Your wife sent me."

"I don't think so." He shifted, and she felt his irritation as well as the imminent cutting off of her air supply again.

A wave of fury swamped her. "No. You men never do think. You indulge in your sordid little affairs and imagine you'll get away with them while the little wifey works her ass off, keeps the house, raises the kids . . ." A picture of her own mom doing just that roared through her mind like a flash fire. "News flash, asshole, the wife's onto you."

"Did my *wife* hire you to kill me?"

What did he think she was? A hit man? "I'm a private investigator. She hired me to gather evidence for a divorce, Einstein."

His eyes had narrowed again and she felt as though he were trying to see right into the thoughts behind her words. "Did my wife hire you herself?"

"No. Her lawyer did."

"What's the lawyer's name?"

"That's confidential. So, now you know why I'm here, how about you produce your lady friend, I'll take a couple of nice photos, and be out of here."

"There is no woman."

She rolled her gaze. The guy was busted. When was he going to realize that and get off her?

"And one more fact you may find interesting." He shifted and his eyes burned into hers.

"Don't tell me. Your wife doesn't understand you?"
She tried to sound confident, but her pulse was jumping.

"I'm not married."

# Chapter Two

Adam almost smiled. The woman's goggle-eyed "What?" was so authentic, he almost believed she thought she'd been sent to spy on a philandering husband.

Almost.

Sending a woman with a spill of blond curls, sea green eyes, and a slim, curvy body to murder him was brilliant.

Except, of course, that her very beauty was what had caused him to notice her at the airport. Then, because he was on the run with secrets his superiors would kill for, he'd kept all his senses alert. And so he'd spotted her pulled over on the road in from the airport, and again when she'd followed him back from the corner store.

But how the hell had they caught up to him so quickly? He'd swear she hadn't been on the plane, and he'd never seen her in Houston. He would have remembered.

He'd called from the airport to cancel his afternoon meeting in D.C., then bought his ticket for San Francisco.

He rolled off the woman, finding it altogether too difficult to think clearly with her soft curves crushed beneath him as though he were making love to her. Her scent teased him and those damn curls had exploded out of their captivity and were tossed all over his pillow like a scatter of gold coins.

She might give him ideas that were hot and intimate, but her gun was cold and businesslike in his hand. Remembering the way she'd tackled him from behind, he kept her gun trained on her while he sank into the single armchair in the room, upholstered in bordello-red velvet.

He'd chosen this place at random off the Internet. How had they found him so quickly?

Once he was off her, the woman sat and turned so she was sitting on the bed, her feet on the floor. "If your wife didn't hire me, then who did?"

"I didn't say you could move." He brandished her gun a bit to remind her he was holding it.

She shook her head. "It's not loaded."

"What kind of assassin carries an unloaded gun?" Any second now he was going to wake up in his own bed and this whole thing would turn out to be a nightmare. Hopefully the last three months would turn out to have been equally imaginary.

"I'm not an assassin. I'm a P.I. And it's not me you have to convince you're not cheating on your wife, so there's little point in this pretense."

"When did 'my wife' contact you?"

"That's privileged—"

"Whatever you're being paid, I'll double it."

She gave him a long, cool look. "I'm getting a thousand bucks for the weekend. I'll take the two in cash." She gave him one of those phony, have-a-nice-day smiles.

"I don't have that kind of money on me. I can write you a check or you can wait until the bank opens in the morning." In fact, he had five thousand in cash, but it was his getaway money and he needed to make it last.

"Thanks anyway. I think I'll pass." She rose. "It's been a real pleasure meeting you, but I'll be on my way."

She bent for her bag once more and, knowing he had to stop her, he reached for his own gun, which he'd unpacked and kept handy, hoping like hell he wouldn't need it.

"This one's loaded."

She stared at him, stared at the gun, and for the first time, he felt her fear. He bit down on any feelings of guilt, knowing he couldn't let her leave his sight. Not before morning.

Still, she remained stubbornly silent.

He did a quick calculation. "You were hired sometime after noon today, your time."

Instead of answering his question, she snapped, "Do you have a license for that thing?"

This had to be the strangest conversation he'd ever had with anyone. "As a matter of fact, I do."

"Do you have any idea how many accidents, even deaths, are caused each year by careless firearm use?"

"Not all of them are accidental. Sit down."

She did, but not before her gaze had swept the area for a possible weapon. Damn it, he was going to have to tie her to the bed. And not for any of the fun reasons.

She crossed her arms under her breasts and glared at him.

"Well? Am I right on the timing?"

"Roughly," she conceded in an icy tone.

He took a moment to check her gun. It was as she'd said. No bullets. Which made his theory that she was an assassin lame at best. Although, maybe her kick was her lethal weapon. He rubbed his back, wondering if she'd bruised a kidney.

He pulled her bag toward him with his foot, waving his own gun at her when he saw her body tensed as though to spring.

And if she did, what was he going to do about it? If

she hadn't figured out by now that he wasn't going to shoot her, she soon would.

He took off his tie. He should have taken the thing off hours ago, but he'd been busy pacing, thinking.

Still holding the gun trained on her, he dug around in his suitcase for a couple more ties.

"I really am sorry about this," he said as he approached her.

"No!" Her eyes widened, and she jumped off the bed and lunged for his gun.

"Are you crazy? Stop it."

They struggled, for a lot longer than they should have, because Adam would neither shoot nor hit the woman. She didn't have the same compunction. He was elbowed, clawed, jabbed, slapped, and punched before he had her tied up on the bed.

While she was squirming, kicking, and generally making his life hell, as well as shamefully turning him on, she rapped her head a good one on one of the posts. He paused to ask if she was okay and she turned her head and sank her teeth into his hand.

"Goddam it, that's the second time you've bitten me. Have you had your rabies shots?"

She glared at him, and he glared right back before going into the bathroom and wetting a face cloth in cold water.

When he returned to the room, she was staring at the ceiling, refusing even to look his way as he approached. He slipped a hand under her head until he found the swelling, and slid the cold cloth under the spot.

"You need that more than I do," she said fiercely, and he realized she was frightened.

Taking a step back, he sank into the chair once more, trying to let her know he wouldn't harm her. "I know. You fight dirty."

One thing puzzled him. "Why didn't you scream?"

Her face reddened. "Don't want a civilian accidentally getting hurt."

More and more he was convinced she hadn't been sent to kill him. Puzzled, he pulled her bag toward him, and now that she was immobile, he took the time to search it properly. There was a cell phone, an electronic notebook, a coil-bound notebook, her purse, and today's paper folded open to the crossword. Half done.

There was also an open box of granola bars and half a bottle of water.

"Stop that. How dare you go through my things?"

Ignoring her, he flipped open the notebook and his own picture stared up at him. A corporate shot. They must have e-mailed it and she'd printed it onto photographic paper. No date or time stamp. Nothing at all written on either side. Still, if the attachment was still on her computer, it could be traced back to the sender. *Evidence.*

Her notebook contained a scribble of illegible shorthand notes and a mileage log. Her electronic notebook was password protected.

A handful of business cards yielded the most information. *Gretchen Wiest, Licensed Private Investigator. Discretion is our business.*

So, it seemed she really was a P.I.

"Gretchen Wiest, is that you?"

She glared at him.

He settled back in his chair. "Look, Gretchen, I'm not any happier about this than you are. I'm going to tell you what I can."

He leaned back and tried to figure out what, exactly, he could tell the hostile stranger currently tied to his bed like the embodiment of a very juicy fantasy. Her shirt had ridden up when they'd struggled, and the sight of her taut belly was giving him ideas he had no business having. He'd pull the shirt down for her, except he didn't want her to know he'd noticed.

"I'm not married. That wasn't my wife's lawyer who hired you. I don't know who it was exactly, but I've got some ideas." He hesitated, and felt a frown pull his brows together. One thing wrestling with a gorgeous feisty woman had done was banish that frown for a few minutes, but now it was back. With Gretchen's entrance into his life, he knew the task ahead had just become more difficult.

"I'm in trouble. I think the people who hired you to follow me are planning for me to meet with a fatal accident. Gretchen, did you report in? Do they know where I am?"

There was a pause and he heard traffic down on the street. A horn honked somewhere. She shook her head. "I was waiting until I saw you with a woman to report."

He let out a relieved breath. "I'm not a criminal. I can't tell you any more for your own safety. I'm sorry," he said again. "I won't hurt you but you'll have to stay here tonight. I can't take the chance that you'll call and give away my whereabouts. I'm leaving San Francisco in the morning. Then you can go free. Tonight, I'll sleep in the chair."

"But my kids." She sounded panicked. "I have to get home for my kids."

Kids? His stomach lurched. He'd assumed she was single. No ring.

He did the one thing he'd sworn he wouldn't. He went for her purse. It was tucked in the bottom of the bag. If she had kids, he wanted to see them. He didn't know one parent who didn't carry photos of their offspring.

In two minutes he knew she was lying. "There are no pictures of kids in here, and your video membership card says 'Miss.' "

"It ought to say 'Ms.' and in case you haven't heard, women have children without husbands. Smart women, anyway."

She had a chip on her shoulder the size of a small country. She must love her work nailing cheating spouses. Story there, but he didn't have time to pursue it.

"If you had kids, you wouldn't put them in danger. You wouldn't let a gun-toting man who ties up women even know of their existence."

She didn't even bother arguing with him. "Why don't you blow town now? Leave me here, and take off if killers are after you."

"I have my reasons. I'm sorry," he said for the third time.

He went to the window and scanned the street carefully, but nothing had changed. He drew the drapes and resumed his seat. The brown paper sack caught his eye. "I almost forgot. Dinner." He pulled out a deli sandwich and a soda. He got a glass from the bathroom and poured half of the soda into it, split the sandwich and placed it on a napkin. "I hope you like chicken salad," he said, placing it on the bedside table. Then he untied her left hand, having noted already that she was right-handed.

She glared at him again, but he was getting used to it. Besides, he thought that if the positions were reversed, he'd be doing some glaring, too.

He was half prepared for her to throw the sandwich and drink at him, but she didn't. She ate and drank. Sensible woman. He liked that.

"So," he said, putting down the gun and picking up his half sandwich. "Do you hate all men or is it just me?"

# Chapter Three

Gretchen jerked awake, startled by the sound of a radio alarm, panicked by a nightmare. It took a second for everything to come back to her, and then she almost wished it hadn't. The nightmare was real.

She glanced over and Adam Stone's eyes flickered open. She watched a grimace of discomfort cross his face and saw his hand go to his neck, bent at an awkward angle on the chair. She hoped it ached like hell.

"Good morning," he said.

"It will be a good morning when you let me go and get the hell out of my life."

She uncurled herself, hating to be so vulnerable before a stranger. As soon as he untied her . . .

Wait a minute. She wasn't much of a morning person, but even her fogged brain could work out that she couldn't have curled up in sleep if her arms and legs were still bound.

"When did you untie me?" She felt even more foolish knowing she could have walked out any time in the night and instead had snoozed until the alarm woke her. Given her track record for the last twenty-four hours, she was going to have to give some serious thought to a career change.

That disturbing glint of humor lurked deep in his eyes again, as though he read her mind and understood her discomfort.

"Come on," he said far too cheerfully. "I'll buy you breakfast."

"Thank you," she said from behind gritted teeth, "but all I want to do is go home."

He glanced at his watch, then winced and rubbed his neck. "What about some coffee?"

"This is ridiculous." She threw off the covers and put her feet on the floor. "I have work to do, a life." She had no idea who this man was—a cheating spouse, a criminal, an innocent man on the run as he claimed, or simply a wacko, but she wanted to part company with him. The sooner the better.

He rubbed his hands over his face and she saw the stubble that shadowed his chin and cheeks. "Okay. I need to get a copy of the e-mail my picture came with. We can stop at your office."

Oh yeah. That was going to happen. Maybe she hadn't been completely on top of her game so far in their short acquaintance, but Mr. Stone was about to discover she had a few surprises in store.

All she had to do was figure out what those were.

Meanwhile, he politely offered her the bathroom first. As she'd discovered last night, the bathroom window was about the size of a postcard. No way of escape.

She was dying for a shower, but the idea of getting naked with Stone in the other room was not a prospect that filled her with glee. She'd wait until she was home.

So she washed, used some of his toothpaste on her finger to brush her teeth, finger-combed her hair, and gave up.

"Okay, here's how we'll do it," he said when she emerged. "You'll drive. First we head for your office, I

grab the e-mail, then you drive me to a place I'll desig-
nate and I disappear from your life. Agreed?"

"I caught a cab from the airport and followed you on
foot."

He rolled his eyes. "Your car's the beige one halfway
down the block. And you've got a ticket."

"Ticket?" She ran to the window, and sure enough,
something white and ominously papery fluttered from
under her windshield wipers. Her professional pride
took another blow. "You even knew my car."

"Hey, if you weren't gorgeous, and I wasn't running
for my life, I wouldn't have noticed."

She scowled out the window. She didn't have time
for gorgeous. Or for the tug of flattery his compliment
elicited.

"Come on," he said.

She did, picking up her bag while he fumbled with
heavy cases and still tried to point the gun at her. She
watched him for a few minutes then stepped forward.
"I'm enjoying the one-man rendition of the Three
Stooges, but if you keep this up, somebody's going to
get shot." She grabbed his flight bag. "We both know
you're not going to kill me. I'll drop you somewhere
public and then we're done with each other. Have a
nice life."

He didn't argue, and slid the gun into a side pocket
in his backpack.

The breakfast he bought her was from a drive-through,
but there was coffee and it was hot so she didn't care.
Truth was, now the night was over and he'd kept his
word, she no longer felt vulnerable. What she felt was
curious. It was probably her insatiable curiosity and love
of solving puzzles that had lured her into this line of
work in the first place.

She wasn't a fool. She'd run background checks on
both Stone and Fisk before taking the case. Stone was a

petroleum engineer and Fisk was a prominent divorce attorney in Houston. She'd never thought to confirm that Stone was married. If he wasn't, or even if he was, why would someone want to kill him?

Once they'd pulled back into traffic, he said, "Okay. Now your office."

She'd already received half her fee up front. Since the client obviously wasn't going to get incriminating pictures of Stone and a woman—unless it was of *her*—then the least she could do was give her client confidentiality.

"I can't—"

"Gretchen, this is important." The way he said her name, as though they were a team, gave her a jolt.

She also realized that she believed him. Well, she was a little skeptical about the running for his life part, but obviously he hadn't met a woman for a wild weekend. She was a fair person; if they'd sent her that photo under false pretenses, she supposed Adam had a right to see it.

"All right," she said. "But I can't go near my office until I've had a shower." She glanced at her watch. It was a few minutes after eight. "I live in a secure building and you will be waiting outside on the street. Got it?"

He made a sound of frustration in his throat, and quickly stifled it. Smart guy. She'd been scared half to death, had precious little sleep, and fast food outlet coffee. She needed a shower, fresh clothes, and deodorant.

"Nice building," he said as she slowed, coming up on her place off Ninth Avenue near Golden Gate Park. He hadn't hurt her, had suffered on an uncomfortable chair all night, and was going to be out of her life in minutes. It made her charitable enough that she was almost friendly.

"It used to be a single-family residence, but now it's been chopped up into apartments. I love it." She glanced up to her bay window on the second floor and felt a puzzled frown pull her brows together as a man appeared briefly at the window. "That's odd," she said. "The super must be in my apartment. I wonder why?"

She glanced at her companion and saw him reaching for his backpack, the nice guy who'd bought her breakfast gone in a heartbeat. "You did call in, didn't you?"

Her face must have given her away.

"Drive! Go on. Get out of here."

"It's probably just a leak or something and the super's in my apartment." But she pulled out into traffic and tried not to floor it. Adam's jitters were catching.

"You can call him from across town." He glanced at her. "Your office."

She nodded. A strange tension gripped her as she drove. As hard as she tried to convince herself there was an innocent reason for the man's silhouette she'd seen, her skin still crawled and she gripped the steering wheel so hard her knuckles ached.

As soon as they got to her office, she'd call the super and find out what was wrong in her apartment. Then she'd give Mr. Stone his e-mail and she'd carry on with her day and hope to hell it was better than yesterday.

But within a block of her office, she knew her day was tanking in the worst way.

The sirens alerted her first. She had to resist the urge to turn down the street and race to where the fire trucks were pulled up outside the remains of her office. The road was barricaded, but it didn't take more than a glance to figure out what had happened.

The fire was all but out. A few dirty gray tendrils of smoke clung to the roof. Water dripped everywhere and a fire hose was still trained on one gaping window; the glass had either blown out or been hacked out.

"Your office window?"

"Yeah."

Adam pulled down a window and yelled to a group of spectators, "What happened?"

"Place burned down in the night."

"Was anyone hurt?" Gretchen asked through numb lips.

"Anybody inside?" Adam asked his informant.

"Don't think so."

"Thanks." He pulled up the window. "Let's get out of here."

She did. The muscles of her legs ached from the strain of not being able to follow her first impulse and gun it out of there. But that, of course, would only bring unwanted attention their way. So she headed away from the destruction at a normal speed.

Adam grabbed his gun and glanced everywhere. "I don't think we're being followed," he said, but she knew it was too early to tell.

"Well," she said on a shuddering sigh, "I now believe that killers are after you."

"Gretchen, I hate to be the one to tell you this, but right now killers aren't just after me. They're after both of us."

"Right." She wasn't stupid, she'd figured that out for herself, but hearing him say the words was not helping. "So, now what?"

"Now, you drop me at a car rental lot and go stay with someone you can trust. Stay out of sight for a few days."

Her fingers began drumming the wheel to the same beat as the fury slamming through her blood. "Hide? You expect me to hide? People I don't even know used me to get to you, trashed my business, did God knows what to my home, and you want me to hide? I don't think so."

"Hey, I know how you feel. But I don't want to be responsible for you getting hurt. Pull into this plaza and over by that mailbox for a second."

She did as he asked, sliding her car in next to a delivery van that was unloading sodas into a corner store. She edged far enough forward that her vehicle would be all but invisible from the road.

From his pocket, Adam pulled a handful of hotel flyers of the kind that were stocked in lobbies and bus stations everywhere. It almost seemed to her that he was playing "eenie, meenie, meinie, mo" with them, flipping through brochures of big hotels on the Las Vegas strip.

He made his choice and pulled a large brown envelope out of his backpack. He had a black pen in an inside pocket, and she watched him address the envelope to himself in care of the Las Vegas hotel.

"I don't suppose you have stamps?" he asked her.

"Not on me."

He dug around in his backpack some more, but came out, not with stamps as she'd half expected, but a baseball cap, which he pulled low over his eyes. He got out of the car, disappeared into the corner store.

She grabbed her cell phone and punched in Fisk's number. She'd tell her client she'd made a mistake and the man she'd followed wasn't Adam Stone. It was too little too late, but she felt she had to try.

She wasn't all that surprised to hear a recorded message telling her that the number was no longer in service. No doubt if she tracked down the real Mr. Fisk, he'd have no idea who she was and his voice would be completely different than the man who'd hired her. And duped her.

The phone was tucked back in her bag when Adam emerged from the store sticking stamps to the envelope, which he then pushed through the slot in the mailbox.

He got back into the car and turned to her.

"Adam? What are you doing?"

He was staring at her, focusing on her mouth. The intensity of his gaze caused her breath to hitch.

"What I've wanted to do since I saw you at the airport," he said, and brought his lips slowly to hers.

He gave her plenty of time to evade, she'd give him that, but the surprising thing was she didn't want to escape his kiss. In fact, she met him halfway.

Perhaps it was accumulated adrenaline from fear, not enough sleep, and seeing her personal and business spaces invaded and destroyed, but there was a lot of pent-up tension in her body and it seemed to explode at once into desire.

She supposed, if they were on the run from death, it was only natural to celebrate life in the most fundamental way. That must have been why she met his hungry kiss with a fierceness that surprised her.

She felt his hands plunge into her hair, tugging lightly so her head tipped back. Her lips opened on a sigh and his tongue plunged inside, hot and demanding.

# Chapter Four

Oh, that man could kiss. His tongue thrust deep into her mouth, stroking, inciting, and somehow soothing her. After all, she reasoned dimly, it was hard to take anything very seriously when you were necking in a parking lot with a man you'd known less than twenty-four hours.

She wound her arms around him and rubbed up against him, needing his solidness and warmth.

With a groan, he pulled away.

"Keep that warm for me," he said with a crooked grin. "I'll be back."

And almost before she'd got her tongue back in her own mouth, he was out of the car and walking away, his backpack slung over one shoulder, his briefcase in the other hand.

She blinked, stunned, as he kept walking, not looking back. He was headed toward a side road. What on earth was he planning to do? The man was crazy and about as conspicuous as a gorgeous guy on the side of a road could be. With his ball cap and fancy briefcase he begged a second glance. She should let him go.

She should simply let him go.

She backed up out of her parking spot and followed him.

She used the electric button to roll down the passenger side window as she drew abreast of him. "Hey. You forgot your luggage."

"I'll be back for it," he said through barely parted lips, staring straight ahead. "Get out of here."

"You won't be back for it if you're dead."

"Quit making a spectacle of both of us and I might survive."

A car honked behind her and then roared around. The driver gave her the finger. "Las Vegas is the other way."

He kept walking.

"You're going to need a car to get there."

"I'll rent one."

"I'm not leaving."

It took another quarter mile, and she was flipped the bird a couple more times, before Adam turned to her with a glare of pure loathing and she knew she'd won. She pulled over ahead of him and he got in.

"Are you completely insane?" he yelled.

"No. I'm mad. And when I get mad I don't hide. It's not my nature."

She wasn't the only one. He was so angry, waves of heat were coming off him. "They'll kill you if they find you."

Yeah, Yeah. If she'd been afraid of danger she would have chosen a different line of work. Besides . . . "I liked that kiss so much I'm hanging around for more."

The way his teeth were grinding together she didn't think kissing was his top priority right now.

She sighed. "I did call in. Right after you got off the plane. Mr. Fisk told me to call again when you checked in to your hotel, but I wanted to wait until I could re-

port that I'd seen you with your supposed lady friend."
She knew she'd put him in great danger, but she didn't
know how much. She recalled Mr. Fisk saying during
the cell conversation, "Airport?" and she could hear
herself responding, "Yes, San Francisco airport."

"They didn't even know which city you were in until I
called, did they?"

He remained silent and still for a moment, then
shook his head.

"I'm sorry."

"You didn't know."

"At least let me drive you to Las Vegas. I might as well
get right out of town. It's probably safer."

He laughed mirthlessly. "Not with me."

She shivered, realizing how very much she wanted to
be with him, on the run or any other way. His kiss had
only confirmed the astonishing sexual chemistry they
had together. Somehow, she'd known it from the first
moment their gazes had connected.

"We'll get on I-5 and be in Las Vegas in about ten
hours," she promised, looking for a place to turn around.

"If your buddy Fisk is who I think he is, he'll have figured out I'm trying to get to the FBI."

She almost slammed on the brakes. "Well, we have
an FBI office right here in town."

"We'd never get there alive. It's the first place they'll
think we're going. I know a guy in Las Vegas. We'll go
there."

It occurred to her there was a lot he wasn't telling
her, and if she was going along with him, risking her life
right alongside his, she'd be changing that soon. But
right now, she was too busy driving and keeping an eye
out for any vehicles that might be too interested in her.

Adam pulled out sunglasses from his pack, then
slumped down in the passenger seat.

"Pass me the scarf and glasses you'll find in my glove compartment," she said.

He did, pulling out the two items she'd requested as well as her road atlas, which he tossed into his lap.

He held the wheel steady while she tied the scarf over her hair in a fifties movie star way and slipped on the dark glasses.

There was silence as she maneuvered her way out of town. She switched on the radio news and soon heard a report about her building fire. Fortunately, it had happened early enough that no one was in the building at the time. Although it was too early for the fire report, an electrical fire was suspected. The word arson was never mentioned.

"I bet your computer mysteriously got fried in the fire," Adam said when the news segued into the weather forecast.

"They burned down a whole building to get rid of an e-mail? Isn't that a little extreme?"

"E-mail, notes, phone numbers. They figured you'd come home and they'd get everything else."

She shivered at his matter-of-fact tone.

Midmorning on a Saturday, the traffic wasn't too bad. Adam glanced into his side mirror almost as often as she checked the rearview mirror, but if there was a tail, they'd yet to spot it.

After flipping through her road atlas, he said, "Take I-580 east and . . . just keep heading east for a while."

"But we can get to Las Vegas much faster—"

"They'll look for us on the main highway. We head for small towns and two-lane roads nobody would ever think we'd take."

"But if we head east, we'll never get to Las Vegas tonight."

"No point getting there before the mail."

"We'll have to spend the night."

"Yeah." And there was a whole lot of nighttime activity packed into a single *yeah*. She shivered, wondering why this virtual stranger appealed to her so much. Well, okay, he was gorgeous and sexy and a whiff of danger clung to him. Her ideal man.

And so she drove east. They drove through Yosemite. She opened her window to suck in the clean, cool air and gaze at the ponderosa pines and big, shaggy cedars. In late autumn, there were few other travelers and no one was following them. A couple of Stellar's jays swooped by, no doubt hoping they'd stop for a picnic and share.

"Sorry, guys," she said quietly, not wanting to wake Adam, who snoozed gently in the passenger seat.

Her soft words must have been enough to wake him anyway, for he started up and glanced around as though for an ambush of crazed Texan killers.

"I have to admit, it seems unlikely that killers would look for us here. Because it *is crazy.*" Her voice rose on the last words, but she didn't care. This whole thing was insane. Her shoulders ached from driving and her companion had snoozed for the last two hours.

"Hey, we can split up anytime."

"Not before I see the assholes who burned my office and invaded my home in jail."

"Then keep driving."

"Why don't we while away the hours with you telling me exactly what is going on?"

There was a long silence, as though he were debating with himself. Finally he said, "I guess I owe you that."

Then he paused again. "I'm a petroleum engineer." Well, she'd backgrounded him and discovered as much. So far he was telling her the truth. "The company I work—*worked*—for in Houston was aggressive, expanding rapidly, the stock price going through the roof. It didn't feel right to me. After the Enron scandal, I started wondering. As other companies lost value and their share prices plummeted, we kept expanding. I don't know, it just seemed too good to be true."

She glanced at him. He hadn't mentioned the company by name, but she knew from her background check that it was a huge Fortune 500 firm with thousands of employees around the world.

"I know, stock price isn't really my area, which is why I didn't listen to my gut for a long time. Then I saw something. A report on a South American field that had been falsified. It was a fluke I even saw the thing. It claimed a huge potential oil field in an area where we'd found none. I know because I wrote the original report."

She glanced over at him. "Wow. What did you do?"

"I kept quiet and started snooping. An old buddy of mine works for the FBI in Las Vegas. I called him. End of story."

"Then why didn't you fly straight there?"

"No flights. I booked at the last minute. Besides, I wanted to throw the dogs off the scent." It wasn't the end of the story, not by a long shot, as she could tell by the way he shifted his body away from her and stared out his window, jaw rigid.

The company was a household name. A rare success story in hard economic times. If it was a house of cards waiting to collapse . . . she thought about the blow to the economy and who knew how many shareholders. "Wow."

"Yeah. Wake me when you want me to take a turn at the wheel," he said, and pulling his cap low and closing his eyes, he settled back once more.

She drove until her back was beyond sore and her stomach growling. They were in a little town off I-395 that she'd never even heard of. There was a strip of motels, a shopping plaza with a Wal-Mart, some fast food places, and a couple of gas stations.

She pulled up in front of the Wal-Mart. "I need to pick up a toothbrush and a few things, stretch my legs, and get something to eat."

He nodded and glanced around. "We might as well stay here tonight. I'll pick up some food and meet you back here."

Twenty minutes later they were arguing.

Adam had not only picked up burgers and fries, but he'd checked them into the Cockerel Motel.

"This place should be called the Cockroach Motel," she complained bitterly, as she gazed around the room. There was a strong smell of antiseptic in the room and stains on the carpet that looked like they were covering up for something worse. The beige walls had yellowed from cigarette smoke and age.

The bed had a dip in the middle visible from where she stood, just inside the entrance, as close to out the door as she could get. And there was a coin box attached to the plastic "wood" headboard.

"I chose it because the parking lot backs onto the highway. We can get out fast if we need to."

"You are getting paranoid." He'd even made her park at the opposite end of the lot from their motel room.

She rolled her head around on her neck, conscious that she was stiff from driving for eight or nine hours. Adam had offered to take the wheel several times, but she knew she'd be more bored as a passenger.

"Come and eat," he said. "It will make you feel better."

Surprisingly, food did make her feel better. She was conscious, as they sat at the small cracked table in the corner, that there was only the one bed, and the way it dipped in the middle, they were going to be intimate whether they liked it or not.

She had a feeling she was going to like it.

Once she'd demolished her burger and half her fries, leaving Adam to finish the rest, and she'd sipped the last of her cola, she said, "I'm going to take a shower."

She grabbed her plastic bag of new stuff and the makeup kit from her trunk. She went into the tiny bathroom. At least it was clean. And the water was hot, pounding against her naked flesh until she tingled. She thought back to the kiss she and Adam had shared earlier and tingled even more.

She soaped thoroughly and even managed to shave her legs with the pink plastic razor she'd purchased. She dried off, applied skin lotion, and pulled on the blue sleep shirt she'd bought. She stared at herself in the scratched mirror and shrugged. Usually when she wanted to seduce a man, she had a few more weapons at her disposal.

When she emerged from the bathroom, Adam's gaze heated as he looked at her, and she felt as sexy as though she were wearing her expensive lingerie and the French perfume she only applied when she wanted sex.

He grabbed his own toiletry bag and almost sprinted for the bathroom. "I'll be fast," he said.

"Oh, I hope not," she muttered to herself.

# Chapter Five

Adam tried to keep his erection under control in the shower, but the damn thing had a mind of its own. He could almost feel it pulling him back toward the other room, where Gretchen waited, and based on the steamy glance she'd sent him, she had more than sleep on her mind.

Washing at the speed of light, he dried himself so fast he left damp patches everywhere and had to force himself to take the time to shave. He didn't want to leave whisker burn on Gretchen's creamy skin.

He opened the door naked to the waist, casually holding his damp towel in front of his distended boxers, and paused at the strange noise. It sounded like a commercial washing machine grinding away.

"Hey, look at this!" Gretchen said.

She sat cross-legged on top of the bed showing acres of tanned leg and grinning at him. She and the bed were both rocking.

If it was possible, the sight made him harder. Her long T-shirt clung lovingly to her form, and from the easy jiggle of her breasts, there was no bra under there.

Even as he crossed to her, the grinding whirr hiccupped to a halt. "Oh, my ride's over."

"Not hardly." He dug into his loose change piled on the side table and stuck in a couple more quarters. She giggled in surprise as the bed started up again.

He watched the sway and jiggle for another minute and decided a mortal man could only take so much.

Shucking his boxers, Adam crawled on behind her, sliding his legs to the outside of hers and snuggling up behind her.

"What are you doing?" she asked somewhat breathlessly.

"Vibrating."

She giggled, but that eased to a sigh when he lifted her heavy tangle of damp hair and kissed her nape. Not even the cheap, bottom-grade motel soap smell could disguise her own spicy-sweet scent. It was in her hair, in the curve of her shoulder. He breathed her in as his hands caught her under the breasts and pulled her in tighter.

His cock, already hard and straining for her, nestled against her vibrating butt while his hands explored her breasts. She moaned and leaned her head back against his shoulder as he molded and teased them, touching and playing with nipples he'd never seen. He wondered what color they were, and couldn't wait to find out.

But not yet.

He planted his hands on her shaking knees and trailed them slowly up her open thighs.

He almost yelled with victory when his questing fingers discovered, not cotton panties, but warm, damp curls. He stroked them a little as she sighed and shifted, then he moved lower to where she was open and hot, slippery with excitement. He dipped his middle finger inside and felt his cock clench. *Soon, buddy,* he promised silently.

He scooped some of her own lubricant and, opening her with his thumb and outside fingers, touched the red hot tip of her with his juicy middle finger. He could have remained like that and let the bed do the rest of the work, but that would have been too easy. And based on the panting he heard, too quick. So he traced a slow, lazy circle around the hard, quivering nub. Around and around.

She raised her hands behind her and grasped the back of his neck, turning to kiss him with sinuous need.

Even their lips were vibrating.

The bed was ridiculous: cheap, noisy, and garish. Like having sex on a carnival ride.

He was so hot, he was about to explode.

Grabbing a condom from where he'd hidden a couple under his wallet on the night table, he readied himself and then lifted Gretchen.

She hovered over him for a minute, resisting impalement, taking him in her hands and holding him against her hot spot. "You're like a human vibrator," she said in a low husky tone.

"I'll be a human volcano in a second. Get on here."

She did, lowering herself hard and fast, her back to his front. The angle was different, the fit of her pussy tight and wonderful. He stripped her shirt from her to enjoy the view of her long, graceful back and to reach all of her, unimpeded.

They were both close enough to the edge that she didn't bother to ride him, just settled back, brought his hand once more to her clit, and let the bed do the rest.

Everything was jiggling, hot, wet, tight, squeezing, tighter yet. Little helpless cries emerged from her throat and she did some shuddering that had nothing to do with the bed.

As orgasm gripped her, her body tightened and milked him until he couldn't stop the explosion that rolled out of him, on and on.

The roar of the bed stopped and his cry of release

was loud in the sudden silence, where he hadn't bothered trying to stifle it. Her own cries were as abandoned.

She turned to face him, her hand clapped—too late—over her mouth. They cracked up together, falling to the bed and laughing like crazies.

"Not a bad ride for a couple of quarters," he said into her ear before kissing the ear, then her cheek, then her throat. He'd have gone for her lips but they both needed to get their breath back.

"They're pink," Adam said.

"Hmm?" She was still floating, feeling far too wonderful for a woman staying in a budget motel, and whose office had burned up that morning.

"Your nipples. I wondered what color they were."

"Oh." If the tingling was any indication, they were getting pinker by the second. Pointier, too. "What else did you wonder?"

"How they'd taste." He leaned over and took them into his mouth, one at a time, doing things with his tongue that had desire drumming in her veins once more.

"This time," he said, raising up until his lips were only a whisper away from hers, "I want to make love face-to-face, so I can watch you when you come."

The sound that came out of her throat was part gasp, part moan, and quickly swallowed when his mouth came down on hers.

Without the racket and jostling of machinery, lying here, naked and staring into each other's eyes was as intimate as anything she'd ever experienced. They'd left the light on, and she could see that his chest hair was as black as that on his head, and that there were a few freckles on his shoulders. Nice shoulders, solid, dependable. As though he carried responsibility with ease. A man you could rely on, she thought.

This time they took time to play and to explore each other's bodies. She discovered he was ticklish when she licked his belly, and that the skin at the side of his ribs was corn silk soft.

And she learned that his cock fit nicely into her fist and when she squeezed the tip, a pearly drop emerged. She rubbed it around the head until it gleamed, and Adam was groaning helplessly.

Since he was currently learning her intimate parts as though he'd be required to draw them from memory, she was so hot herself she had little sympathy to spare.

Still, she didn't want him coming until he was deep inside her, so she reached for a new condom and took her sweet time rolling it on.

She was feeling very much in control of things when she felt herself flipped on her back so fast and so hard it reminded her of the first time they'd met, when he'd tossed her to the bed and jumped on top of her. Then she'd been scared, now she was . . . not scared.

"Enough play. I need you now."

She blinked up at him, trying not to squirm. "Okay."

He held her gaze with his blue, blue one and entered her as though he were entering a cathedral, quietly and reverently.

Okay, now she was scared. No woman should feel so intimately connected to a man she'd just met. That spelled danger.

She shouldn't look into his eyes while he loved her so sweetly; that was more dangerous still. She should crack a joke, change positions, she should . . . With a quiet sigh, she arched her hips to take him deeper, increasing the connection between them.

She gasped at the heat that flared, each slow, deliberate stroke driving her both higher and yet deeper into something that was outside her experience. He felt it, too, she was certain. His gaze was hot with more than sexual desire.

"Adam, I . . ."

But what she'd planned to say, she had no idea, and after a second's silence, he gripped her hips, locking their bodies more tightly together. She reached down and cupped his balls, squeezing gently.

"Oh my God," he cried. "I can't—" His cry was cut off by a groan as his entire body clenched and shuddered.

It was that uncontrolled rocking against her that set her off, her hips jerking hard against his as the tremors ripped through her and a sob of pure ecstasy poured from her mouth.

But, for all the writhing and trembling coming from both of them, neither broke eye contact.

It seemed Adam had slept only minutes when something woke him.

"Get up. Adam, get up." Gretchen's voice was tense and urgent. It was the tone as much as the words that had him blinking to full alertness.

She stood beside the bed, her hand ice cold as she shook his shoulder.

"What is it?"

"Two men. Hanging around my car."

He didn't say a word, but scrambled out of bed to the window. Through the blinds, he saw them. They were circling; one was bent and staring into the windows. And it didn't look like they were car shopping. "Shit."

"Could be car thieves," she said, but he knew from her tone she didn't believe that.

There were much better cars in the lot.

"Start packing," she said.

"What are you doing?"

She had the phone in her hand. "Calling nine-one-one. The cops should keep those guys busy while we sneak out of here."

He nodded, appreciating that she didn't freak at danger but used her brains. He stuffed a few clothes, his toiletries, his wallet, and his gun into his backpack, and picked up his briefcase—which held copies of everything he'd mailed to Vegas, plus the complete South American reports, and some footage he'd shot himself in Venezuela knowing he'd have to leave the rest of his stuff.

She made her call, hanging up without giving any personal information, then stepped into her jeans, tucked in her T-shirt, and stuffed her few things in her bag.

"What are they doing now?" she asked Adam, who'd swapped positions with her and was peering through a crack in the blinds.

"They're either breaking into your car or rigging it to explode. I can't tell."

"Oh, great. My home invaded, office blown up, now my car," she mumbled, grabbing her toothbrush and toiletry bag from the bathroom. "What next?"

"They kill us."

"It was a rhetorical question."

"Here come the cops. Come on."

Their door faced the parking lot, and the very last thing Gretchen wanted to do was barge on out there to join the hired thugs. But they couldn't hide in the room; they had to get out.

Adam pulled the door open an inch and she crowded under his arm so she could peer out as well. The two dark hulking shapes were doing something to her car, all right. The police cruiser turned in to the motel parking lot, and as the headlights pierced the gloom, they briefly highlighted the two men who did not look like ordinary car thieves. They wore dark suits and carried their tools in a bulky leather briefcase.

As they were panicked into action, Adam said, "Let's go."

He pulled the door open and she slipped out, hoping neither cop nor robber would glance over a shoulder and see her and Adam so painfully exposed.

He grabbed her hand and they ran the length of the motel, in the opposite direction of the commotion.

They rounded the side of the motel, out of sight, and pulled up against the pollution-gray siding. The highway stretched in front of them, brightly lit and relatively quiet at two A.M. "We could hitchhike," Adam said, gesturing to the highway.

"We might get picked up, all right," she said, pulling him back against the siding as a dark sedan came toward them.

It wasn't just that the car itself looked like a prop from a *Godfather* movie, and had her stomach sinking, but that the driver looked like one of the extras. In the gleam from the overhead streetlights, she had the impression of a big head, hulking shoulders, and no neck. The car slowed, and even though the driver didn't bother with a turn signal, the vehicle started to turn into the lot.

The flashing police lights changed the driver's mind right quick. He straightened the car, and, as he did, his headlights strobed over her and Adam. There was no possible way he hadn't seen them.

Could their luck get any worse?

The car swerved toward them, and for a second she was frozen there until she felt her arm almost tugged out of its socket as Adam hauled her into a sprint.

She'd wondered, back when she first took her training, what it would feel like to run for her life.

Now she knew.

It felt like one of those dreams in which the faceless monster is chasing, and you run and run but you can't ever run fast enough.

They dodged behind the motel to the miserable sliver of ancient asphalt that housed the dumpsters. She felt like a fox trapped between two packs of baying hounds. On her left was the sinister shadow of the sedan with Bull Neck following them. On the right, police officers were in noisy pursuit of the two guys who'd been messing with her car.

Adam scrambled up on top of one malodorous dumpster and held out a hand for her. She grabbed it and he hauled her up. From there they could step onto a cinderblock wall that separated the motel from a convenience store/gas station.

He bent his knees, ready to jump, but she stopped him. "There are police over there. They can help us."

He shook his head. "No time. I've got to get to Las Vegas. You go if you want. Get back to your life."

Since her entire life had either been blown up, invaded, or tampered with in some fashion, it wasn't all that exciting a prospect. Besides, she was in too deep now to give up. And the thought of Adam continuing on without her didn't impress her in the least.

"I'll see this through," she decided, launching herself off the wall to make a bone-jarring landing at the edge of the convenience store property. She just managed to prevent herself from toppling onto a heap of scattered dented and rusting beer cans, crushed, empty cigarette packets, and candy wrappers.

"Maybe we could go into the convenience store and—"

"Good idea, go."

The black sedan turned into the gas station even as she took the first step toward the brightly lit squat building. Adam didn't move.

"Come on. Don't be a hero!" she cried.

"I'll slow him down." Adam reached into his back pocket, and she knew damn well he was going for his gun, just as the driver's side of the sedan opened.

"No." She grabbed his arm and pointed with her free hand. "Look!"

A camper van the size of an oil tanker swung in from the other entrance and pulled into the bay opposite the sedan. A couple of seniors were visible, and there was a wheel cover with *I ♥ Grandpa* affixed to the front.

And God bless Grandpa, she thought, as Bull Neck swiftly tucked his firearm away. This time it was Gretchen's turn to yank Adam's arm, pulling him into a run. They sprinted what seemed like half a mile to the end of the camper and around the back of it.

She scanned the vicinity, but with pursuit so close, there was only one option. Still holding Adam's hand, she ran out into the highway.

Even with sparse middle-of-the-night traffic, they took their lives into their hands. Still, she figured, better the possibility of death and maiming in a roadway than the certainty of it from the men chasing them.

They made the other side and she glanced back, but with the bulk of Grandpa's camper in the way, she couldn't see the black sedan.

"You must be awfully important," she mumbled as he pulled her down the embankment and into a thicket of some kind of scrubby bush. They crouched and ran until the sound of a siren split the air. Both scrambled back up the embankment and peeped over.

"I like the look of that," Adam said as the black sedan roared past them with the quiet purr of a very powerful motor. One rear door was flapping open and she could see the tumble of dark bulk in the backseat, one arm fishing out for the door handle. "He must have caught up with the other two guys."

The car flashed past, closely followed by two black and whites with sirens screaming. "I hope they get caught."

"Me, too. But don't count on it."

It was a reprieve, if only a short one. She was so happy, she took her first deep breath and then had it sucked right out of her when Adam grabbed her for a long, hard kiss.

She responded, thrusting her fingers in his hair, touching his shoulders, his back, squeezing his butt, and pulling him hard against her. It was so good to feel him alive and whole.

She pulled away unwillingly.

"Come on," he said. "We've got to get out of here."

"How did they follow us and we didn't even notice them?" She'd kept a vigilant eye out as she'd driven and she'd have sworn they weren't followed.

"I don't think they did. Did you use your credit card to buy your things?"

"Cash."

He said nothing, and she groaned. "They must have found my car records at the office. Shit!"

"Hey." He pulled her back against him. "We're going to beat them. We are going to win. Come on. We'll start walking. Maybe when we get to the next town we can steal a car."

"Good plan."

It was a shitty plan, and they both knew that, but they didn't have a lot of options.

They walked.

It wasn't too bad. Her bag with the essentials stuffed in it wasn't too heavy. There was a half-moon, so they could see in the long sections between overhead lights, and Adam seemed so safe and normal somehow that she couldn't entirely believe they were in danger. For a P.I., she'd known little enough of that.

They didn't talk; both were too busy listening for vehicles. The only sound was of their shoes scuffling and the breeze blowing through ancient pines. Occasionally she'd hear a rustle of some nocturnal animal or the hoot of an owl. Once an animal, a coyote or a wolverine, dashed across the road.

Perhaps it was the fear, but she was aware of everything. Every sound, the smell of dust and oil, the feel of the pavement beneath her feet, the breeze against her cheeks and in her hair, the feel of Adam's hand, so solid and warm holding her own.

She wanted to throw him down and make love to him, right here, simply so she could enjoy incorporating every super-sensitive nerve in her body.

They couldn't, of course. The business of staying alive was too much on their minds. But if they got out of this, she promised herself she'd do things that would have Adam on his knees thanking her.

She wove scenarios in her head as they walked, deciding it was more pleasant to plan sex than to imagine what would happen if they were caught.

Adam's hand grew warmer in hers, almost as though her thoughts and fantasies were communicating themselves. It was amazing, but there was a kind of lovemaking going on between their joined hands that was making her wet with anticipation.

Twice they dove for cover and her heart pounded in terror as a vehicle drove by. One was a dusty old pickup truck, the other a small, fast sports car.

After an hour of walking, they sighted a gas station/rest stop and she breathed a sigh of relief. Her bladder was full and she fantasized about hot coffee.

A couple of long-haul rigs were parked over to one side for the night, and a tour bus was refueling.

"There's some kind of tour pulled in here," she said, in case he'd missed it. "It should be safe to use the washroom and grab some food. We could be walking for a while."

"It's dangerous to be—"

"It's more dangerous to make me pee in the bushes. Believe me, you don't want to do that."

A ghost of a smirk flitted across his face. "All right. But keep your ears open. If I see anything I don't like, I'll hoot like an owl and you meet me out back, behind the dumpster."

"You're not coming in?"

He shook his head. "If they come snooping—and they will—they'll ask about a couple, not a woman alone."

A shiver crossed her back. "I'll be fast."

But it wasn't as easy as she'd imagined. When she followed directions for the ladies' room, she discovered a line. She blinked as though it were a hallucination. It was three in the morning in a rest stop at the foot of the Sierra Nevadas. How could there be a line for the bathroom?

She shook her head, but the sea of pastel-colored jackets and polyester trousers didn't disappear.

Her feeling of disorientation intensified when one of the women, who reminded her vaguely of her own grandmother, turned to her with a smile and said, "I hope I get lucky in Las Vegas."

# Chapter Six

It was hopeless. Adam knew it in his gut. He was going to die, gunned down ignominiously on a two-bit highway and probably included as a grim robbery statistic.

That was bad enough, but the truth burned like acid through his vitals. They wouldn't be satisfied with silencing him. They'd take Gretchen, too.

Two innocent lives forfeited, and those bastards would get away with one of the biggest stock scams in history. Unless a miracle happened, he and Gretchen were toast.

Without wheels, they didn't stand a hope of getting away.

Wait a minute. He shook his head, knowing fatigue had dulled his brain. There were wheels out front. He had a gun. They could hijack one of the massive long-haul trucks.

Trying to appear casual, he strolled toward the two rigs. As he did so, he passed the tour bus.

"Warm evening." The words made him start. He glanced up to find the driver leaning against the bus enjoying a quiet smoke. The scent of burning tobacco should have clued him in that he wasn't alone, but he'd been too busy focusing on the rigs.

"Yeah," he answered, and stopped. Might as well find out how long he'd have to wait until the bus left so he could get on with his hijack.

"Are you driving through the night?" As in, *How the hell long are you going to be here?*

"Yep. I do this trip four times a month. Seniors, mostly. The scenic circle tour. From here we drive straight through to Las Vegas."

"Las Vegas?" he said. It shouldn't have been a surprise, but the idea of anyone but him and Gretchen going to Las Vegas seemed amazing. "When do you pull out?"

The driver checked his watch. Adam saw the pale green glow of the numbers. "About half an hour."

"That's where we're going." Easy. Easy, he told himself, thinking fast. Hitching a ride on a tour bus of seniors was not only easier than stealing a rig, but no one would think to look for them here. "Our car broke down back a way."

"You're driving all night, too?"

Was it his imagination or did he hear slight suspicion?

He gave a short laugh. "My girlfriend suddenly decided she wanted to get married. Like, right now. So we loaded the car and headed out. We're planning to get married tomorrow." He ran a finger under the collar of his T-shirt as though the words were choking him. It wasn't for the driver's benefit. He couldn't help himself.

The cigarette tip glowed red, and the driver chuckled as he exhaled. "Las Vegas gets its share of those. Hundred and fifteen thousand weddings a year. They come from all over." He tossed his cigarette and Adam watched it arc to the ground. "Your girlfriend knocked up?"

Adam thought about Gretchen for an instant, and imagined that tough, capable woman growing round with his child. The idea made him grin. "Yeah. You haven't got a couple of spare seats on the bus, have you?"

The driver hesitated. No doubt this was against company rules.

"I'd pay cash," Adam said. "I got some out of the bank. Figured I'd need a good stake for the tables." He grinned, man to man. "Hope I win. My girlfriend wants to start a college fund for the kid."

"We-ell, I don't normally pick up on the road, but since you're stuck." The driver spread his hands. "A hundred bucks each."

"Great. Thanks, man, you're really helping us out."

Adam couldn't wait to see Gretchen's expression when she found out that in the last few minutes they'd become engaged and he'd impregnated her.

Adam tried to ignore the prickle of unease at the back of his neck as the minutes ticked by. He'd handed over the cash, no mention of tickets or receipts had been made, and he wanted nothing more than to get on the friggin' bus and get out of here.

After about a quarter of an hour of small talk, an old couple tottered out of the door of the complex. Seconds later a trio of old ladies.

Within five minutes, they were swarming like so many white-haired bees back into the hive, as they congregated round the open door into the bus and one by one climbed into it, some spry, some arthritic.

Adam had taken a step toward the building to look for Gretchen when she emerged chatting to a couple of old women. One with a walking stick leaned on Gretchen's arm as though they were relatives or old friends. He stood there blinking as she spotted him. Her other hand held a tray with two take-out coffees and a couple of Danishes.

With a significant glance at him, she said, "Oh look, Sadie and Verna. There he is. Hi, *honey.*"

She'd obviously come up with the same idea he had. "Hey, darling," he replied.

"I was just telling these ladies that we're on our way to Las Vegas." She dropped her gaze and wouldn't look at him. "To get married."

"That's right," he told them cheerfully. "I'm hoping we can get the King himself to marry us."

"Oh, Elvis. How romantic."

"Are you in the family way, honey?" asked her new friend Sadie.

"Of course—"

"Of course she is," he said loudly, enjoying Gretchen's sudden blush and the glare she sent him.


"How dare you make me pregnant!" Gretchen whispered in a furious undertone as they snuggled together in two high-backed padded seats near the back of the bus.

It wasn't a popular place to sit, as it was across from the rear exit, and drafty, as one of Gretchen's new friends had warned her. But being close to the exit held enough advantages to overlook a hurricane coming through the rear door.

Within minutes of them boarding, it became clear that their story was being whispered throughout the bus. Heads turned and they were checked out, slyly by some, and with nods and smiles by others.

Adam felt the least they could do was act out the part of eager lovers he'd forced them into. Besides, there were hours to kill until they got to Las Vegas, and the skin of Gretchen's throat was so soft. When he kissed her there, she sighed and her curls tickled his face.

In spite of the number of hearing aids in the vicinity, and the roar of the bus engine, he wasn't taking any chances on being overheard.

He ran his lips up the column of her throat and bit the lobe of her ear. He tried not to let her shiver of reaction arouse him as he pressed his lips to her ear. "These guys are all staying at the same hotel. When the bus pulls up, get out with them and get yourself a room. False name. Pay cash." He stuffed some bills in the pocket of her jeans.

She dropped light kisses of her own on his jaw and cheeks. "And what will you do?" she whispered as softly as he had.

"Pick up the stuff and go straight to the FBI."

"It's Sunday. Not open to the public."

"I've got Wilks's home number. He'll meet me there."

"Is he the one you knew in college?"

"Yes."

"You trust him?"

He nodded. "That's why I chose him."

After a while, the glances and whispering stopped. Knitted slippers were donned, along with some of those night masks movie stars wore. He smiled. These were obviously experienced bus travelers.

"You should get some sleep," he said to Gretchen. "I'll keep watch."

She nodded, but her eyes stayed open. Finally she said, "Why didn't you tell someone in Houston what you suspected? The authorities?"

"I told a company vice president I trusted." His voice sounded odd, and he dropped his head as his fingers played with the button of her sweater.

"And the VP didn't believe you?"

"I think she believed me enough to tell someone she shouldn't have. She's dead."

Gretchen's eyes went wide. "What?"

"Car accident. Hit-and-run. Terrible tragedy. These things happen. That's when I knew I had to get out of there and fast."

"You think it wasn't an accident?"

"I knew her. Barbara would have started checking. She probably asked questions. Maybe she found something. All I know is two days after I met with her and told her my suspicions, she died. If she told them there was a whistle-blower, she didn't mention me by name or I'd be dead, but it was only a matter of time until they caught up with me. I decided to get out first."

She must have heard the guilt and pain in his voice, for she hugged him to her like a mother comforting a hurting child. "Adam, I'm so sorry."

"The only thing I can do for her now is to bring those bastards down."

One of her blond curls tickled his nose, so he scooped it out of the way, resisting the impulse to bury his face in her hair. Maybe he just wanted to escape the memories, maybe he knew he and Gretchen didn't have much time together, but he wanted her with a fierceness that had him shifting against the seat.

While they held each other, he kissed her ear, her hair, the curve of her throat. Based on her shallow breathing and the pulse jumping under his lips, she was similarly afflicted.

"I'm not staying in the hotel alone. I'll come with you. Cover your back. Two heads—"

"No." His voice was sharper than he'd intended and a couple of heads turned. "No," he repeated in a softer tone. He ran a hand over her hair, enjoying the wild bounce and curl—her hair suited her. It had personality, life, and it most certainly had a mind of its own.

He'd entangled her in this mess and already caused her more than enough trouble. Now he needed to keep her safe, not because of his guilt over Barbara, although that was certainly part of it, but because he knew he wouldn't be able to concentrate on keeping himself alive if he was also worried about Gretchen. He stared deeply into her gorgeous green eyes, realizing quite suddenly that he was no longer pretending to be a lovesick fool.

They hadn't known each other more than forty-eight hours and yet they'd achieved an intimacy he'd never found with another woman. He supposed running for your lives together could speed up the getting-to-know-you process considerably.

He glanced away, out the window, where stars burned in the blackness of the predawn sky.

They had a few hours left before they reached Las Vegas. Then, who knew? He wanted something to take away with him, the way a knight heading for the jousting field might ask for a token of his lady's affection and keep it near his heart. "Tell me a secret," he said.

"A secret?"

Down toward the front, somebody was snoring. He glanced up and noted how many passengers had now slipped sleep masks over their faces, changed their shoes for slippers, snuggled under the blankets provided, and were sound asleep.

He had the impression that everyone on the bus was asleep but him, Gretchen, and presumably the driver.

"Something you've never told anyone."

"Hmmm." She picked up his hand and toyed with his fingers. "Okay. I have a thing I do that's kind of embarrassing, and you can never tell anyone."

He nodded solemnly.

"If I have to do something I'm uptight about—" She shot him a glance and put a hand over her eyes. "I can't believe I'm telling you this. I have these Ben Wa balls. I put them inside me and it . . . I don't know, centers me, I guess. Instead of being all nervous, I'm conscious of my power as a woman."

Oh, he was conscious of it, too. He ached to go where those Ben Wa balls had been.

"Okay, my turn," she said. "How'd you lose your virginity?"

"By having sex with a girl." She shot him a glare and he grinned. "Jillian MacFarlane. She was a high jumper, had these amazing legs. We were sixteen and each other's first. I used to climb up this trellis outside her window with clematis tangled all over it. No kidding, the sight of those big purple flowers still gives me a boner."

So did being this close to Gretchen. He stroked her arm, let his hand brush her breast, and felt her shiver. The slight vibration of the bus reminded him of that foolish vibrating bed which only further tightened his groin.

"Strangest place you've ever done it?" he asked.

"The aquarium, in front of the piranha tank."

"Good one."

"Thanks. I dated a marine biologist who worked there. We snuck in one night. It was magic. How about you?"

"Back of a bus," he whispered to her, and slipped his hand under her shirt. "On the way to Las Vegas. It was dark and quiet, just the hum of the bus engine, outside the night sky and the black mountains and desert stretching for miles."

She blinked at him and drew an unsteady breath as he unfolded the blanket from the back of his seat and spread it over them.

"Are you sleepy?" he whispered.

"No."

"Excited?"

"Yes."

Her jeans zipper opened soundlessly, masked by the quiet rumble of the bus engine. He stroked her belly and felt it quiver, then reached into her jeans, under her panties, and discovered that their conversation had turned her on as much as it had him.

He smiled and began to stroke her until she started making nudging motions with her hips.

"I want you inside me," she said, in case he was having trouble interpreting her body language.

Careful to remain quiet, he finessed a condom from the pack at his feet. Pulling his own jeans down to his knees he quickly prepared himself, fumbling a little under the blanket.

He turned to her and found she'd wiggled her jeans down, too. He stroked her, loving the feel of her bare skin.

Grasping her hips, he turned her away from him. "You have a beautiful ass," he told her, wishing he could see it. He could touch it, though, and he did, stroking the curve of her hip and the round softness of her butt until she started to pant. Already, in their short acquaintance, he was able to judge her arousal level by her breathing.

She arched her back, nudging back against him until he obliged her, thrusting smoothly into her, finding her hot, tight, and wet, just as he'd remembered.

"One day, I want to make love to you on something that doesn't vibrate," he whispered.

She chuckled softly. "I like it. The motion adds a certain something."

"Think of me as your personal Ben Wa balls," he said, and began to thrust. "I'm going to relax you, and you should definitely be reminded of your female power."

"I have power over you?" She turned her head over her shoulder to address him.

"I am your slave."

He loved that they were fully clothed, and from the waist up perfectly respectable. Since he couldn't see her naked torso, or caress it, he relied on his memories of how she'd looked in the cheap motel room, her skin pink and fragrant, her breasts pert and bouncy, the small, pointy nipples a deep rose.

If he couldn't caress her upper body, he'd make do with the lower, and once more slipped his hand between her legs.

Even over the noise of the bus, he heard her gasp. He longed to kiss her, to plunge his tongue deep inside and suck her cries into himself. He wanted to taste and touch her everywhere, lick and pleasure her until she was limp and spent. But he couldn't. He could, however, enjoy what they had going right now.

Bracing his palm against her pubis, he held her tight against him while he thrust, letting his fingers play over her. His middle finger found her clit, hard and already close to bursting. He spread her own wetness over her and then held his finger on that magic spot, barely moving it, for the shuddering motion of the bus acted a bit like the vibrating bed in the motel.

Under the blanket, her hands reached back to grasp his hips. She was shuddering inside, outside; he felt his own tremors building, the flood rolling up from deep inside him, thundering through his cock and into her. He'd wanted to wait for her, but . . . even as he had the thought, he felt her jerk and clutch against him, knowing his climax had triggered hers. She turned her head, their bodies still joined, and smiled at him. He smiled back and reached forward to kiss her, deep and sweet.

Reluctantly, he withdrew from her, tidied himself, and slipped into the tiny bathroom to dispose of the condom.

When he returned, she was asleep. He put an arm around her and she snuggled against his chest. "I love you," she mumbled.

He gazed down at the tumbled blond curls and dropped a kiss on top. She was asleep, of course, and not responsible for her words, but he liked the sound of them just the same.

He settled back, keeping his bag with the gun in it

within easy reach, his briefcase nudging his foot. The chances that the Three Stooges would search for him on a bus tour of seniors were slim, but he couldn't afford to sleep.

# Chapter Seven

Gretchen woke with a start. She'd been dreaming about Adam, which was likely because her head was lying on his chest, and sometime in sleep she'd turned so her nose poked into the hollow of his chest. She was literally breathing him in; no wonder she was dreaming about him. Of course, that didn't explain why her dreams had been so erotic—or perhaps it did.

He got to her in the most elemental way.

Blinking slowly, she glanced up to find him gazing right back at her, as dark and sexy as her dreams.

There was a general shifting and rustling throughout the bus. "What's going on?" she asked, pulling herself away from the comfy warmth and gazing about with gathering wariness.

"Last stop before Vegas."

She blinked and glanced at her watch. "It's six in the morning."

"Yeah."

"How do these old people have the stamina?"

"Hell if I know," he said, stretching out his shoulders. "Come on. Let's get some coffee."

She turned to stare out the window. They'd pulled into another gas station complex complete with restaurant and shops. She searched anxiously for a black sedan in the parking area but there wasn't one. Still, that didn't mean it wouldn't turn up. "Are you sure it's safe?"

"Safer than in here like sitting ducks."

"Right." Her eyes felt gritty from lack of sleep and her mind was fuzzy. Coffee. "Must have coffee."

They hauled to their feet, then stumbled out of the bus with the old folks. She hunched into her jacket and hoped the baseball cap she'd added hid her face, just in case anyone was watching them.

She felt Adam's tension when he bumped into her from behind. Still, there were no scary dudes in the vicinity, or in the coffee shop where their fellow passengers piled in. The morning was overcast. Damn. She'd missed dawn. It was probably spectacular.

The coffee shop was almost deserted. Their fellow bus travelers began pulling tables together with practiced ease, as though they'd done it hundreds of times. She glanced at Adam, and he shrugged. If she and Adam skulked off into a corner, she supposed they'd only be more conspicuous, as well as offending a lot of perfectly nice seniors.

Adam lent a hand pulling tables into a long line, and soon they were all sitting together and a cheerful waitress with improbable red hair was pouring steaming coffee.

"What's the seniors' breakfast special?" asked Norm, the unofficial group leader, and Gretchen realized she was hungry. Before she knew quite how it happened, she was enjoying her first seniors' breakfast special.

She'd barely dug into her scrambled eggs when Norm barked down the table, "So, I hear you kids are getting married."

If Norm wasn't ex-military, she'd eat her "I ♥ Nevada" baseball cap. Adam must have sensed the same thing, for he answered, "Yes, sir."

If he told anyone else she was pregnant he was going to be wearing his coffee, and maybe he realized that, for with the briefest of glances her way, he said, "We're both big Elvis fans."

Norm nodded and bit into a sausage patty. "Going for the Love Me Tender package?"

"I was thinking the Jailhouse Rock package," he said with a foolish, lovesick grin, looping an arm around her. "Now I'm tying myself to the old ball and chain."

"Keep it up, you'll be after the Heartbreak Hotel divorce," she said, shrugging off his arm.

"Oh, they are darling!" exclaimed Sadie, the one who'd adopted her outside the rest room and who planned to get lucky by winning at the tables. "I just love weddings. What time is the ceremony?"

Gretchen swallowed before she could choke. "We haven't, uh, booked one yet," Adam said.

"Really? But the Elvis weddings are very popular. What if they're all booked up?"

"We like to be spontaneous," said Adam, who was scratching at his neck as though he had hives. "The way I look at it, if it's meant to be, they'll have a spot."

Norm chuckled. "I got married in Las Vegas myself. Had thirty-seven happy years with my wife." He shook his head, sadly.

A moment passed, and Gretchen felt her heart stir.

"What are you wearing for your wedding, honey?" asked a lady halfway down the table.

Since Gretchen had the clothes on her back, plus a blue nightshirt, an extra T-shirt, and two pairs of underpants left in her brand new pack of three, there was only one answer. "I'll pick something up when we get there," she said, forcing a smile to her face.

"Well, don't forget something old, something new— that will be your bridal gown, of course—something borrowed, and something blue." The birdsong voice had Gretchen shifting uncomfortably on the hard wooden seat. Damn Adam for putting her in the position of lying to an entire busload of grandparents.

"I think they must be hard up for cash," a woman with a hearing aid the size of a lemon said in a penetrating whisper to her husband across the table.

There was some general nodding, and Gretchen felt her cheeks heat, as though she and Adam were the deadbeat kids none of them had ever been saddled with.

"No, really—"

"Where you staying tonight? I hope you've got a nice place picked out for your honeymoon?" Norm said, looking at Adam as though if he said the wrong thing, he'd have to drop and give him fifty push-ups.

"Yes, sir. We're at . . . I forget the name of the place. I liked the look of the fountains outside."

"Poor things. You can see they've got no money. And I hear she's P.G.," Hearing Aid bellowed, pointing to her own belly and miming pregnancy, as though her words could possibly be misunderstood.

"Probably forgot to use a condom!" her husband yelled back.

"You're having more trouble with your colon? You should have said something."

"Condom," the man shouted loud enough that they could hear him in Canada. "I bet they forgot to use a condom."

Gretchen couldn't take any more. Feeling as though the heat of her own embarrassment was going to fry her on the spot, she said, "Excuse me" and rose hastily. "I have to use the washroom."

"Morning sickness, I bet," said Hearing Aid to her even deafer friend. "I was like that with my first, Ernestine.

Eat, vomit, eat, vomit. My husband used to say I should just go dump my breakfast in the toilet and not waste my time eating it." She chortled merrily.

"You got a job, son?"

As Gretchen reached the washroom door, she heard Adam's answer. "Not at the moment, sir."

By the time they got back on the bus, Gretchen almost thought she'd rather face the hit men than another meal with the well-meaning bus mates.


"I don't like the look of that whispering going on up there," Adam said after they'd been on the road half an hour or so.

She knew what he meant. A group of passengers was huddled, Norm at the center. It seemed everyone was awake now for the day. She wouldn't have paid them any notice except that one or another would glance back at her and Adam every once in a while, as though they were the subject of conversation.

"I bet he's going to give me a man-to-man talk on my responsibilities now I'm going to be a family man."

"Or a lecture on birth control."

He groaned. "I never got through that one with my old man. I couldn't go through it with Norm barking at me about the reproductive system."

She tried not to snicker and failed miserably. "It's your own fault. Are you sorry now that you knocked me up?"

He stared at her oddly for a moment before saying, "I guess I'll survive a lecture."

As they closed in on Las Vegas, Gretchen felt the knot of tension between her shoulder blades and in her neck.

This was it.

The bus pulled up at a three-star hotel on the strip

where the group was staying. They must have been pretty excited about the gambling or shows, because there was enough giggling and whispering up front for a school bus.

The group filed out of the front door; since they'd been the only ones at the back, she and Adam came down the steps last.

"I'll slip away," Adam said as they rose from their seats. "You grab a room. I'll call you on your cell when I can."

The parking lot smelled hot and dusty, and she knew he was not going to make it easy for her to accompany him, but she was determined.

Even as she tried to marshal her arguments, she was distracted by the giggling and pointing.

"Surprise!" their bus mates yelled in unison.

Blinking, she followed the pointing fingers to a brightly shining, primrose yellow limousine. She was puzzled until she saw the name emblazoned on the door: *The Elvis Chapel.*

Standing beside the open rear door, and looking remarkably like Elvis—if Elvis had been a hundred pounds heavier and Greek—was the driver.

# Chapter Eight

"We clubbed together and got you the Love Me Tender package," said Sadie, glowing with excitement. "You don't have to worry about a thing. And it won't cost you a cent. We decided we'd like to help you youngsters— and the little one on the way—to get a good start in life."

"Oh, well, thank you," Gretchen mumbled, feeling like the biggest jerk around, "but we couldn't—"

"What Gretchen's trying to say is thank you. You've helped us out of a real jam," Adam said, pushing her toward the limo with enough force that she almost sprawled.

She turned to stare at Adam in surprise, wondering if two minutes in this hot parking lot had given him sunstroke. He nudged his chin and she turned to see a familiar black sedan pulling in behind the bus.

Oh no.

She hustled into the limo. Adam followed, and before they could stop them, Norm and Sadie and Verna piled in with them.

The door shut, the driver got in, and they were off. If there was any doubt of their standing out, even in the glitz and noise of Las Vegas, that was put to rest when the engine started and "Viva Las Vegas" blared out of the speakers inside the cab—and from the megaphone mounted on top of the limo.

"Doesn't the driver look just like Elvis?" Sadie cried.

"The sideburns are good," Gretchen managed, wishing for once that she actually had bullets to load into her gun. If the sedan caught up with them, at least she'd be able to help protect the three seniors. How on earth had the hired thugs found them? She glanced at Adam and the way he was frowning, he was wondering the same.

"First, we're going to the Clark County Marriage License Bureau on Third, to get the license. Norm reminded us you'll need to do that. The ceremony is set for two o'clock. Norm organized it all with his cell phone. And I can tell you never guessed a thing!"

"No," she managed weakly. "We never did." Norm must have been something in the military. She bet he could launch an invasion given fifteen minutes and a cell phone.

"Then you'll go off for your honeymoon and we'll all still be in time for happy hour at the hotel."

As Sadie was talking, Gretchen had gazed fearfully out of the tinted windows, but, amazingly, the black sedan stayed with the bus. She supposed it was just too absurd for hired hit men to imagine anyone would make their getaway in a daffodil yellow stretch limo belting out "Viva Las Vegas."

"Thank you, Elvis!" Adam said, unknowingly echoing her thoughts as he removed his hand from his backpack. Norm glanced at him sharply but didn't say anything.

"And thank you all," Gretchen said to their new friends. She was touched by their thoughtfulness, as well as horrified at the awkward situation in which she now found herself. "It's like having a busload of fairy godmothers and fathers."

"Oh, well, we all liked the idea of helping you two get started. Plus, it gives us some excitement. I hope you don't mind if we all come to the wedding?"

Gretchen's smile developed a sudden case of rigor mortis. She and Adam were going to ditch the limo long before the service, but she hated the idea of hurting all these nice people's feelings.

What were they going to do? She glanced at Adam, but he was no help, looking as perplexed as she felt.

"Well, thank you," she said. "That's very nice. But maybe you should check first in case we get cold feet at the last minute. I mean"—she laughed, slightly hysterically—"this whole wedding thing was awfully sudden."

"I said you were being kind of impulsive, didn't I, hon," Adam said, patting her knee. She knew he was acting, but she still wanted to slap him. No one, but no one, called her *hon*.

Sadie shook her head fondly. "My youngest was like you. She almost didn't get married. I stuck to her like glue on her wedding day just to make her go through with it. I'll do the same with you." Here she patted Adam on the knee. "Don't you worry. Your lady will be there."

Gretchen shot Adam a glance of appeal. If she was being strong-armed to the altar then he was going to have to do the jilting.

Never having contemplated the matter before, she was amazed at how simple it was to get married. A bored clerk took their thirty-five dollars—which Norm would have paid, and a red-faced Adam insisted he could handle—and gave them a form which took less than ten minutes to complete. Before they knew it, they had a license, which Norm put in his pocket.

"For safekeeping," he said, and winked. He was getting as much of a charge out of this wedding nonsense as Sadie.

From there, the lemon limo serenaded them with "Blue Suede Shoes" to the chapel.

"I'm as excited as if it were my own wedding," Sadie said.

"It's still early, so Elvis's voice will be nice and fresh." If the Greek Elvis was going to be marrying them, Gretchen imagined "Love Me Tender" accompanied by the Bouzouki and wedding toasts drunk in ouzo. She closed her eyes on the vision of "My Big Fat Greek *Elvis* Wedding."

Greek Elvis opened the limo door and Gretchen found her knees were trembling as she climbed out.

She glanced up at her phony bridegroom as he held the door for her to pass through and she saw amusement dancing in his eyes. He thought this was funny? Then he gave her the ghost of a wink and she started to relax. He obviously had a plan.

He leaned close as though to kiss her, and said, "Play along." Then he did kiss her. Even through her nerves and the surreal haze that surrounded her sleep-deprived senses, she still felt the mule-kick of attraction. If she'd known him longer, if he weren't on the run for his life, if . . .

What on earth was she thinking? She shook her head and her curls bounced in her face like so many light slaps. *Pull yourself together.* Of course she wouldn't marry Adam if she weren't being forced into it by a parcel of well-intentioned and extremely stubborn seniors.

Adam held the bag containing his gun close to his chest as he scanned the area, and she almost giggled with latent hysteria. Talk about a shotgun wedding.

The foyer had two banks of slot machines, and a couple of newlyweds were pushing quarters in faster than they could lose them.

"Now," Sadie said, pulling her attention away from the binging and bonging of the machines, "the men will sort out the details. There's a bride's dressing room down this way." She pointed to a sign.

The faint hope Gretchen cherished of her new friends giving her any privacy was soon squelched. They followed her in as full of giggles and excitement as any bridesmaids. Gretchen was suddenly filled with affection and gave them each a warm hug when they were alone in the room. It wasn't large, but there was a closet, an ornate settee, a huge makeup table complete with vanity lighting, and a washroom with shower. Sadly, however, it had no window she could climb out.

"We've got half an hour," said Sadie. "Let's get started."

"I need a shower," Gretchen said, feeling she could cope with this nightmare better if she was at least clean.

While she let the hot water pound over her, Gretchen realized her stomach was full of butterflies. She was nervous about the hit men catching up with them, nervous about ditching Norm and Sadie and the rest. Nervous about the damn wedding.

From her bag she pulled out clean underwear—white cotton panties and a white bra. Not exactly the lingerie she'd imagined herself wearing for her wedding. Oh, well, at least it was clean. There was also a clean T-shirt in there, which she'd have to wear with her jeans.

She emerged from the bathroom feeling somewhat calmer, her wet hair already corkscrewing around her face, and stopped with a start.

A dress lay on the gold and white settee. "We're sorry it's not a real wedding dress, but it's Verna's and it's new. She always dresses far too young for her age, but will she listen?" Sadie shook her head. "That's your something blue."

"I may be old but I don't have to dress like it," said Verna, and those were the first words she'd managed since they'd left the bus.

"It's a beautiful dress," Gretchen said. And it was. It wasn't exactly white tulle, but the soft blue cotton halter dress with big purple and green flowers on it was cheerful and fun.

"Come and sit at the vanity, honey. Verna's a retired hairdresser. She'll get you all fixed up."

"I am so excited. I haven't done a bride in—oh, it must be fifteen years." Verna laughed gaily, already combing out Gretchen's wet hair, while Gretchen smiled faintly and noticed how pale her reflection looked—and tried to remember what hair styles had been popular fifteen years ago. She had a strong feeling she was about to be reminded.

"Oh, I wish I had my hot rollers. I do a great Farrah Fawcett. At least I used to. With your hair, you could be one of Charlie's Angels themselves, yes, you could."

*Oh goodie.*

Verna chatted all through the hair and makeup, as though once allowed to speak she couldn't shut up, but the result wasn't anything as bad as Gretchen had feared. Without the hot rollers, Verna had been forced to simply blow-dry Gretchen's hair into natural waves, and then she'd pulled the front pieces back and tied them with a piece of ribbon she found in her purse.

The two women insisted on helping her into the dress, which was only slightly loose at the waist, and when she'd taken off her bra, it really looked pretty good.

"Shoes," said Sadie, staring at Gretchen's bare feet. "Oh my gosh. We forgot about shoes."

Gretchen glanced at her beat-up Nikes and didn't think they made quite the right statement—although, being running shoes, perhaps they did. "It's okay, really. They'll look kind of funky."

"No, no. Here, try mine," Verna said, slipping off her white vinyl thongs studded with plastic jewels.

"Oh, but I can't take your shoes."

"They go better with your dress than those old sneakers. There's a ruby missing on the left sandal, but I don't suppose anybody will notice."

Verna was so insistent that Gretchen slipped her feet into the sandals, still warm from Verna's feet. They were a couple of sizes large, but if she curled her toes when she walked they stayed on okay.

Sadie glanced at her watch and nodded with pleasure. "And five minutes to spare."

There was a knock on the door and Sadie answered. She didn't open the door wide, but Gretchen heard Norm's voice. Then Sadie shut the door and turned, holding out a bouquet of white silk roses. "For the bride."

Gretchen felt her eyes fill. She wanted to think it was guilt but really it was just plain gratitude. "You are my fairy godmothers," she said, hugging them both once more.

"Nonsense," said Sadie, sniffing. "You're all set. You've got something old—that's us." She giggled. "Something new, the bouquet, something borrowed"—she pointed to the shoes—"and something blue." She swept her hand in the direction of the dress.

"Ready?"

Gretchen took a deep breath and tried to give them a big, confident smile. Adam better come up with something, and fast.

The bridal party, such as it was, left the comparative safety and seclusion of the dressing room and made its way toward the chapel itself.

Sadie grabbed Gretchen's hand as they hit the main foyer. "Come on. Let's put in a dollar for good luck. Maybe you'll win enough for the baby's college fund."

She was dragged to the front of the foyer where all the slot machines were wedding-themed.

Gretchen stuck the dollar Sadie handed her into a slot and pulled the handle.

Out of the corner of her eye, she saw a black sedan drive past outside. There must be hundreds, thousands of black sedans in Las Vegas. She wouldn't let it get to her.

Still, she groaned.

"Never mind, honey," Sadie said, glancing over her shoulder at the bride, bouquet, and cherry that showed in the slot machine window. "You're marrying the man you love and starting a family. That's all the luck you need."

Goosebumps line-danced up and down Gretchen's arms as she watched the sedan turn the corner. "The air conditioning's pretty cool down here. I think I'll head in."

"Okay. I lost my dollar, too," Sadie said.

Worse, Sadie and the rest of them were going to lose whatever investment they'd made in the Love Me Tender package. She'd make sure and reimburse them for the money, but she knew nothing could replace the joy they'd all taken in giving two broke young strangers with a baby on the way a wedding to remember.

She strode down the corridor, wondering exactly how she was going to sabotage her own wedding.

# Chapter Nine

When they got to the chapel, the men of the party were already there along with everyone else from the bus.

Gretchen tried to smile for the fifty or so seniors offering congratulations and hugs, but her gaze went immediately to Adam and her heart shuddered in her chest.

He wore his jeans, a clean white T-shirt that she assumed was his, and a jacket that certainly was not. It was a double-breasted navy blazer that belonged to a cruise ship captain or a lounge singer. But somehow, the effect of the whole outfit was stunning. He was so tall, his hair so black, his eyes so piercing a blue, and when he smiled at her, his slightly crooked grin caused a combination of heat and longing to wash over her.

"Go to your man, honey," Sadie said, giving her a little push.

*Her man.* Well, for now, for today, and for however long this crazy adventure lasted, she supposed he was her man.

She stepped forward. Adam held out his hand and she took it, finding it reassuringly warm and steady. He gave her fingers a slight squeeze, and she wasn't sure if it was simply to make her feel better or because he had a plan and she didn't have to worry. She strongly hoped it was the latter.

The piped in music was all Elvis, all the time. The carpet was the color of bubble gum, the walls some kind of shiny blond wood, and there were plastic palm trees and a white plastic trellis with silk roses in assorted colors spiraling up each side. To the left of that was a pulpit, and beside it was a microphone on a stand and a white guitar.

She'd barely finished looking around her when the King himself appeared. Not Greek Elvis this time, but Las Vegas Elvis. He'd dim any bride with his pure white pantsuit covered in flashing rhinestones.

This man was a pretty good Las Vegas Elvis, she decided, right down to the white scarf, the blue black sideburns, and the flop of black hair across his brow. When he emerged from a door behind the pulpit, everyone broke into applause. He said, "Thank you. Thank you very much," and she thought, *All right.*

For an Elvis fan having a fake wedding, she supposed that an Elvis impersonator presiding over the ceremony added a perfect touch of irony.

"Would the happy couple step forward, please," he said, wasting no time, and she realized there wasn't going to be much preamble. There weren't even pews or seats for the guests. This was the wedding version of the drive-through.

Norm handed Elvis their license while Adam led Gretchen to stand before the pulpit, one of her hands tucked in his grasp. She clutched her bouquet so hard that if there'd been real roses in there, with real thorns, she'd have been stabbed to pieces.

A loud sniffling erupted behind her, coming from Sadie's direction. Gretchen knew just how she felt. She wanted to do some sobbing herself.

"Dearly beloved," came the familiar words in the

even more familiar drawl, and her hand jerked inside Adam's clasp. He squeezed again reassuringly, and moved a little closer to her so their bodies were touching.

"Do you, Adam Ezra Stone, take Gretchen Louise Wiest to be your lawfully wedded wife?"

Even as she thought, *Wow, Ezra, tough one*—and could imagine how his real wife would address him by his middle name when she was mad at him—she waited, tensed, for Adam Ezra Stone to reject her in front of Elvis, God, and everybody.

Adam turned and gazed down at her with the strangest expression in his eyes and said, "I do."

She blinked at him. *What?* Well, she sure as hell wasn't going to be the one looking like a jerk in front of all these nice people.

Now it was her turn. "Do you, Gretchen Louise Wiest, take Adam Ezra Stone to be your lawfully wedded husband?"

Silence heavy as eternity seemed to weight her tongue. She had to say no, she wouldn't make a mockery of her first wedding—but this was Elvis, for Pete's sake. You didn't say no to Elvis. And Norm and Sadie and the rest. She glanced up and found she couldn't say no to Adam either. So she said, "I do," her voice low and trembling, then dragged in a breath as though someone had squeezed the valve on her air supply hose.

Her palm was tingling and she was pretty sure it was because her hands were sweating.

Oh Lord. She'd started out to track a cheating spouse—she'd never intended to marry him herself! Elvis needed to speed things up because the room was beginning to spin and she really, really needed to stick her head between her knees.

Then there was the thing about anyone knowing of any impediment as to why they couldn't get married, and she breathed again, knowing Adam must have set somebody up to stop the wedding. But the silence was broken only by the sniffles of Sadie and the distant chirping of a slot machine. Sounded like somebody'd won the jackpot.

Then Elvis continued. No one had stopped the wedding. If somebody didn't do something fast, then Elvis was going to say—

"I now pronounce you man and wife. You may kiss the bride."

Even as her lips fell open in shock, Adam leaned in to kiss her. A short, shocking contact of his mouth against hers. Then he hugged her to him, whispering in her ear, not words of love or an apology for not stopping the wedding, but words that made her feel even more faint.

"Larry, Moe, and Curly found us. You head through the door Elvis came in and I'll deal with these clowns. Go!"

He gave her a little push toward the pulpit while Elvis picked up his guitar and began crooning "Love Me Tender."

She couldn't move. Larry, Moe, and Curly? That must have been them in the sedan she'd seen earlier. But how could they have found them? She didn't have time to work it out. She couldn't leave Adam to fight off three killers. Besides, he was the one who needed to get away and pick up his evidence. She was trained in self-defense. She could probably hold them off long enough for everyone to get out.

She glanced back at the three burly guys in dark suits. There wasn't a full neck between the three of them.

Okay, maybe holding them off single-handed wasn't going to happen.

"Those men must be here for the next wedding," Sadie murmured nervously, standing close to Gretchen. "How rude of them not to wait."

Behind them, the first verse of "Love Me Tender" melted into the second. She saw the three tough guys spreading out and felt the hairs rise on the back of her neck. They couldn't let Sadie and Norm and the rest get caught in the middle of something ugly.

Gretchen began to herd the ladies toward the Elvis door behind the pulpit. The singer watched them, but kept on performing.

Norm walked up to the hulking tough in the middle. "What is it you want?"

"We don't want no trouble, sir."

"There's a wedding going on," Norm said in his drill sergeant voice. "You'll have to wait outside."

"We're here for Adam Stone. He's under arrest."

Norm neither backed off nor raised so much as a hair. "On what charge?"

"Murder."

"Where's your warrant?"

"It's . . . ah . . . in the car."

"Which agency are you with?"

The burly guy in the middle clenched his fists and glared. "Look, sir, this here's official business."

All eyes were on the small drama, including those of the other two stooges, and Adam took advantage of their lapse in concentration to slide behind the one closest to him.

Dropping her bouquet, Gretchen picked up one of the urns holding a flower arrangement. It was plastic, and not as heavy as she'd hoped, but it would have to do. She assumed Adam would make the first move, but she was wrong. It was Norm. His arm, skinny and gnarled but still ropy with muscle, snaked out and grabbed the gun from the holster of the chief stooge.

"Why you old—" Even as Bull Neck lunged at Norm, the old man twisted and executed some kind of fancy martial arts move.

And then all hell broke loose. Adam jumped the second stooge from behind at the same moment Gretchen whacked the third one as hard as she could with the plastic flowerpot. Silk flowers exploded from the pot. The big guy grunted and then turned on her with an ugly expression.

She tried to call up all her karate training, wishing she had a better weapon.

Soon, she realized that she did have a weapon, and a pretty heavy duty one. A busload of pissed-off senior citizens.

Sadie jumped onto the big guy's back like a flea onto a Saint Bernard, wrapped her arms around his neck, and squeezed.

While he was grabbing at the age-spotted arms, Verna whacked him in the knees with her walking stick and Gretchen launched herself at him with a banshee wail and her best kick to the midsection. He threw off Sadie, stumbled and cursed at the walking stick, and Gretchen's kick bounced off his belly like a kid off a trampoline.

He reached for his ankle and drew a knife. The gleam of deadly steel flashed as he closed in on her.

"No, Gretchen!" Adam yelled, too far away to help. He ran forward, but there was no way he could get to her in time. She backed slowly away, her only hope being that she could find some shelter and throw herself behind it.

In her peripheral vision she caught a blinding flash of white, and then heard a discordant crash as a white guitar came smashing down on the head of stooge number three, wielded by Elvis himself. The thug's eyes rolled once before he toppled to the floor, unconscious.

Elvis shrugged off their thanks.

"Nobody messes with my chapel."

Adam glanced at Norm, efficiently hog-tying his man. All three were still out cold, and in the absence of handcuffs, the gold curtain cords with the elaborate tassels were doing the job.

The man Adam recognized as the driver of the black sedan groaned, opened his eyes, glanced around, muttered an obscenity, and shut his eyes again.

They were in a smaller, currently vacant chapel. Another wedding had been scheduled right after Adam and Gretchen's, and while the men dragged out the three unconscious men, the women pitched in to put the chapel back to rights.

Elvis retreated to his private anteroom for a new guitar, and the ladies cleaned house until the chapel looked neater than it had when they'd arrived. The flowers in the urn were better arranged, too, thanks to one of the bus ladies who turned out to be a retired florist.

"You ex-military?" Adam finally asked Norm.

"Yep. Twenty years in the marines, then I got out. Went to work for the FBI."

That explained a lot. "How are you so sure I'm the good guy and these are the bad guys?"

Norm flashed him an expressive glance. "Only crooks wear suits that bad."

"Norm."

The older man rocked back on his heels. "You work where I've worked, you get a feel for people and a nose for trouble. You stepped on that bus and trouble stepped on with you. I watched you looking over your shoulder, obviously worried about your gal. I wasn't sure who you were expecting until these turkeys showed up."

Adam nodded. "Thanks. I've been in contact with

Special Agent Wilks out of the Las Vegas office. I have to pick up some stuff I mailed to myself, incriminating evidence on my former employer, and deliver it to him."

Norm nodded. "You want me to come with you and watch your back?"

"No. I want you to make sure my wife gets to the hotel safely. Call Wilks and tell him to have somebody pick up these guys." He handed Norm the card with all of Wilks's numbers on it.

At the words *my wife*, Norm sent him an enigmatic glance but didn't say a word. Which was good. Adam didn't feel like explaining.

Norm pulled out a cell phone and started punching numbers. In his other hand he held the gun he'd liberated earlier. He looked as though he'd be only too glad to shoot his three charges if they gave him half an excuse.

Satisfied, Adam opened the door to leave and bashed smack into Gretchen coming in. It was the first time he'd touched her since they'd held hands during the wedding ceremony.

Now, he didn't stop to think or to worry about the dozen or so busybodies watching eagerly, he just gathered her in his arms and kissed her long and hard.

She melted against him and he felt the contours of her body, the soft skin of her bare back, the plump fullness of her unfettered breasts pressing against his chest. Best of all, he felt her heart beating against him, reassuringly alive.

He imagined he'd have nightmares for the rest of his life about that one dreadful minute when the hit man had advanced on her with a knife and he knew he couldn't reach her in time.

He ran his hands over her shoulders and down her arms to take both her hands in a loose clasp.

"Hey, what's this thing?" Norm's voice had them turning to where he held a device that looked like a kid's electronic game. "I found it in this guy's pocket."

"Oh, my God," Gretchen exclaimed, "that's a hand held GPS monitor. That's how they found us again and again. They've been tracking you, Adam."

"Tracking me?"

"Sure. It's easy enough to plant a transmitter. I put one on you myself the first day we met."

He'd deal with that one later. Was it possible he'd been tracked by his employer? He shook his head slowly. "But no one in Houston even knew who the whistle-blower was until I went AWOL. If they'd known, they wouldn't have bothered with a transmitter. I'd be dead."

The three of them, Norm, Gretchen and he stared at one another, the three thugs and the device. "Wait a minute," said Gretchen, snapping her fingers. "Your brief-case. *The briefcase with the discreet company logo.* Where did you get it?"

"It was a gift from the board of directors. All the executives got them about a year ago. It's a real status symbol around Houston." He glanced at the monitoring device that Norm still held and then at his briefcase, which had never left his sight since he'd taken off. "You're saying there's some kind of tracking device in there?"

Gretchen nodded. "They must track their executives the way some companies track their fleet vehicles, only the targeted employees don't know anything about it. It's highly unethical, but I'll bet every employee of importance is being tracked. Those gizmos can tell where you've been and how long you've stayed there. That's why the thugs didn't bother following the Elvis limo.

They knew they could pick you up whenever it was convenient."

Adam rubbed his forehead. "If they knew where I was all the time, then why did they hire you to follow me?"

"Probably for extra insurance. In case you dumped the briefcase."

"Which I should have. Damn it, I was in such a hurry I wasn't thinking. He glared at the briefcase which had almost got him and Gretchen killed. "It must be built into the lining somehow. I'll get some tools and we'll get that sucker out of there. Destroy it."

"No, son, don't do that," said Norm, who'd been looking at the device in his hand as though he might want one for Christmas. "Turn it over to your FBI buddy. They may be able to use that briefcase to pull some more insects into the web."

The old man chuckled, obviously delighted to be back in the game. "Tell you what, take everything you need out of there and I'll take the briefcase to the bus station and put it in a locker. We don't want your old work pals knowing you've been to the feds."

Adam shook his head. "I'm not putting you in danger. Or should I say, not again. I'll do it."

"Are you kidding? These turkeys won't be calling in to say they've been nabbed." Norm nodded his chin to the trio on the floor. "I'll drop the case off in the bus station and then swing by the FBI office and meet you there." He rubbed his hands. "I haven't had this much fun since I retired."

Adam glanced questioningly at Gretchen who nodded. "Norm's right, Adam. His plan works."

"Okay," he said, knowing the faster they got going, the sooner justice would prevail. "You go to the hotel with the others. I'll meet you there."

He tried to step around her but she blocked his way. "Oh no, you're not."

"But—"

"I was hired to follow you and I'm not near done yet."

# Chapter Ten

"It's good to finally get this in the right hands," Adam said as he presented a thick brown envelope to Special Agent Chet Wilks, an unremarkable-looking man in a department store brown suit, wearing glasses and a bland expression belied by the hopeful gleam in his eyes.

He dumped out the envelope and Gretchen was able to see what she and Adam had almost been killed for. A sheaf of documents, two computer disks, a roll of film, and a small tape, like the kind from a personal video camera, tumbled to the neat desktop.

"You were able to obtain everything I asked for?"

"Pretty much. I mailed myself the originals," Adam said, pointing to the photocopied document. "They should be here tomorrow."

Wilks nodded, still emotionless, but he was tapping the sheaf of papers against the desktop as though he couldn't wait to dive in. "I'd like to interview you today, Adam," he said, glancing at his watch. "Say an hour or two to get the basics. We'll go over everything here." He gestured to the items littering his desktop. "And talk again tomorrow."

"What about Gretchen?"

"Ms. Wiest, another agent will interview you separately about the events of the last few days."

She nodded. "All right."

They were taken to separate interview rooms and she recalled, as best she could, everything that had happened from the moment the man calling himself Mrs. Stone's lawyer had contacted her.

Of course, she left out anything intimate between herself and Adam, but she didn't suppose that would remain private for long.

At the end of the interview, she was escorted back to Wilks's office to wait for Adam. She could have simply left, but she had to arrange with him about the divorce. She smiled to herself. Las Vegas saw its share of quickie weddings and divorces, but this was going to be a record.

Adam emerged sometime later and her heart flip-flopped at the sight of him. He looked tired, and she was conscious of a desire to rub his stiff shoulders and kiss everything better.

Oh man, they'd better get that divorce fast before she got any more silly ideas.

"I understand congratulations are in order, Mrs. Stone," Wilks said, offering his hand.

"Oh, well, I'm not—"

"She's not taking my name, Wilks. Get with the modern age."

"Right. Well, I'll let you two get back to . . ." He cleared his throat. "I'll see you tomorrow. Is noon too early?"

"We'll be here," Adam said, and held out his hand to her. She was so shocked that he hadn't told Wilks the truth about their fake wedding that she took it.

An agent drove them to the hotel—not the one where the bus tour was staying, but to one of the new, grand hotels on the strip. They entered the lobby, with its slot machines, in-house theater, restaurants, bars, and scantily clad waitresses everywhere. She was so busy looking around that they were at the elevators before she realized they hadn't passed the registration desk.

"Don't we need to check in?" What was going to happen now they didn't have to share a room? Now they weren't on the run for their lives? Would he still want her?

Would she still want him? She sneaked a glance at him under her lashes, and those poetic Irish looks called to her. The deep blue color of his eyes mesmerized her. The answer was obvious. Yes. She wanted him.

"Wilks arranged it."

She wasn't going to ask if he'd booked one room or two. She wasn't going to make a federal case out of it either way. She'd simply relax and go with the flow.

Yep. Relax. She was so relaxed her knees had locked and her shoulder blades felt welded to her spine.

Adam spent the time in the elevator fiddling with one of the buttons on that foolish blazer he still wore. It wasn't a long ride, but it was filled with unspoken thoughts. Soon they exited the elevator and she followed him.

He opened a door and held it for her to enter first. She loved his manners. In fact, there was a lot to love about Adam Stone. Once they were inside, she blinked. It was a huge room, with the biggest four-poster she'd ever seen. A fireplace flickered in a corner and on the balcony outside was a steaming whirlpool spa that gave her ideas involving Adam, herself, and a lot of hot frothing water.

A big basket containing fruit and snacks sat on a low table by the bed, along with champagne cooling in an ice bucket and two champagne flutes.

"This is . . . this must be . . ."

"The bridal suite."

She put a hand to her forehead. "Oh no. Those sweet old people. They even booked us the bridal suite."

Adam turned and rested his hands on her shoulders. "No. I booked it. It's not every day a person gets married. I thought we should spend our wedding night in style."

"You booked it? But . . . but . . . we're getting divorced, aren't we?"

His eyes glowed, blue and mysterious. "This is still our wedding night," he said, "and I intend to kiss the bride." He found the tie to her halter dress and pulled, and the soft cotton slid to her feet without so much as a sigh, leaving her in nothing but white panties and plastic jeweled sandals.

"I intend to kiss the bride all over."

He started with her lips. A deep drugging kiss that had her clinging to him, ship's captain blazer and all. She dug under it and his shirt to find warm, taut skin, running her hands up and down his back.

He dragged the blazer off and tossed it in the general direction of a chair, then peeled off his T-shirt. Oh, he felt so good. So absolutely right. She snuggled against him, buried her nose in his chest hair and drew in his scent, put her tongue out and tasted his flavor. She felt his heart beating beneath her lips, loved the taste and scent and essence of him. Loved feeling him blessedly alive and safe, and—for tonight at least—hers.

She walked her fingers down the center line of his belly to his jeans and unbuckled his belt. She traced his contours and damn near scorched her palm. That boy wanted out of those jeans, and bad.

Only too happy to oblige, she unzipped him carefully and slipped her hand inside to grasp him, warm and hard and wonderful.

"I need you now," she managed to articulate.

"It's our wedding night, I wanted to go slowly," he managed between panting breaths, "but I don't think I can."

"No."

She pulled her hand back out of his waistband and he had those jeans off so fast it was like he had supernatural powers. Leaving jeans, jockeys, socks, and cotton T-shirt heaped on the floor, he rose, naked, and stepped toward her, an expression on his face of such concentrated lust that she almost stepped back in self-preservation.

She didn't, though. She was more excited than she ever remembered being. He reached for her and she watched his hand, dark and lean, approach the needy, greedy core of her and just skim the front of her panties. Panties that were perfect for playing tennis or grocery shopping but were about as far from her idea of wedding night lingerie as . . . well, as her wedding was from typical.

"I wish I were wearing white silk and lace," she whispered.

"I like these just fine," he said, and cupped her so she moaned. He dropped to his knees and pulled her panties down her legs so she could step free of them. He remained squatting, gazing up at her. "Like unwrapping a plain brown paper package and finding a fantastic gift."

It was the craziest damn thing, but she felt her eyes sting. His words might be a little corny, but they were very sweet. She'd never seen this side of him before.

He rose slowly, his eyeballs about three inches from her body the entire trip, and she felt both nervous and vulnerable.

Something was different tonight. He was different. She was different. Everything was different.

He smiled down at her, taking her face in his hands. "I am so looking forward to making love with you in a normal bed that doesn't rumble and quake, without the threat of death constantly hanging over our heads."

"Me, too," she agreed dreamily. There were agents assigned to protect them, probably outside the door even now.

He twitched back the luxurious gold brocade bedspread, tumbled her onto the bed, and followed.

The sheets were cool and smooth at her back, Adam warm and furry against her front. Then she forgot about warm, cold, back, or front, for he was kissing her breasts—licking, sucking, teasing until she was squirming.

"I thought you said you were in a hurry," she gasped.

"This is me in a hurry," he said, smiling down in a way that made her want to smack him, except she was feeling so loose right now, she didn't think she could lift her hand.

Her body writhed shamelessly beneath him, her legs had fallen open of their own accord, and her hips were pumping. What did the man need? A neon sign? "I'm ready," she cried. "I want you inside me, now."

"I'm busy," he said indistinctly, and moved down, licking the underside of each breast before moving to her heaving diaphragm and then her belly, making long licking strokes that left trails of goosebumps.

He'd solved the problem of divorce, she realized. He was simply going to kill her on her wedding night instead!

By the time his tongue was tracing the triangle of hair, she was beyond words. Sighs, moans, the odd gurgle, she had plenty of those, but an actual word was beyond her powers.

Then he crawled between her thighs, spread her with his thumbs, and licked her just *there* and she lost even the moan and gurgle capability. Every nerve, every impulse was centered in that magical spot beneath his tongue.

Thankfully, he didn't tease her anymore, but built her up until she believed that only his hands, firm on her hips, kept her earthbound. A few more strokes of his tongue and she felt as though she'd burst those fetters, as well. Pleasure gripped her, roared through her, and spasm after spasm, so intense it shocked her, hurtled through her body.

It wasn't enough, it wasn't nearly enough. Even as the shock waves receded, she felt fresh tremors begin to rock her. She was open, greedy, desperate to be filled.

Adam kissed his way back up her body, leaving lip prints of her own wetness on her flesh. When he kissed her lips, she tasted herself on him, then he deepened the kiss and she tasted both their flavors, mingling on her tongue and becoming something new.

When, at last, he entered her, her voice came back. Moans, cries, and even words returned as he buried himself to the hilt, his hips rocking against hers.

He raised up just enough to stare down into her eyes as he thrust. She wanted to look away; the intimacy was so intense it frightened her.

She knew in that moment that she couldn't walk away from this and not be scarred—couldn't walk away from him and not be broken. Heartbreak, however, was for the morning. For now he was hers and that had to be enough.

He was moving, each slow thrust taking him impossibly deep into her body, into her heart. He reached up for her hands and twined his fingers with hers. Her legs wrapped around his as he increased the rhythm and she followed as though they were dancing to an unheard beat.

Their fingers were entwined, their gazes meshed, her legs wrapped around his, and his cock was as deep inside her as he could thrust it, and still she felt him reaching deeper.

Connecting. Maybe the whole Elvis thing had been hokey, but she felt as married as though their union had been blessed in an ancient cathedral. They were joined in some elemental way she couldn't have imagined existed three days ago.

She loved him.

The truth rippled through her, clenching her throat even as an orgasm clenched her intimate muscles. "I . . . I . . ." No, she couldn't say it, couldn't tell him, not when they'd be parting so soon. But what she didn't say in words, she said with every other part of her. Her blood sang with it: *I love you.* Her eyes telegraphed the same message. Her body drummed it against his hips. And if he understood the unspoken language of sighs, it was there on her lips.

She felt the increase of concentration in his gaze and his body, as though he'd received and understood her message, as though he were saying it right back to her with every part of him. Then his control snapped, and he jerked and shuddered inside her, which set her off again, so they cried out together, rocked by an orgasm so strong she expected a tsunami to result.

He collapsed against her, damp and spent, and she stroked his hair, tears welling, while he panted against her neck.

"Want some champagne?" he said a few minutes later, when their breath was pretty much back to normal.

"Mmm."

"We'd better eat something, too." His eyes glinted at her with sexy promises. "You need to keep up your strength."

And just like that, the desire she thought was spent spiraled up through her belly.

Gretchen awoke feeling a smile tug at her lips. A broad shaft of sunlight had her blinking and realizing they never got around to closing the curtains.

Even as she stretched, enjoying the feel of being well loved, reality hit her with a physical pain. After the greatest wedding night in history, she was getting divorced today.

She shifted, and as she did, her body brushed the warm nakedness of Adam. Love, lust, and sadness tangled together in her throat. She watched him, still sleeping, and took the time to memorize his features. She remembered the first time she'd seen him, not long ago, but a lifetime ago if feelings could be measured like time.

She'd been right in her first assessment. He had the eyes of a poet, the nose of a fighter, and the mouth of a lover. She'd seen all those sides of him in the last few days, and so much more. He was all the heroes she hadn't believed existed.

Odd that she'd first believed him an adulterer, for she now knew he was the rare kind of man who valued integrity above everything. Of course, his integrity almost got him killed, and her, too, but it had also caused her to fall in love with him. He was a man she could trust with her life and her heart.

But not a man who could pretend. When he loved, it would be forever, that she knew. Until that happened, no woman could claim him, any more than she could claim the gold signet ring he'd stuck on her finger as a real wedding ring.

Beneath her gaze she saw his eyes flicker and didn't deny herself the pleasure of watching him wake.

He blinked, the gorgeous black lashes lifting like a curtain to reveal the dark blue gleam of his eyes. He blinked again, and then his gaze fell on her face and he smiled up at her. "Morning."

Even though her heart was breaking, she couldn't help but smile back. "Morning."

He stretched, and she wished she could turn back

the clock and start last night all over again. They'd made love until dawn, watching the sun come up from the whirlpool. And the sunrise had been spectacular. No wonder they'd slept in.

"How about breakfast in bed?"

"We don't have time. We have to see Special Agent Wilks at noon, and before that we have to get divorced." It broke her heart to say it, but she had to let Adam know she wasn't holding him to a promise made under duress.

He stacked his hands behind his head and regarded her. "Or we could stay married."

"Why would we do that?" The words were shocked out of her.

"Well, let's see." He scratched his chest and appeared to ponder. "If we skip the divorce, we've got time for breakfast in bed. I love you. And those nice old people bought us the wedding for a present. Seems churlish to reject it."

Her heart was beating so hard her ribs were in danger. "What was the middle reason again?"

He grinned at her, and she wondered if there was any high like being the recipient of that grin. "I love you. I know it's crazy. These things aren't supposed to happen so fast, but I was in love with you before I knew it."

Tears were welling so fast she couldn't prevent them overflowing and spilling down her cheeks. "I love you, too. But it *is* crazy. Love can't possibly work that fast."

"We've already trusted each other with our lives. Isn't that what marriage is about?" He cupped her cheek and kissed her softly. "I thought we'd have a wedding reception here at the hotel and invite the bus tour people. They'd get a kick out of that."

"I don't know, I . . . It's awfully sudden."

His grin was a dare. "This is Las Vegas. Let's take a chance."

"Well, the wedding night was pretty spectacular," she said, laughing through her tears. "I guess I'm willing to gamble with the rest of my life."

And she crawled on top of him and got started.

Please turn the page for an exciting preview of
DRIVE ME CRAZY
by Nancy Warren.
Available at bookstores.

*Help*. She had to get help. There was a phone in her office, but she wasn't near brave enough to hang around having a tête-a-tête with a corpse while she waited for the police. She'd run next door and get Tom Perkins. He'd know what to do.

*Run* being the operative word.

She took off at a sprint. She barreled through the library, rounding the corner so fast she put out a hand to hang onto an end cap and knocked *Interior Decorating for Beginners, Third Edition* onto the floor.

It was an indication of her level of panic that she didn't even consider pausing to reshelve the book sprawled untidily on the floor, but kept running.

Only to smack into something warm and hard.

That grabbed her.

She screamed, horror-movie visions of psycho killers overcoming her common sense. Strong arms tightened, and she bucked and struggled wildly. Kicking, scratching, squirming—fright lending her supernatural strength.

Her fist connected with flesh in a satisfyingly deep jab.

Immediately, the arms released her. "Ow! Alex! It's me. Duncan Forbes. Hey, what's wrong?"

The voice. She knew the voice. As the words penetrated the veil of terror covering her senses, she stopped struggling and drew a deep breath, focusing on the strong, rugged planes of the face in front of her. She'd think about how foolish she'd acted later. For now, even a book defacer was a comforting presence in comparison to a psychotic murderer.

"He's dead," she said in a small voice, pointing, ashamed to note that her entire arm trembled.

"Dead? Who's dead?"

"The man. On the floor. Between Art and Home Decorating."

Duncan Forbes didn't look all that shocked by her explanation. He had, she realized, eyes that had seen everything, broad shoulders that encouraged a woman to lay her head—and her problems—there. There was a solidness to him. If there was trouble he'd get to the bottom of it. A fight to be fought, he'd fight it. A dead man on the floor, he'd deal with it.

For a woman who already had too much weight on her own shoulders, such a man looked tempting indeed.

Duncan Forbes gave her arms a brisk rub. "You okay?"

She nodded. *Liar.*

"Wait here," he said and headed off to investigate. Now that Duncan Forbes was here, she didn't feel such a strong urge to run, and she realized she couldn't leave her post. Forcing herself to march back through the door and into the library, she walked straight to her office and phoned the sergeant.

"Tom's across the street getting donuts," his cheerful secretary told her. "He'll just be a minute. Want him to call you?"

"No. Ask him to come straight over. I'm closing the library so he'll have to use his master key or knock."

"Oh, my gosh! You didn't close that time you had pneumonia. Were you all robbed?"

If Alex told gossipy Raenne there was a dead man in her library, the entire county would know about it long before Tom made his choice between cream-filled and sprinkles.

"No. We weren't robbed. There's a . . . situation I'd like his advice about."

"Is there anything I—"

*God no.* "No. Tell Tom to bring me over a cinnamon sugar." The very idea of a donut was enough to make her gag, but her request would squelch Reanne's curiosity.

She locked up the library, then reluctantly went back to the dead man.

As she dragged her feet back to the spot, she braced herself to face a deceased man face down on her floor, but even so she suffered a second shock.

"What are you doing?" she shrieked.

So much for her ridiculous fantasy that a man who scribbled on library books could be counted on in an emergency. The fool had flipped the corpse onto its back.

"I was checking to make sure he was dead."

Oh. The man had no pulse and felt like a slab of granite. That had been good enough for her. "Is he?"

Duncan Forbes glanced up. "Oh, yeah."

Something about the way he spoke made her look at the body again, and the minute she did so she wished she hadn't.

"Oh, God. He was . . . he was . . ." She slapped a hand over her mouth as nausea choked her.

Ignoring her distress, Forbes calmly completed her sentence. "Murdered. Yes. Recognize him?"

She forced herself to look at the man, really look at him. "No." She swallowed. If the stranger could be matter-of-fact, so could she. "Why would anybody murder a man inside a library? It doesn't make sense."

He shook his head. "Nobody did."

"What? You think he killed himself in here?" She glanced around. "Where's the gun?"

"He was murdered all right. But not here."

How did Forbes know that? Who was he anyway? Two stangers came into her library within twenty-four hours, one live and one dead. Could it be a coincidence? Damn, she wished Tom would hurry. As one of the only bachelors in town young enough to sport a good head of hair and his own teeth, Tom was popular and prey to matchmakers of every description. She supposed even getting donuts involved chit chat—especially since Val at the donut shop had a single daughter she'd been trying to fix him up with for years.

Meanwhile, Alex was stuck in here. For all she knew, the live stranger had killed the dead one. She rubbed her chilled arms. "I called the police."

"Good."

We don't think you will want to miss Lori Foster's
THE SECRET LIFE OF BRYAN
available now.
Here's a sneak peek.

She left the bar and grill thinking to search out another pay phone nearby. The rain continued to fall, and the wind was blowing it against the building fronts, leaving the narrow streets almost deserted. Earlier, when she'd arrived to get Leigh, she'd seen other women she suspected to be working the streets, too. She'd wanted to talk to them, but apparently, the weather had chased them all away.

Huddling under the faded, tattered awning of the bar, Shay folded her arms around herself and debated what to do next.

That's when she saw him.

And once seeing him, no way could she look away.

The man, seeming oblivious to the storm, stood in front of a small, gaudy barroom on the opposite side of the street. Blinking lights surrounded him, forming a soft glow, giving him the look of a dark, too serious angel.

Despite the rain, his shoulders weren't hunched, but were straight and wide, his posture confident, even arrogant. Long legs were fitted into snug, well worn jeans, braced apart as if preparing for battle, though Shay doubted anyone would dare to oppose him. She knew she wouldn't.

He stood facing her, staring at her in intense concentration. Although she couldn't see his eyes, she knew he looked directly at her, that somehow he *could* see her eyes. It was the oddest feeling, like comfortable familiarity, but with the excitement of the unknown.

Rain blew in her face and she remembered to close to her mouth before she drowned. As it was, steam surely rose from her head. She felt flushed from head to toe.

In an effort to see him more clearly, she wiped the rain from her cheeks and eyes—and belatedly remembered her makeup. She probably looked a fright now, but she wouldn't turn tail and run because of it. She wasn't sure she could leave.

There was no sense of danger, no alarm, only a thrill of awareness that ran bone deep, leaving her breathless and edgy as she instinctively responded to it. Her emotions had been rioting since the call had come in from Leigh. She'd suffered anxiety and urgency, then anger and remorse, all powerful emotions, only now they were being transformed into something much more exhilarating.

The man took a calm, measured step toward her, then another, straight into the storm. His movements were unhurried but determined, and Shay had the feeling he didn't want to spook her with his approach. Her stomach curled in response, her cheeks flaming. She wasn't afraid, but then, she rarely did feel fear. Not anymore.

Once, long ago when she'd been a child, she'd lived in fear. But she'd gotten over that with a vengeance, and now she kept it at bay with bossiness and a will of iron.

At least, that's what her parents claimed.

Shivering, Shay attempted to smooth her wind-blown hair, then walked out to meet him halfway. Leaving the scant protection of the rough-brick building, she immediately felt the rain soak through to her bones.

His step faltered as she started toward him, and when the neon lights flashed again, she finally saw his eyes. They were such a dark brown as to almost look black. They were intense and direct, scrutinizing her in a most uncomfortable way.

Shay stopped, staring back, breathless and uncertain. His eyes narrowed and his gaze dropped, skimming down the length of her body as she stood in a pool of reddish light.

Shay didn't dare to move. When he looked up again, he seemed almost . . . angry. But why? He hadn't wanted her to greet him?

She scowled and started forward, intent on asking him. She didn't get a chance to move before a deafening crack rattled the air and a blinding burst of electrical light seared the dark night. One entire side of the street—her side—fell into blackness and Shay knew the lightning must have struck a transformer. The darkness was absolute, the lights from across the street not quite penetrating that far, making it impossible to see, making her more aware of the noises around her, more aware of the man approaching the shadows with her.

The sounds of people leaving the many bars, the hush of excitement as darkness gave leave to wicked possibilities, was nearly drowned out by the raw severity of the storm. Shay turned to look behind her and knew that men hovered in the doorways.

Her skin prickled with dread. Safe within a building was not the same as being outside in a horrendous storm during a blackout. She hadn't lost all common sense, and she knew the situation could turn lethal. Crossing the street into the light became a priority, but as she jerked about to do just that, she managed only one step before she slammed into a solid wall of warm muscle.

Large, firm hands closed on her upper arms and held her steady when she would have staggered back. Her own hands lifted to brace against a wide chest. Muscles leaped beneath her fingertips and she stilled.

Then a voice, so close she felt the warmth of his breath and smelled the clean scent of damp male skin, whispered into her ear. "It's not safe here. Come with me. Now."

Wow. Not a question, but a command, and a very tempting one—if she were an idiot. Even before she lifted her gaze, her heart tripping with a mixture of anticipation and excitement, she knew it was him.

Across the street, one of the bars turned on floodlights, probably in the hopes of scaring away any looters. The illumination fanned out over the wet pavement and filtered onto the opposite sidewalk, providing a soft glow. Through the pelting rain, Shay stared at the man, able to make out his features for the first time. And Lord, was he incredible.

This close, she could see the golden chips in his dark eyes, and his thick, almost feminine lashes. Combined, they should have softened his gaze, but didn't. He was too intense to be softened in any way.

Dark brows were lowered in an expression of grim concentration. His cheekbones were high, his jaw lean with an edge of hardness. Tall, broad shouldered, clean and very commanding, he was a direct counterpoint to most of the men she'd seen in the area, men who skulked about, their postures either humbled or belligerent.

This man was enough to make a woman swoon—if she was the type inclined to such things. But Shay had no intention of closing her eyes for a single instant. He might very well disappear if she did.

## MY THIEF
by *New York Times* bestselling author
MaryJanice Davidson

John Crusher is hauled into his hotel room only to come face-to-face with a stunning redhead who orders him to strip. And when the room service is this superb, what's a guy to do but show his appreciation . . .

## HOT AND BOTHERED
by *USA Today* and *Essence* bestselling author
Kayla Perrin

Marrying Trey Arnold after a whirlwind romance was the dumbest thing Jenna Maxwell ever did. Divorce is the simple solution, but once she sees Trey's sexy smile again, things get complicated . . . and very, very hot . . .

## MURPHY'S LAW
by *USA Today* bestselling author Morgan Leigh

Kat Murphy is in love with her lawyer boss Sam Parrish. Fearing his heart may never heal from his wife's death, she quits her job and heads for the beach. And when Sam follows, the sensual heat they generate is out of this world.

## I LOVE BAD BOYS

*They are the men of our wildest dreams. With just a look, they can jump-start our deepest desires. So, crack open the cover . . . and discover men who can't be tamed . . .*

## HER CRAVING
by *New York Times* bestselling author Lori Foster

Shy Becky Harte has decided to explore her wicked side. Being spotted in a sex shop by her secret object of desire, George Westin, was not part of the plan. George is intrigued at her purchases, and he'd love to teach the blushing Becky a thing or two about surrender. But when fantasy becomes reality, it's the not-so-innocent Becky calling the shots . . .

## NAUGHTY BY NIGHT
by *USA Today* bestselling author Janelle Denison

Since they were teenagers, sparks have flown between Chloe Anderson and Gabe Mackenzie. Now, Gabe is back in town, and a friendly poker game is turning into a game of seduction. The stakes: their wildest desires. Leave it to the irrepressible Chloe to turn the poker tables on Gabe. Now she has him at her mercy for four nights—and they've got six years of pent-up passion to make up for . . .

## . . . AND WHEN THEY WERE BAD
by *USA Today* bestselling author Donna Kauffman

For Cameron James IV, a vacation at the private Caribbean club Intimacies is his chance to find his inner wild man. In real life, Allison Walker is a computer nerd with a successful firm, but at Intimacies, she's in over her head—until she meets Cam. And though Cam is looking to shuck his nice guy image with a wanton woman, it's the nice girl he's just met who's about to bring out the wickedness in him . . .

# BAD BOYS NEXT EXIT

*Forget the straight-and-narrow. When it comes to the uncharted off-ramp of desire, these sexy bad boys can show you exactly where to get off . . .*

## MELTDOWN
### by Shannon McKenna

Jane Duvall wants to bag a big account for her head-hunting firm, even if it means stealing an employee from under sexy hotel CEO Michael "Mac" McNamara's nose. To find out what game the luscious Jane is playing, Mac's going to give her a private tour of the hotel's finest suite, where she can take whatever she wants from him—and he'll give everything he's got in the process . . .

## EXPOSED
### by *USA Today* bestselling author Donna Kauffman

It's Christmas Eve and Delilah Hudson is on a train stranded by a blizzard. At least she can snap a few pictures . . . if she can elude the gorgeous passenger who claims to be interested in her "equipment." Something about Delilah has photographer Austin Morgan feeling hungry for more. And once they're alone, Austin can't wait to see what develops . . .

## PURE GINGER
### by E.C Sheedy

Ginger Cameron is a P.R. pro who has wasted too much time on the hey-baby, great-sex, see-ya kind of guy. From now on she's a serious woman who sleeps alone. Cal Beaumann wants to hire Ginger, and he's convinced there's more to her than orthopedic shoes and industrial-strength underwear. And if anyone is skilled at penetrating defenses, it's Cal . . .

*Put on your blinker, and make the turn toward sheer temptation . . .*

**BAD BOYS ONLINE**
by Erin McCarthy

*Take a little time to reboot, 'cause these sly guys give a whole new meaning to on-site tech support . . .*

"Debut author Erin McCarthy pens a sizzling anthology that triples our reading pleasure! She superbly combines wicked humor with red-hot passion."
—*Romantic Times*

### HARD DRIVE

Mack Stone can't believe he's just walked in on the delilcious Kindra Hill in *computer flagrante delicto* in her office. When Kindar claims to prefer an online affair to the complication of a relationship, Mack convinces Kindra to grant him twelve hours to turn every erotic e-mail into a hot reality and prove that there's no substitute for the real thing . . .

### USER FRIENDLY

Computer guru Evan Barrett can solve any tech problem, but the sight of Halley Connors's lovely head pasted onto some woman's nude body—courtesy of a hacker determined to derail her catering Web site—has him in a cold sweat. Now, as they work overtime to save the business, Evan realizes that not every fire needs putting out so quickly . . . and some require very little stoking to catch . . .

## PRESS ANY KEY

To Jared Kinkaid, the only way to keep his mind—and his hands—off his luscious co-worker Candy Appleton is to insult or ignore her at every turn, until his boss signs them both up for online counseling. But when they mistakenly enroll in sensual couples counseling instead, Jared and Candy's shock turns to pleasure as they each deliver some hands-on therapy of their own . . .

# Thrilling Romance from
# Meryl Sawyer